Collins
Classroom
Classics

D0525691

OTHELLO

The Alexander Text

William Shakespeare

Edited by Peter Alexander
General editor R.B. Kennedy
With an introduction, theme and character index
and textual notes by Gareth Calway

William Collins' dream of knowledge for all began with the publication of his first book in 1819.

A self-educated mill worker, he not only enriched millions of lives, but also founded a flourishing publishing house. Today, staying true to this spirit, Collins books are packed with inspiration, innovation and practical expertise. They place you at the centre of a world of possibility and give you exactly what you need to explore it.

Collins. Freedom to teach.
Published by Collins
An imprint of HarperCollins*Publishers*
The News Building
1 London Bridge Street
London
SE1 9GF

Browse the complete Collins catalogue at
www.collins.co.uk

HarperCollins*Publishers*
1st Floor, Watermarque Building, Ringsend Road
Dublin 4, Ireland

The Alexander Text of the *Complete Works of William Shakespeare* was first published in 1951
© HarperCollins*Publishers* Limited 2020

10 9 8 7 6 5 4 3 2

ISBN 978-0-00-840046-0

All rights reserved. No part of this publication may be reproduced, stored in a retrieval system, or transmitted in any form by any means, electronic, mechanical, photocopying, recording or otherwise, without the prior written permission of the Publisher or a licence permitting restricted copying in the United Kingdom issued by the Copyright Licensing Agency Ltd, Barnard's Inn, 86 Fetter Lane, London, EC4A 1EN.

British Library Cataloguing-in-Publication Data
A catalogue record for this publication is available from the British Library.

Text edited by Professor Peter Alexander
General Editor: R.B. Kennedy
Author of the introduction, theme and character index and textual notes: Gareth Calway
With many thanks to expert reviewer Chris Green
Cover designers: The Big Mountain and Ken Vail Graphic Design
Typesetter: whitefox
Printed and Bound in the UK using 100% Renewable Electricity at CPI Group (UK) Ltd

MIX
Paper from
responsible sources
FSC
www.fsc.org
FSC™ C007454

This book is produced from independently certified FSC™ paper
to ensure responsible forest management.

For more information visit: www.harpercollins.co.uk/green

The publishers gratefully acknowledge the permission granted to reproduce the copyright material in this book. Every effort has been made to trace copyright holders and to obtain their permission for the use of copyright material. The publishers will gladly receive any information enabling them to rectify any error or omission at the first opportunity.

Contents

Introduction

People get worked up about *Othello*. Scholars like A.C. Bradley and M.R. Ridley have called it Shakespeare's 'best play'[1] – 'his most painfully exciting and most terrible',[2] his 'most nearly intolerable',[3] most *Greek* tragedy. It spotlights his only Black hero and 'by far the most romantic (and poetic) figure among Shakespeare's heroes'.[4] *Othello* is also legendary in the theatre for the number of times audience members have warned the onstage characters or cried out their sympathy, horror or hatred. At a production in Williamsburg, USA, in 1750, the Cherokee Emperor and Empress sent servants onstage to stop the killing. The French novelist Stendhal reported that in 1822, a soldier standing guard in a Baltimore theatre shot the actor playing Othello lest a (Black man) 'kill a white woman'.[5]

The play shockingly dramatises the silencing of women within a patriarchal society. Desdemona at first speaks her mind freely, but once married she begins only to *re*act to men's actions and accusations and becomes their object (a handkerchief, handed about). Emilia's ordinary 'housewife' experiences, which Iago views so contemptuously, portray the silenced woman on another level. It is because Emilia fears Iago and wants his approval that she gives him the trophy of Desdemona's handkerchief. The 'courtesan' Bianca, who sells her company to wealthy patrons, provides an important contrast for the audience: her character's sexual nature is too readily condemned as shameful and dishonest, yet for Iago *every* woman (even Emilia his wife) is an untrustworthy 'strumpet' and for Othello, in his murderous rages, even Desdemona is.

'Inappropriate' marriages (for example, of an older man to a younger woman)[6] had, since the 1300s, incited the community protest known as *charivari*.[7] This is the noisy festival riot we see, led by Iago, in Act 1, Scene 1, not just because an older man has married a younger woman but through *racial* difference: Iago describes Othello as 'an old black ram' and his

bride, Desdemona, as a 'white ewe' (Act 1, Scene 1, lines 89–90).
As so often in Shakespeare, a marriage threatens the existing
social order. In a comedy, the marriage's triumph over such
opposition would provide a happy ending. In *Othello*, the
marriage marks a new start, and the old order's protests against
it are led by a racist malcontent (Iago) who ends the play
universally condemned as a 'devil' and a 'villain'. Audiences
must ponder whether the tragic ending of the play endorses
the *charivari* by punishing the interracial marriage or whether
a potentially better world has been destroyed by this 'devil'.

Othello is also Shakespeare's most shocking version of his
signature theme: political naïvety versus worldliness. The
worldly-wise, cynical and devious character (here, Iago)
outwits naïvely 'Christian' ones (here, Desdemona, Othello
and Cassio). General Othello's 'My life upon her faith! –
Honest Iago' (Act 1, Scene 3, line 294) fuses *in the same line*
both architect and victim of his inability to distinguish
appearance from reality, as well as the tragic flaw of his 'free
and open nature / That thinks men honest that but seem to
be so' (lines 395–396). Shakespeare's ideal ruler (represented
in *Othello* by the Duke) is the moral figure who learns not to
judge the world by his own goodness but to see *through* the
disguised wickedness of others.

Yet what seems to have shocked audiences most is Iago's
malignity and *why* he dedicates himself with such relentless
zeal to the destruction of 'the Moor'. His soliloquies seek
endlessly for motives (racial hatred, misogyny, jealousy, self-
interest, being cuckolded, loathing) for his malignity. He
resembles the Devil in the medieval morality plays[8] in his
existential envy of human grace. The Devil terrified audiences
in Shakespeare's time and Iago's 'demi-devil' continues to
unsettle audiences today; the urge to cry out 'Don't trust him,
mate' (as some 19th-century audiences apparently advised
Othello) remains.

Issues in context
Texts tend to engage with and reflect the conventions and
assumptions of their time. But this is not the same as saying

they *endorse* them. One of the reasons Shakespeare's plays continue to be held in such high esteem and take on new meanings for every generation is that they can be seen to humanise and challenge stereotypes. Shakespeare's Black hero has a tragic nobility not present in the play's source (Cinthio's *Hecatommithi*, published in 1565). The motif of a daughter (Desdemona) falling in love against her father's orders is a constant pattern in Shakespeare's plays (think about Juliet, Cordelia, Jessica, Hermia, Miranda) and seems designed to engage the audience's approval even if tragic consequences ensue. In this regard, Jacobean stereotypes in *Othello* are as much questioned as represented.

Race

There are no 'grey areas' in *Othello* when it comes to skin colour. 'Black' invariably has negative connotations and 'white' (or 'fair') positive ones. 'An old black ram / Is tupping your white ewe' sets this racist tone early on (Act 1, Scene 1, lines 89–90), and even the Duke's supposedly civilised reassurance to Brabantio that 'Your son-in-law is far more fair than black' reinforces it (Act 1, Scene 3, line 290). Thereafter 'black' is used by Iago to denote the 'fair' Desdemona's female sexual organs, alleged impurity and dirtied name, and Othello's lack of social grace, racially defined social disadvantage and hellish vengeance. 'Fair' is used 22 times in the play, mostly to describe Desdemona as a shining positive ('my fair warrior' – Act 2, Scene 1, line 179) *or* (often) to describe the *appearance* of goodness and innocence behind which she hides her alleged moral 'blackness'. Iago's 'black Othello' (Act 2, Scene 3, line 27) trades on the connotations of the word as 'having or demonstrating evil intent; malignant, deadly; sinister'[9] and is reinforced by senator Brabantio's 'sooty bosom' during his rants about (black) magic carrying off his daughter (Act 1, Scene 2, line 71). Shakespeare's text never challenges these black/white distinctions embedded in the English language, but it does show the *White* Venetian Iago unleashing the moral darkness, not the Black General Othello, entrusted by the Senate with a key post in Cyprus and with his marriage approved by the Duke.

Shakespeare set two plays in Renaissance Venice: *Othello* and *The Merchant of Venice*. The great bustling port was perhaps *the* world-centre of Shakespeare's time, a pivot of world travel and trade and of the exciting but uneasy interaction between Christian Europe and Arab, Asian and African worlds. Shakespeare's hero is definitely 'black' (the text repeatedly emphasises this) but he is also named the 'Moor' of Venice and identified with 'Barbary', meaning both the coast of North Africa (Berber + Araby) and (from a European perspective) 'the land of the barbarians' so he is in effect ambiguously portrayed as both African *and* Arab (though a Christian convert). Shakespeare brings these outsiders (Jews, Africans, Moors) centre-stage in a famously rich and exciting European location, not too different from Christian England. That he presents them with some sympathy is unusual for his time but typical of Shakespeare. However, the degree to which these 'outsider' characters are presented sympathetically by Shakespeare remains a matter of intense critical debate. Emma Smith notes that 'Most contemporary critics have been more comfortable arguing that the play interrogates racism and racist categories, and that it shows us an Othello whose race is significant not because it makes him essentially savage, but because it exposes him to the terrible psychic vulnerability of being an outsider.' However, Smith argues that the play is 'marked by its own institutional racism'; 'in focusing our attention on Iago [...] it makes us complicit in the Moor's downfall.' Ultimately, the debate around representations of Othello 'tells us more about racial attitudes now than then'.[10]

Writers are products of their age but Shakespeare's attitudes to his hero seem more humane than those of his main source, the Italian author Cinthio (1504–1573). In Cinthio's *Hecatommithi*, an unnamed ensign undermines a Moor's recent marriage by saying, in a line Shakespeare avoided, 'The woman has come to dislike your blackness.'[11] She ('Disdemona', a Greek word meaning 'ill-fated') points the moral of the story for Italian ladies: don't marry against your parents' wishes or outside of your culture and ethnicity. Cinthio's ensign and 'Moor' bludgeon her to death with sand-filled socks and, in a vendetta narrative (avoided by Shakespeare) the Moor is hunted to death. By contrast, Shakespeare's *named* Moor (Othello) is a *royal*, educated, experienced African promoted into the White European ruling class.[12]

The same cannot be said for Shakespeare's references to 'the Turk', a term that for centuries connoted an 'Ottomite' barbarism threatening Christian civilisation. This perception draws on the context of the 1570 conquest of Cyprus, a Venetian-held island, by the Ottoman Empire, which marked the start of the Fourth Ottoman-Venetian War (1570–3). The 'Ottoman Wars' – between various states within Christian Europe and the Muslim Turks of the Ottoman Empire – began in the late 13th and lasted until the 20th century. The almost mythical fear of 'The Turk' which permeated Christian Europe is doubtless based in such military action, as the wars were perceived in Europe as the conflict between civilisation and barbarism. An understanding of this historical conflict helps to contextualise the conflicts and tensions that play out in *Othello*, and the often generalised and derogatory use of the term 'Turk' throughout the play. 'The Turk' remains offstage throughout the play but Brabantio equates the 'Moor of Venice' (Othello) with the 'Turk of Cyprus' (Act 1, Scene 3, line 210). In Cyprus, breaking up a drunken brawl, *our* Moor of Venice asks, 'Are we turn'd Turks...?' (Act 2, Scene 3, line 158); in this period the phrase meant not just abandoning one's Christianity for Islam but reverting to savagery, betraying all human values. Othello's final self-divided service to Venice is to kill *himself* as a 'turban'd Turk' (Act 5, Scene 2, line 366).

Women and gender

Desdemona was documented in 1660 as the first character to be played by an actress rather than by a boy in women's clothing.[13] Since ancient Greece, men had acted female roles, so this Desdemona was a landmark moment in the history of Western theatre. It meant that Shakespeare's play took on a naturalism he never saw. Some audience members found it shocking to stage a woman for the public gaze like this: an epilogue written for the play around 1660 criticised such contemporary objections as likening an actress to a sex worker and thereby reproducing Othello's mistake about Desdemona.

Ideal human virtues like Meekness, Patience and Charity, Mercy, Truth, Righteousness and Peace were typically represented in medieval morality plays as 'sweet ladies' and sisters.[14] Elizabethan and Jacobean audiences would have been familiar with such representations, though also used to contemporary playwrights like Christopher Marlowe and Shakespeare refining these 'types' so that they were also more like 'real' people. More recent critics have found abstract ideal humanity presented in Desdemona[15]; some have even found Christ-like qualities in Othello's reference to her as the 'pearl' the 'base Indian' threw away and in her (perhaps impossibly) forgiving resurrection speech (Act 5, Scene 2, lines 360 and 129–132). But Desdemona is not always/only this ideal: she is also a rebellious daughter and engages with Iago in light-hearted innuendo as she waits for the storm-tossed Othello on the quay in Act 2, Scene 1. She takes a lively interest in good-looking young men and is an enthusiastic advocate for Cassio when he falls out of favour with her husband. She rows with, and challenges, Othello, and only as he becomes bewilderingly hostile does she begin to lose confidence and fear the passions she knows he struggles to control. After he hits her and verbally abuses her, calling her a 'cunning whore of Venice' (Act 4, Scene 2, line 94), she begins to doubt herself and to not want to live without his favour and love.

Emilia, her maid, has much more cynical expectations of men, no doubt based on her marriage to Iago. For most of the play she accepts men's limitations and does not judge her husband for his (unsubstantiated) suspicions of her adultery with Othello; she feebly seeks his favour by disloyally procuring him her mistress's handkerchief and takes Iago's word that Bianca is female 'trash' involved in a murder attempt. But Emilia develops: she makes an impassioned speech in favour of the rights of wives in Act 4, Scene 3, recognises Desdemona's virtue and, in her death scene, finally sees through Iago to a tragic truth.

Bianca works as a courtesan – a 'paid female companion' with wealthy and upper-class clients – so does not have Desdemona's innocence of the world, but she is genuinely in love with Cassio. Like Desdemona, she is silenced and blamed for something she hasn't done. We, as the audience, bear witness to her personal worth, integrity and – in a different sense – innocence (of the murder attempt and of being 'trash' or a 'strumpet').

As in Greek tragedy, these three women collectively voice – and stage – a range of real female social concerns, including rights within marriage. Shakespeare's theatre gave a public forum for such female voices (symbolically written and acted by males) in a society in which they were often otherwise publicly excluded.

Manhood and masculine power

This is a gentleman's world. The Duke is its model Renaissance ruler and Othello its brilliant general; its Senate is all-male. Montano is an esteemed governor of Cyprus but replaced when martial law (under a better soldier, Othello) is required. Ludovico is a model courtier who provides the Venetian contrast for Othello's descent into savagery in Cyprus. The Florentine nobleman, Cassio – not quite the upper-class fool that Roderigo is but in some ways his twin – is fast-tracked to promotion (by Othello to lieutenant and later by the Senate to general) while his 'senior' Iago is overlooked. Being a professional warrior can get you to the top (even if you're an outsider) as long as you're royal or noble – and Iago isn't. This invites the audience to ponder how far Iago's revenge on this elitist world is justified. Shakespeare himself was not part of the establishment by birth and was called 'an upstart crow' for the success he achieved by hard work and merit.[16]

The text is ambivalent about marriage and manhood. Othello is delighted to be married but Iago clearly expresses a contrary view: the misogynistic assumption that men are happier when 'free' of the 'shackles' of women. Othello's pre-domesticated, pre-Desdemona 'unhoused free' masculinity is evoked, in majestic language, as raw, fearless, fathomless and wild (Act 1, Scene 2, line 26). Desdemona falls in love with his tales of it; Iago admires and yet envies it – he may be especially jealous of a woman taming it. Exploiting Othello's insecurity about and inexperience of this 'domestication' through marriage, he plays on Othello's fear of being cuckolded and emasculated. 'Are you a man?' he taunts his superior officer in Act 3, Scene 3 (line 377). He also repeatedly and deviously emphasises the promiscuous sexuality with which Venetian women were associated. Iago is a misogynist and totally cynical about women, but he relentlessly insinuates their corruption and deception for a reason: to precipitate Othello's downfall. For Othello, marriage is a new venture, which doubly emphasises his outsider status, something his perceived rival Cassio's *apparent* ease with women would aggravate. Yet if a test of true 'manhood' includes the ability to maintain a successful relationship with a woman, even Cassio fails.

Tragedy

While tragedy for us is a literary genre, for the ancient Athenians who invented it, the word had its roots in ritual sacrifice and meant 'goat song'.[17] For the ancient Greeks, tragedy was religious festival and a civic duty, non-attendance at which was punishable with fines. Theatres (the Greek word for 'witnessing') were large open-air stadiums that combined the functions of town hall (where dramatic speeches were given on key issues), law court and temple. The Greek philosopher Aristotle said tragedy must deal with people of high social rank falling into misfortune because of a *hamartia* (a 'fatal flaw') or error of judgment (such as *hybris*, 'insolent pride').[18] The plot must feature one or more *peripetea* (surprising downturns of fortune or, more accurately, disasters resulting from well-meant actions) and an *anagnorisis* (a final recognition of some unwelcome truth). Shakespeare's tragedies, even this unusually domestic one, are Greek in this way.[19]

In Shakespeare's day, whole regions (Norfolk, for instance) had their interests represented in national councils by one 'great' man (in Norfolk's case, the Duke of Norfolk). In a Greek tragedy, a great man (of noble birth) is punished, and by his symbolic sacrifice, the watching city is purged of its 'sins'. Shakespeare uses this tragic convention and his audience would have recognised it, but they would also have recognised the way he enriches it (or, to some, dilutes it with comedy and other material). In this way, we have Othello as both the universal 'great man' of tragedy and a particular suffering human being. Commenting on the downfall of Othello, the critic F.R. Leavis regretted that, instead of a tragic *anagnorisis* (recognition), we get the 'pathetic self-dramatization' of a sentimentalist who has learned nothing.[20] Yet perhaps such criticism overlooks Othello's social function as the sacrificial tragic hero and dismisses his 'goat song' as self-pitying 'bleating'. A properly 'tragic' reading of the play might see it as a conduit through which Elizabethan audiences could witness society's sins of racism, misogyny, elitism, hypocrisy, violence, denial, jealousy, rage, and hatred and, through Othello's death, feel 'purged' of them.

Writing, dramatic structure and techniques
Setting
The dual setting of the play in a city (Venice) and a wild place (the island outpost of Cyprus) is a familiar trope in Shakespeare. Shakespeare uses Venice to represent civilisation, government, reason and law. In Act 1, Scene 3, the violent forces, excited passions of fathers and lovers, race-hatred and street-brawling anarchy that Iago unleashes (and even the hint of self-abandonment behind the magnificent rolling speeches of Othello) are held in check by the ranked Senate in rich robes and symbols of office and their simple statements. As Brabantio puts it, 'This is Venice; / My house is not a grange' (Act 1, Scene 1, lines 106–107).[21]

Beyond Venice is the invader-barbarism of the general enemy: the 'Turk'. Othello reports his experience of this racially defined wilderness where cannibals eat each other and in which he was once enslaved, with its 'high seas, and howling winds' and treacherously hidden 'gutter'd rocks, and congregated sands' that would 'enclog the guiltless keel' (Act 2, Scene 1, lines 67–69). Cyprus, through a terrible storm, is a far frontier against this 'Turk'. But there is also divine wisdom in those wild hills, the 'Rough quarries, rocks and hills whose heads touch heaven' (Act 1, Scene 3, line 141). In Cyprus, Othello faces this encounter with (his) wild nature without the order of Venice to support him. He, like many Shakespearean heroes, must carry Christian civilisation and marriage through the wild and return (if he can) with a deeper self-knowledge to Venice. The way his jealousy-provoked 'bloody thoughts' of revenge overwhelm him like the 'icy current and compulsive course' of the Pontic, Propontic and Hellespontic seas (Act 3, Scene 3, lines 462 and 459) before he kneels to make his cosmic vow (lines 465–466) is one example of the awesome powers of wild nature below his Venetian-'civilised' surface.[22] If he could harness this wild nature, he would be self-wise indeed.

He fails. But is it Othello's 'inner Turk' that derails him, as some commentators explore or the 'civilised' Venetian without (i.e. Iago)?[23] Othello finally recognises his folly and bears tragic witness to the truth of Desdemona's goodness, paying for this self-knowledge with his life. Iago will recognise nothing. Discontented with his place in the social order, he destroys all order, military and marital, by stoking anarchic passions in all: Roderigo, Brabantio, Othello, Cassio. In Venice, his attempts to create chaos were frustrated by Othello's calm management of himself and by the onstage lighted Senate chamber. In the dark outpost streets of Cyprus, Iago's anarchy runs riot and society falls apart: drunken Venetians cut one another down and marriage becomes domestic abuse. As Lodovico comments after witnessing Othello strike his wife, 'This would not be believ'd in Venice' (Act 4, Scene 1, line 243).

Language and imagery

While Shakespeare's grandiloquence is varied with a range of poetic language and registers for the many human situations he depicts, his characters are not presented *as if* they are real people: they do not speak 'realistically'. The three opening scenes of *Othello* alone range from formal elaborately patterned speeches to a portrayal (in verse) of swift colloquial dialogue. But Shakespeare's basic medium is poetry in iambic pentameter: speech musically organised into lines of ten syllables in a regular beat, *occasionally* varied for special effects, which would have astonished Elizabethans if used in ordinary conversation. This doesn't mean that the play fails to be a 'realistic' representation of real life (it is deeply so) only that it does not pretend to *be* real life, as 'realism' does.[24]

'Decoding' Shakespeare is not translating his Tudor language into literal modern English; it is noticing the suggestions and effects of his poetry. So when Desdemona says to Emilia of Othello in Act 3, Scene 3 that she will 'watch him tame' (line 23), she is comparing him with a wild hawk and the audience should notice Othello unconsciously developing the same hawk-taming imagery about *her* later in the scene. Othello ominously speculates that his wife is untameable and that he will let her go. The fact that each lover thinks of the other as a wild bird of prey emphasises both the (tragic) grandeur of their relationship and its imminent destruction.

Othello is conveyed in images drawn from wild, unconfined nature. When he says, 'But that I love the gentle Desdemona, / I would not my unhoused free condition / Put into circumscription and confine / For the seas' worth' (Act 1, Scene 2, lines 25–28), he emphasises the undomesticated freedom of his pre-married state. This emphasis on his 'unconfined' and 'uncircumscribed' nature links with Roderigo's insult that Othello is 'an extravagant and wheeling stranger' (Act 1, Scene 1, line 137). Othello is portrayed as a force of Nature, a natural inhabitant of the world's great spaces, which (he says) only his powerful love for Desdemona could have 'tamed'. However, the epithet 'gentle' by which he identifies Desdemona, making it part of her name, indicates he lacks much real knowledge of her and perhaps makes naïve (possibly army-bred) assumptions about women. By Act 3, he is thinking of her as an untameable female hawk: this *could* be because his view has been changed by Iago's insinuations but perhaps, too, his independent Venetian lady was always wilder than his 'gentle' assumes.

Plot versus character

In Shakespeare's other major tragedies – *Hamlet, King Lear, Antony and Cleopatra* and *Macbeth* – he puts character before plot. We ask, 'What kind of people are these and how will they have changed by the end?' In *Othello*, we ask plot-driven questions: 'What will the next move be?' or 'Will he/she see the danger before it is too late?' And once the plot is established, it is relentless, advancing 'without appreciable pause and with accelerating speed towards the catastrophe'.[25] It is also, as Aristotle recommended, remorselessly simple. An ensign – a junior rank of officer in the armed forces – expecting promotion to lieutenant and furious when another man is promoted before him plans revenge on the general and his rival. He persuades the general that his wife has committed adultery with the new lieutenant. As a result, the general kills his wife and then himself. The ensign disastrously fails in the second part of his plan: his plot is exposed, the lieutenant is *further* promoted (to general) and the ensign faces trial and torture.

Yet would any old ensign plot with Iago's murderous fanaticism to avenge a missed promotion, based on such passionate envy of human happiness? Is it not in fact Iago's extreme *character* that drives the plot? Could any ensign *except* Iago successfully dupe so many people: Othello, Cassio, Roderigo, Desdemona, Montano – even his own wife? Or would a different general (the Venetian Duke perhaps) have been so easily duped as Othello? Is it also the *character* of Othello – and his (and Desdemona's) naïvety – that make the plot work out as it does? If Iago and Othello are exceptional rather than typical, then perhaps character flaws *are* more important than the plot that reveals them.[26]

Structure

Othello is the most compact (and therefore potentially, the most intense) of all the great tragedies, with only 13 characters

(*Hamlet* has 25, *King Lear* 20, *Antony and Cleopatra* 33). *Othello* hurtles without a sub-plot at increasing speed to its catastrophe. Oddly, the antagonist Iago has more lines than the protagonist, and his frequent soliloquies to the audience situate *him* rather than Othello as its 'narrator'. Might this then be Iago's tragedy, *his* brilliant but deeply flawed self-revealing? In this sense perhaps Iago is an anti-protagonist, an anti-hero, a 'satan' in the sense of adversary, whose story is merely the negation of Othello's.[27] It is worth noting that the word 'devil' recurs twenty times in the play, following Iago and his schemes around without ever being applied to their real source.

Act 1 (up to Scene 3, line 290) could be a one-act comedy, the play Shakespeare might have made in a different mood or for a different theatrical need. All the racist abuse of the (unnamed, misrepresented) central character, all the society's ignorant ritual opposition to a interracial marriage and all Iago's vicious envy is *refuted* by Othello's calm and majestic entry and a grateful Venetian state honouring him with a position of trust. Many critics have noted the extreme structural shift in the middle of *Othello*, after which the seeds of jealousy planted by Iago explode out of all proportion to the 'real' events within the world of the play. Jan Kott described this as a dispute between two world views: Iago's that the world is vile, consisting of fools and villains; Othello's that it is full of noble and beautiful people, bound by love and loyalty.[28] Iago successfully imposes his negative view on the other characters, hiding the strings by which he pulls them and making all the evil he sees in himself true for the characters around him. In this sense, the play is structured as a progression of worldviews. Part of the resolution is Othello's *half*-rejection of the supernatural explanation of Iago as 'devil' in Act 5, Scene 2: 'but that's a fable', demanding instead a human *as much as* a diabolical explanation of this '*demi*-devil': 'Why he hath thus ensnar'd my soul and body?' (lines 298 and 314–315).[29]

Interpreting the play

Othello has never disappeared from the stage and enjoys a high critical reputation. As Alvin Kernan notes, 'When Shakespeare wrote *Othello* in c.1604, his knowledge of human nature and his ability to dramatize it in language and action were at their height.'[30] The play has been interpreted by four centuries of critics and theatre practitioners in multiple ways.

Audiences and producers have always engaged with the issues about race presented in *Othello* and responses range from the deeply racist to the Black-empowering and beyond. The Jacobean practice was to have a White actor play Othello in 'blackface'. In 1818, the Shakespeare scholar and Romantic poet, Samuel Taylor Coleridge insisted that Othello, until then played in blackface, should be light-skinned (beginning the 'bronze age of Othello'[31]), perhaps conditioned by his age's experience of Black Africans as more often enslaved than royal. The first instances of its Black hero being played by Black actors occurred in, and shocked, the early 19th century. This became normal practice during the 1960s but raised the problem of a single Black character being made to represent *all* Black men. If Black actors were originally prevented from playing Othello by the colour of their skin and later seized the role as part of the Civil Rights empowerment,[32] some now began to believe it was the last role a Black actor should play. The Oxford University educated, classically trained, Black British RSC actor Hugh Quarshie (born 1954) said he had seen more productions of *Othello* than any other play by Shakespeare and after his 'interest in watching white men imitate black men waned' he wanted to see productions with Black actors in the role but worried that 'if a black actor plays Othello does he not risk making racial stereotypes seem legitimate and even true?'[33]

By the early 18th century, many of Desdemona's scenes and any reference by its 'pure' leading lady to sex (even bedsheets) was cut. This left only a 'willow' figure willing to die at her husband's hands. As Carol Carlisle commented, 'No ambitious actress would attempt to build her reputation on the drooping, wavering creature.'[34] Fanny Kemble briefly bucked this trend in 1848 by having her Desdemona fight back on her deathbed. By the late 1960s, Ellen Terry argued that 'a great tragic actress with a strong personality and a strong method is much better suited to [the role], for Desdemona is strong, not weak.'[35] Millennial productions (including the National Theatre 2013 and 2015 RSC) have reverted to presenting Desdemona as strong but extremely young, naïve and in love for the first time. There is a textual basis for this age difference between Othello and Desdemona (she is called 'young' or 'young maid' several times; he is called 'old') but some feminists believe it circumvents the exploration of male–female power issues by making Desdemona a sort of child-bride.

As Othello's life, and the tall stories he has made of it, ends in self-execution for his tragic folly, he interprets it – in fact directs the retelling of it – as a tale 'Of one that lov'd not wisely, but too well' (Act 5, Scene 2, line 357). Directors and readers of the play are left by Shakespeare to decide exactly how they will 'these unlucky deeds relate' (line 354) in the theatres and in their own minds.

Shakespeare's theatre

An Elizabethan playhouse. Note the apron stage protruding into the auditorium, the space below it, the inner room at the rear of the stage, the gallery above the inner stage, the canopy over the main stage, and the absence of a roof over the audience.

William Shakespeare (1564–1616) was a man rooted in theatre. He began his career as an actor, so had an actor's sense of which speeches would be effective on stage and how plays could be delivered with maximum impact. When writing plays, he worked directly with his company, the Lord Chamberlain's Men, so it is likely that he took on board feedback from other actors.

The Globe Theatre in London, where most of Shakespeare's plays were first performed, opened in 1599. By this time, Shakespeare was a man of theatrical influence and a shareholder in The Globe. However, the idea of a permanent theatre in London was relatively new: the city's first theatre was built in 1576. Theatres were becoming an important source of entertainment, but they were also places where radical ideas were explored. Indeed, the Puritans, who began to dominate English politics from the 1630s, considered plays to be subversive and passed a law closing theatres down in September 1642.

To get a good idea of what Shakespeare's theatre was like, we can look at the new Globe Theatre, which opened in 1997 on the site of the original, on the south bank of the Thames. It was built from plans drawn from painstaking research and used Elizabethan materials and building methods, though with added safety features such as fire exits and sprinklers.

The Globe building was circular – in Shakespeare's *Henry V* it is described as a 'wooden O',[36] with a stage raised on a 'scaffold'[37] (in the modern Globe Theatre, the stage is at adult chest height). The stage stuck out into the circular yard, known as the Pit, surrounded on three sides by the audience. There was probably a curtained-off area to the rear of the stage, (used for Othello and Iago's 'withdrawals'), and a gallery above that was used by musicians, and for such occasional central scenes as 1Gentleman on lookout above the Cyprus quay (Act 2, Scene 1, lines 1–4).

A ticket to stand in the Pit cost a penny (about £1 in today's money) so ordinary working people could afford to attend. Audience members in the Pit were known as groundlings; a number of characters in Shakespeare's plays make disparaging remarks about them. Around the Pit, forming the walls of the theatre, were more expensive seats on three levels. Access to these seats cost at least double the entrance to the Pit, and a box in a prime position cost considerably more. Shakespeare's audiences therefore represented a full cross-section of Elizabethan society. Indeed, King James I was the patron of Shakespeare's theatre company and attended performances at court.

A thatched roof covered the seating areas and the stage, but the central Pit was open to the weather. There was no artificial lighting, so performances usually started in the early afternoon. The atmosphere at times was probably quite rowdy; the groundlings would form a lively crowd, eating and drinking during performances and voicing their opinions about the events of the play. Does *Othello* start with a loud argument partly to get their attention?

Productions in the theatre had very little in the way of sets, making scene changes quick and easy. Actors could descend from above or use the stage trapdoor for entrances and exits. Costumes showed little regard for historical accuracy. Wealthy patrons sometimes handed down resplendent robes to actors playing noblemen and royalty; occasionally, companies spent considerable sums on costumes; there could be rudimentary armour or improvised togas for Roman characters. Yet everything was an approximation: in *Henry V*, the Chorus appeals to the audience's imagination to make up for the lack of numbers in battle scenes, asking 'Piece out our imperfections with your thoughts.'[38]

While the visual elements in Shakespeare's plays were simple, the words held great importance. Shakespearean audiences would speak of going to *hear* a play rather than to see one (the Latin root of the word *audience* means 'to hear'). Although many audience members in the Pit would have been illiterate, England had a long tradition of oral storytelling. Listeners loved words and paid careful attention to them, which is why Shakespeare's plays are full of rich verbal imagery and extensive word play.

In Shakespeare's time, all actors were male and boys played female parts, which perhaps explains why women characters dress up as boys to disguise themselves in a number of Shakespeare's comedies, such as *Twelfth Night* and *As You Like It*. Adult comic actors probably played older comic women, such as Juliet's nurse. Actors needed a wide range of skills and were expected to be able to fence, sing, dance and play musical instruments. We know from *Hamlet*, however, that Shakespeare did not appreciate over-the-top actors spoiling his plays: Hamlet tells a group of travelling actors they should 'not saw the air too much with your hand,'[39] as this would lead an actor to tear 'a passion to tatters.'[40]

The Globe was one of several London theatres, and not all of them were outdoors. Indoor theatres were lit by candles and could make use of sets, allowing designers to produce elaborate scenic designs on backcloths for plays with music known as masques. In 1608 Shakespeare's company took over the indoor Blackfriars Theatre The Blackfriars' rectangular auditorium with the stage at the shorter end was a very different design. Here, Gentleman's lookout might have been in a box (post seat) above the 'tiring house'.

When studying a play by Shakespeare, think how scenes might originally have been performed and how the simple apron stage might have been used. Consider how the cruder comic scenes would have appealed to the groundlings, at times a few inches from the actors, and how elaborate and intimate elements of plays such as the lighted Senate chamber and bedroom scene in *Othello*, would have benefited from the facilities of the Blackfriars Theatre. By staging plays at Blackfriars and at Court, Shakespeare was also catering to a more educated, wealthy audience than the groundlings in the Pit, suggesting how widely his plays were admired.

Endnotes

1   Ridley, M.R. 'Introduction', *Othello,* Arden, 1958, p.xiv. Ridley flips Bradley's famous judgment about *King Lear* as Shakespeare's 'greatest work but not ... the best of his plays', judging *Othello 'Not* his greatest work but (much) his best *play.'*

2   Bradley, A.C. *Shakespearean Tragedy*, Macmillan, 1904, p.176.

3   Ibid., p.179.

4   Ibid., p.187. Bradley also esteems Iago as Shakespeare's greatest villain and Desdemona as his 'most pathetic' (i.e. most poignant) heroine.

5   Thompson, Ayanna (ed.) 'Introduction', *Othello*, Arden 2017, p. 42.

6   'Inappropriate' marriages included those to domestic abusers, widowers considered too old for their second wives, and husbands not able to control their wives.

7   A pan-European carnival 'disturbance' (abusive language, pot-clashing, horn-blowing, noise and violence) with an appointed ringleader. Shakespeare's audiences would have instantly recognised this important social and cultural context and identified the ringleader as Iago. The wrongdoer was punished with mock serenades, effigy burnings, ritual drownings and even violence.

8   The Devil (or Vice, his representative on Earth) is often a grimly humorous yet supernatural, demon-like character in medieval drama, competing with angels and symbolic Virtues for possession of the human soul.

9   Oxford English Dictionary, www.oed.com.

10 Smith, Emma. *This is Shakespeare*, Penguin Books, 2020, pp.211–16.

11 Giraldi Cinthio, *Gli Hecatommithi,* published in Mondovi, Italy, 1565.

12 Othello was a popular role with audiences and sympathetically played. An elegy written for Shakespeare's own leading actor Richard Burbage in 1619 mentions that when (Burbage) played the 'grievéd Moor, made jealous by a slave' he 'moved the heart' (Furness, H.H. (ed.) *Othello*, New Valorum Edition, 1886). The Andalusian Muslim author Hasan ibn Muhammad al-Wazzan (c 1485–1554) seems to have influenced Othello's backstory. Hasan's popular 'Geographical History of Africa,' translated into English in 1600, became a standard text about the region and may as such have helped shape some of the details of Othello's past experiences in north and west Africa. More directly, Hasan himself, a well born, educated and experienced African man captured by pirates in the Mediterranean and brought to Europe, where he rose into the ranks of the White ruling class, echoes some key elements of Othello's story.

13 It was documented by Edmund Malone, writing in 1660; possibly Desdemona was played by Margaret Hughes – she certainly played her in the same company later.

14 Morality plays, with characters representing Virtues or Vices, were typically staged outside as entertainments with a moral message for the common people. Their high point was the 15th and 16th centuries.

15 'It is necessary to know that Desdemona represents particular human values, love or charity (and forgiveness) in order to avoid making the [mistake] of searching for some tragic flaw in her' (Kernan, Alvin. 'Introduction', *Othello*, Signet Shakespeare, 1963, p.xxxv).

16 By Robert Greene, a 'University Wit' educated at Cambridge (but with a degree from Oxford as well) in *Greene's Groats-Worth of Wit*, published 1592.

17 From *tragos* meaning 'he-goat' and *aeidein* meaning 'to sing'.

18 Comedy dealt with the lower classes.

19   A five-act play is structured as follows: exposition; rising action; crisis point or climax; falling action; denouement/resolution.

20   Leavis, F.R. *The Common Pursuit,* Penguin Books, 1962, pp. 150–151.

21   He means his house is not some remote farm dwelling which the law cannot protect as it can a house in town.

22   Some readers see this vow as specifically Islamic, and as the moment Othello turns (or reverts to) 'Turk'. Either way, the point about cosmic *grandeur* stands.

23   Viktus, Daniel J. 'Turning Turk in Othello: The Conversion and Damnation of the Moor', *Shakespeare Quarterly,* Vol. 48, No. 2 (Summer, 1997), pp.145–176. Also Arthos, John. 'The fall of Othello', *Shakespeare Quarterly,* Vol. 9, No. 2 (Spring, 1958), pp.93–104.

24   Characters in a realist novel (for example, *Pride and Prejudice* or *Jane Eyre)* are just as artificial as the characters in a tragedy (or the puppets in a Punch and Judy show); they are just presented *as if* they are 'real'. They 'think' and speak in prose sentences and often in a closer approximation to 'real time'.

25   Bradley, A.C. *Shakespearean Tragedy*, Macmillan, 1904, p.177.

26   Aristotle says of this objection: 'Tragedy is an imitation not of persons but of *action and life* … It is in our actions that human beings are happy or the reverse, not in a study of our characters.' In other words, in *Othello* we witness human misery as we experience it in life, *in action.* In Act 1 up to line 290, the villain loses and the 'good' characters get a happy ending; the tragic plot had not *yet* unfolded their tragic flaws through misfortune, reversals and recognitions.

27   Oxford English Dictionary, www.oed.com. The Hebrew word satan means adversary, plotter.

28   Kott, Jan. *Shakespeare Our Contemporary*, Methuen, 1965.

29   Demi means 'half'. Othello insists that Iago's malignancy is as much human as supernatural.

30   Kernan, Alvin. 'Introduction', *Othello,* Signet Shakespeare, 1963, p.xxiii.

31   After Coleridge's objection to Othello being 'black', actors began playing him as a Moor or 'Arab' and the colour of the make-up lightened accordingly (to 'bronze').

32   The Civil Rights and Black Power movements campaigned for social justice and racial equality in the United States during the 1950s, 60s and 70s.

33   Quarshie, Hugh. *Second Thoughts about Othello*, Chipping Camden, 1999. When Quarshie finally played Othello for the RSC in 2009, he did so opposite a Black Iago.

34   Carlisle, Carol. *Shakespeare from the Greenroom*, Chapel Hill, 1969.

35   Terry, Ellen. *Four Lectures on Shakespeare*, Benjamin Blom Inc., 1969, p.129.

36   Shakespeare, William. *Complete Works of William Shakespeare*, HarperCollins Publishers, 1994, p.590.

37   Ibid., p.590.

38   Ibid., p.590.

39   Ibid., p.1101.

40   Ibid., p.1101.

Further reading

Bradley, A.C. *Shakespearean Tragedy*, Macmillan and Co., 1904.

Bristol, M.D. 'Charivari and the comedy of abjection in *Othello*', *Renaissance Drama XXI*, 1990.

Calway, Gareth. 'Introduction', *The Tempest (CSEC edition)*, Collins, 2017, pp.7–14.

Coles, Jane. (ed.) *Othello (Cambridge School Shakespeare)*, CUP, 2014.

Day, Roger. *Shakespeare, Aphra Benn and the Canon*, Routledge, 1996.

Kernan, Alvin. (ed.) 'Introduction', *Othello*, Signet, 1963.

Kott, J. *Shakespeare our Contemporary*, Methuen, 1967.

Leavis, F.R. *The Common Pursuit*, Chatto and Windus, 1952.

Margolies, D. *Monsters of the Deep: Social Dissolution in Shakspeare's Tragedies*, Manchester University Press, 1992.

Melville, Alexandra, 'Character analysis: Iago in *Othello*', *Discovering Literature: Shakespeare and Renaissance*, British Library, www.bl.uk/shakespeare/articles/character-analysis-iago-in-othello.

Quarshie, Hugh, 'Playing Othello', *Discovering Literature: Shakespeare and Renaissance*, British Library, www.bl.uk/shakespeare/articles/Playing-Othello.

Ridley, M.R. (ed.) 'Introduction', *Othello*, Arden, 1958.

Thompson, Ayanna. (ed.) 'Introduction, *Othello*, Arden, 2017.
Vaughan, V.M. 'Critical Approaches to Othello', *Discovering Literature: Shakespeare and Renaissance,* British Library, www.bl.uk/shakespeare/articles/Critical-approaches-to-Othello.

Timeline

Very little indeed is known about Shakespeare's private life: the facts included here are almost the only indisputable ones. The dates of Shakespeare's plays are those on which they were first produced.

1558	Queen Elizabeth crowned.	
1564	Christopher Marlowe born.	William Shakespeare born, 23 April, baptised 26 April.
1567	Mary, Queen of Scots, deposed. James VI (later James I of England) crowned King of Scotland.	
1572	Lord Leicester's Company (of players) licensed; later called Lord Strange's, then the Lord Chamberlain's and finally (under James), the King's Men.	
1573	John Donne born.	
1574	The Common Council of London directs that all plays and playhouses in London must be licensed.	
1576	James Burbage builds the first public playhouse, The Theatre, at Shoreditch, outside the walls of the City.	
1577	Francis Drake begins his voyage round the world (completed 1580). *Holinshed's Chronicles of England, Scotland and Ireland* published (which Shakespeare later used extensively).	
1582		Shakespeare married to Anne Hathaway.

1583	The Queen's Company founded by royal warrant.	Shakespeare's daughter, Susanna, born.
1585		Shakespeare's twins, Hamnet and Judith, born.
1587	Mary, Queen of Scots, beheaded. Marlowe's *Tamburlaine (Part I)* first staged.	
1588	Defeat at the Spanish Armada. Marlowe's *Tamburlaine (Part II)* first staged.	
1589	Marlowe's *Jew of Malta* and Kyd's *Spanish Tragedy* (a 'revenge tragedy' and one of the most popular plays of Elizabethan times) produced.	
1590	Spenser's *Faerie Queene* (Books I-III) published.	
1592	Marlowe's *Doctor Faustus* and *Edward II* first staged. Witchcraft trials in Scotland. Robert Greene, a rival playwright, refers to Shakespeare as 'an upstart crow' and 'the only Shake-scene in a country'.	*Titus Andronicus* *Henry VI, Parts I, II* and *III* *Richard III*
1593	London theatres closed by the plague. Christopher Marlowe killed in a Deptford tavern.	*Two Gentlemen of Verona* *The Comedy of Errors* *The Taming of the Shrew* *Love's Labour's Lost*
1594	Shakespeare's company becomes The Lord Chamberlain's Men.	
1595	Raleigh's first expedition to Guiana. Last expedition of Drake and Hawkins (both died).	*Romeo and Juliet* *Richard II* *A Midsummer Night's Dream*
1596	Spenser's *Faerie Queene* (Books IV-VI) published. James Burbage buys rooms at Blackfriars and begins to convert them into a theatre.	*King John* *The Merchant of Venice* Shakespeare's son Hamnet dies. Shakespeare's father is granted a coat of arms.

1597	James Burbage dies. His son, Richard, a famous actor, turns the Blackfriars Theatre into a private playhouse.	*Henry IV (Part I)* Shakespeare buys and redecorates New Place at Stratford.
1598	Death of Philip II of Spain.	*Henry IV (Part II)* *Much Ado About Nothing*
1599	Death of Edmund Spenser. The Globe Theatre completed at Bankside by Richard and Cuthbert Burbage.	*Henry V* *Julius Caesar* *As You Like It*
1600	Fortune Theatre built at Cripplegate. East India Company founded for the extension of English trade and influence in the East. The Children of the Chapel begin to use the hall at Blackfriars.	*Merry Wives of Windsor* *Troilus and Cressida*
1601		*Hamlet*
1602	Sir Thomas Bodley's library opens at Oxford.	*Twelfth Night*
1603	Death of Queen Elizabeth. James I comes to the throne. Shakespeare's company becomes The King's Men. Raleigh tried, condemned and sent to the Tower.	
1604	Treaty of peace with Spain.	*Measure for Measure* *Othello* *All's Well That Ends Well*
1605	The Gunpowder Plot: an attempt by a group of Catholics to blow up the Houses of Parliament.	
1606	Guy Fawkes and other plotters executed.	*Macbeth* *King Lear*
1607	Virginia, in America, colonised.	*Antony and Cleopatra* *Timon of Athens* *Coriolanus* Shakespeare's daughter, Susanna, married to Dr John Hall.

1608	The company of the Children of the Chapel Royal (who had performed at Blackfriars for ten years) is disbanded. John Milton born.	Richard Burbage leases the Blackfriars Theatre to six of his fellow actors, including Shakespeare. *Pericles, Prince of Tyre*
1609		Shakespeare's *Sonnets* published.
1610		*Cymbeline*
1611	Chapman completes his great translation of the *Iliad*, the story of Troy. Authorised Version of the Bible published.	*A Winter's Tale* *The Tempest*
1612	Webster's *The White Devil* first staged.	
1613	Globe Theatre burnt down during a performance of *Henry VIII* (the firing of a small cannon set fire to the thatched roof). Webster's *The Duchess of Malfi* first staged.	*Henry VIII* *Two Noble Kinsman* Shakespeare buys a house at Blackfriars.
1614	Globe Theatre rebuilt in 'far finer manner than before'.	
1616	Ben Jonson publishes his plays in one volume.	Shakespeare's daughter, Judith, marries Thomas Quiney. Death of Shakespeare on his birthday, 23 April.
1623	Publication of the Folio edition of Shakepeare's plays.	Death of Anne Shakespeare (née Hathaway).

OTHELLO

Prefatory note

This Shakespeare play uses the full Alexander text. By keeping in mind the fact that the language has changed considerably in four hundred years, as have customs, jokes, and stage conventions, the editors have aimed at helping the modern reader – whether English is their mother tongue or not – to grasp the full significance of the play. The Notes, intended primarily for examination candidates, are presented in a simple, direct style. The needs of those unfamiliar with British culture have been specially considered.

Since quiet study of the printed word is unlikely to bring fully to life plays that were written directly for the public theatre, attention has been drawn to dramatic effects which are important in performance. The editors see Shakespeare's plays as living works of art which can be enjoyed today on stage, film and television in many parts of the world.

LIST OF CHARACTERS

Duke Of Venice	a Senator, father to Desdemona
Brabantio	
Other Senators	
Gratiano	brother to Brabantio, two noble Venetians
Lodovico	kinsman to Brabantio
Othello	the Moor, in the service of Venice
Cassio	his honourable Lieutenant
Iago	his Ancient, a villain
Roderigo	a gull'd Venetian gentleman
Montano	Governor of Cyprus, before Othello
Clown servant to Othello	
Desdemona	daughter to Brabantio, and wife to Othello
Emilia	wife to Iago
Bianca	a courtezan, in love with Cassio

Gentlemen of Cyprus, Sailors, Officers, a Messenger, Musicians, a Herald, and Attendants etc.

The Scene: Venice; Cyprus.

ACT 1 SCENE 1

The play begins with a middle-ranking soldier (Iago) and a showy Venetian gentleman (Roderigo) arguing. Roderigo complains that Iago has loyally served a shared unnamed enemy ('him' – line 7) who has overlooked Iago for a military promotion to lieutenant, despite Iago's seniority. This unnamed man is also Roderigo's successful rival for a fine lady (Desdemona), whom he has now married. Iago's male pride is comically offended by Roderigo's suggestion that he lacks self-interest; he retorts that he's planning revenge while pretending to be loyal to 'the Moor' (line 40). Iago then leads a riotous protest against the marriage, which provokes the bride's father (Brabantio) to lodge an official complaint to the authorities about his daughter's disobedient marriage to a Black man.

1. *Tush* an exclamation of impatient contempt. The two men are having a violent argument.

4. *'Sblood* a blasphemous oath ('God's blood'). Iago's social status and failure to be promoted clearly infuriate him; he might almost spit the 'you' in line 4 (see note on line 7).

6. *Abhor me* hate me, i.e. *if* you can't trust me. Iago means that Roderigo should listen to learn why he, Roderigo, *can* trust Iago (the irony being that Iago is completely untrustworthy).

7. *Thou* you; like '*tu*' in French, less socially respectful in Shakespeare's time than 'you'.

13. *bombast circumstance* fancy explanations.

16. *certes* a fancy way of saying 'certainly'. Iago is mocking Othello's pretensions by using pompous language here (see also *Forsooth*, line 19).

19–20. *a great arithmetician … Cassio, a Florentine* Iago dismisses Cassio as having no experience (of war) despite his learning.

20. *damn'd in a fair wife* Iago is sneering at Cassio's associations with women (see also *spinster*, line 24) as a contrast to the male-only army world. In fact, Shakespeare changed his source, Cinthio, to make Cassio single, which is important to the plot later.

25. *toged* the robe of a senator, another sneering swipe at those who appointed Cassio, i.e. politicians without Iago's experience of war.

ACT 1
SCENE 1

Venice. A street.

[Enter RODERIGO *and* IAGO.*]*

Roderigo
    Tush, never tell me; I take it much unkindly
    That you, Iago, who has had my purse
    As if the strings were thine, shouldst know of this.

Iago
    'Sblood, but you will not hear me.
    If ever I did dream of such a matter,   5
    Abhor me.

Roderigo
    Thou told'st me thou didst hold him in thy hate.

Iago
    Despise me if I do not. Three great ones of the city,
    In personal suit to make me his lieutenant,
    Off-capp'd to him; and, by the faith of man,   10
    I know my price, I am worth no worse a place.
    But he, as loving his own pride and purposes,
    Evades them with a bombast circumstance
    Horribly stuff'd with epithets of war;
    And, in conclusion,   15
    Nonsuits my mediators; 'For, certes,' says he
    'I have already chose my officer'.
    And what was he?
    Forsooth, a great arithmetician,
    One Michael Cassio, a Florentine,   20
    A fellow almost damn'd in a fair wife,
    That never set a squadron in the field,
    Nor the division of a battle knows
    More than a spinster; unless the bookish theoric,
    Wherein the toged consuls can propose   25

26. *prattle* idle talk.

27–9. *had the election … on other grounds* Cassio was chosen, not the proven warrior Iago, veteran of battlefields in Rhodes, Cyprus, etc.

30. *be-lee'd* (of a sailing ship) the wind literally taken out of its sails by being obstructed by ('under the lee' of) an enemy ship.

31. *debitor and creditor … counter-caster* devices for counting, or the (non-action) man who calculates on such a device; variations on the 'arithmetician' insult of line 19.

33. *his Moorship's* more sneering at Othello's pretensions, a put-down combining 'His Lordship' (or 'His Worship') with 'Moor'. In Shakespeare's time 'Moor' had a number of different meanings: a Muslim person, someone from Africa, and an atheist, among others. Shakespeare's text repeatedly emphasises this (see, for example, line Act 1, Scene 1, line 89: *an old black ram*; Act 1, Scene 2, line 71: *sooty bosom*; Act 3, Scene 3, lines 390–391 *black/ As mine own face*).

33. *ancient* standard bearer; today a sort of regimental sergeant, the given rank Iago feels is beneath him, especially combined with the sneering *his Moorship's*.

36–7. *Preferment goes by letter … old gradation* promotion is decided by favouritism and recommendations from powerful men, not by seniority.

45–6. *knee-crooking … obsequious bondage* grovelling and fawning behaviour intended to gain the approval of someone important.

48. *nought but provender* just enough to live on.
48. *cashier'd* forcibly retired.

50–4. *trimm'd in forms and visages … Do themselves homage* pretend to serve their masters while in fact looking after their own interests. Iago admires such self-servers and scorns those truly loyal; Shakespeare's play invites us to consider whether Iago is against his society's declared values in this, or representative of how its individuals truly feel and act.

As masterly as he – mere prattle, without practice,
Is all his soldiership. But he, sir, had the election;
And I, of whom his eyes had seen the proof
At Rhodes, at Cyprus, and on other grounds,
Christian and heathen, must be be-lee'd and calm'd   30
By debitor and creditor – this counter-caster,
He, in good time, must his lieutenant be,
And I, God bless the mark! his Moorship's ancient.

Roderigo

By heaven, I rather would have been his hangman!

Iago

Why, there's no remedy; 'tis the curse of service: 35
Preferment goes by letter and affection,
Not by the old gradation, where each second
Stood heir to the first. Now, sir, be judge yourself
Whether I in any just term am affin'd
To love the Moor.

Roderigo

                I would not follow him, then.   40

Iago

O, sir, content you.
I follow him to serve my turn upon him:
We cannot all be masters, nor all masters
Cannot be truly follow'd. You shall mark
Many a duteous and knee-crooking knave   45
That, doting on his own obsequious bondage,
Wears out his time, much like his master's ass,
For nought but provender; and when he's old,
   cashier'd.
Whip me such honest knaves. Others there are
Who, trimm'd in forms and visages of duty,   50
Keep yet their hearts attending on themselves;
And, throwing but shows of service on their lords,
Do well thrive by 'em and, when they have lin'd
   their coats,
Do themselves homage – these fellows have some
   soul;

61. *for my peculiar end* for my own private purpose.

64. *compliment extern* outward (external) show.

66. *daws* jackdaws. The jackdaw is a bird in the crow family and a symbol of foolishness.

67. *thick-lips* a viciously hostile and racist 'naming' of Othello, whose actual name does not appear until Act 1, Scene 3, line 48 (*Valiant Othello*).

76. *timorous* frightening.

[BRABANTIO appears above at a window] This stage direction suggests the use of a small upper stage above and behind the main platform stage, representing the upper storey of an Elizabethan house.

And such a one do I profess myself.   55
For, sir,
It is as sure as you are Roderigo,
Were I the Moor, I would not be Iago.
In following him I follow but myself –
Heaven is my judge, not I for love and duty,   60
But seeming so for my peculiar end.
For when my outward action doth demonstrate
The native act and figure of my heart
In compliment extern, 'tis not long after
But I will wear my heart upon my sleeve   65
For daws to peck at: I am not what I am.

Roderigo
What a full fortune does the thick-lips owe,
If he can carry't thus!

Iago
                        Call up her father.
Rouse him, make after him, poison his delight,
Proclaim him in the streets; incense her kinsmen,   70
And, though he in a fertile climate dwell,
Plague him with flies; though that his joy be joy,
Yet throw such changes of vexation on't
As it may lose some colour.

Roderigo
Here is her father's house. I'll call aloud.   75

Iago
Do, with like timorous accent and dire yell
As when, by night and negligence, the fire
Is spied in populous cities.

Roderigo
What, ho, Brabantio! Signior Brabantio, ho!

Iago
Awake! What, ho, Brabantio! Thieves, thieves,   80
    thieves!
Look to your house, your daughter, and your bags.
Thieves! thieves!

[BRABANTIO appears above at a window.]

7

87. *Zounds* Christ's wounds (a swearing exclamation).

89. *black* See note on line 33.

89–90. *an old black ram ... your white ewe* Rams were an emblem of lechery, 'tupping' is Iago's typically reductive word for the consummation of a marriage, and 'black ram' is a racist slur on Othello's ethnicity. This is the first reference to the age difference between Othello and Desdemona and suggests the comedy tradition where an unfaithful young wife makes a fool of her old husband (see the Introduction, p.iv); Iago will make a tragedy out of this suggestion. The contrast between the 'white ewe' and the 'old black ram' is designed for maximum upset of the father, painting his daughter as a pure, innocent victim (see also lines 111–114).

91. *snorting citizens* sleeping (snoring) residents of the city.

92. *grandsire* grandfather; i.e. the devil (insultingly meaning Othello) will bear children on his daughter.

97. *charg'd* ordered.

100. *distempering draughts* unsettling drinks (alcohol).

101. *malicious bravery* disorderly, alcohol-fuelled behaviour.

102. *start* disturb, disrupt.

Brabantio

    What is the reason of this terrible summons?

    What is the matter there?

Roderigo

    Signior, is all your family within?   85

Iago

    Are your doors lock'd?

Brabantio

                   Why, wherefore ask you this?

Iago

    Zounds, sir, you're robb'd; for shame, put on your

        gown;

    Your heart is burst; you have lost half your soul.

    Even now, now, very now, an old black ram

    Is tupping your white ewe. Arise, arise;   90

    Awake the snorting citizens with the bell,

    Or else the devil will make a grandsire of you.

    Arise, I say.

Brabantio

              What, have you lost your wits?

Roderigo

    Most reverend signior, do you know my voice?

Brabantio

    Not I; what are you?   95

Roderigo

    My name is Roderigo.

Brabantio

                The worser welcome!

    I have charg'd thee not to haunt about my doors;

    In honest plainness thou hast heard me say

    My daughter is not for thee; and now, in madness,

    Being full of supper and distempering draughts,   100

    Upon malicious bravery dost thou come

    To start my quiet.

Roderigo

    Sir, sir, sir –

104–5. *My spirit and my place … bitter to thee* I am a senator so have the power to punish you.

107. *grange* an isolated house in the country (therefore vulnerable to burglaries).

112–14. *cover'd with a Barbary horse … gennets for germans* a continuation of the spiteful mocking of Othello's heritage and the stoking of Brabantio's racist fears. This sequence presents his daughter's marriage as a mating between beasts and suggests that the offspring of the union will be animals ('Barbary' refers to the north (Berber–Arab) coast of Africa; *coursers* are racehorses; *gennets* are Spanish horses; 'germans' here means offspring).
115. *profane* foul-speaking.

117. *the beast with two backs* a derogatory term for sexual intercourse, from the French *faisoient la bese a deux doz* (a term used by the French writer Rabelais, whom Shakespeare knew); its use here reflects Iago's typically offensive and reductive view of sexual love.
118. *Thou art a villain / You are – a Senator* Iago manages to make the traditionally respectful 'You' and 'Senator' mirror Brabantio's insulting 'Thou' and 'villain.' Iago has been put in his inferior social place and responds, as always, by combining an *appearance* of respect for social rank with an envy and inner contempt for it. (Even calling a social *equal* a 'villain' would lead to a duel, so Iago could be toying with his superior's expectations here. There might be a dramatic pause before he says 'Senator'.)

Brabantio

              But thou must needs be sure
My spirit and my place have in their power
To make this bitter to thee.

Roderigo

                      Patience, good sir.   105

Brabantio

What tell'st thou me of robbing? This is Venice;
My house is not a grange.

Roderigo

                  Most grave Brabantio,
In simple and pure soul I come to you.

Iago

Zounds, sir, you are one of those that will not serve
God if the devil bid you. Because we come to do you 110
service, and you think we are ruffians, you'll have your
daughter cover'd with a Barbary horse; you'll have your
nephews neigh to you; you'll have coursers for cousins
and gennets for germans.

Brabantio

What profane wretch art thou?   115

Iago

I am one, sir, that comes to tell you your daughter and
the Moor are now making the beast with two backs.

Brabantio

Thou art a villain.

Iago

               You are – a Senator.

Brabantio

This thou shalt answer; I know thee, Roderigo.

Roderigo

Sir, I will answer anything. But I beseech you,   120
If't be your pleasure and most wise consent –
As partly I find it is – that your fair daughter,
At this odd-even and dull watch o' th' night,
Transported with no worse nor better guard

125. *knave of common hire* a male servant.

125. *gondolier* one who propels a gondola (a boat with high-pointed ends, a kind of water-taxi) on the canals of Venice. Roderigo is snobbishly playing on Brabantio's fears about the 'low' nightlife his lady-daughter is encountering through her association with Othello.

126. *gross clasps of a lascivious Moor* Roderigo picks up and reinforces Iago's racist fear-mongering here by linking Othello's ethnicity to sexual threat. He has a willing audience in Brabantio, who is racist and angry at his daughter's lack of obedience and so ready to fear the worst. Roderigo, as Othello's love rival for Desdemona, is a ready puppet for Iago – but this is an early indication of Iago's ability to put his ideas into other people's heads and mouths. Later he will almost write the speeches and direct the actions of characters less easy to persuade than Roderigo and Brabantio, notably Othello himself.

128. *bold and saucy wrongs* insolent (insulting and disrespectful) invasions of Brabantio's privacy.

136. *an extravagant and wheeling stranger* a vagrant wanderer from outside Venice; a soldier of fortune. Roderigo's words are meant as yet another xenophobic insult, but this provides the first hint of something exciting and gloriously free-wheeling about Othello as a world-straddling hero. Tragedy requires a noble protagonist, and nothing remotely noble has been revealed about Othello through his enemies' descriptions until now.

141. *Strike on the tinder* striking a spark onto tinder (a dry substance that catches fire easily) to provide torch-light.

148. *check* constraint

152. *fathom* ability, worth, grasp, depth. The depth of the sea is measured in fathoms, but the word is also used for measuring or understanding profound matters or people; Othello is frequently identified in the text with the sea and as a titanic natural force.

But with a knave of common hire, a gondolier,   125
To the gross clasps of a lascivious Moor –
If this be known to you, and your allowance,
We then have done you bold and saucy wrongs;
But if you know not this, my manners tell me
We have your wrong rebuke. Do not believe   130
That, from the sense of all civility,
I thus would play and trifle with your reverence.
Your daughter, if you have not given her leave,
I say again, hath made a gross revolt;
Tying her duty, beauty, wit, and fortunes,   135
In an extravagant and wheeling stranger
Of here and everywhere. Straight satisfy yourself.
If she be in her chamber or your house,
Let loose on me the justice of the state
For thus deluding you.   140

Brabantio

Strike on the tinder, ho! Give me a taper; call up all
    my people.
This accident is not unlike my dream.
Belief of it oppresses me already.
Light, I say; light!

               [Exit from above.]

Iago

              Farewell; for I must leave you.
It seems not meet nor wholesome to my place   145
To be producted – as if I stay I shall –
Against the Moor; for I do know the state,
However this may gall him with some check,
Cannot with safety cast him; for he's embark'd
With such loud reason to the Cyprus wars,   150
Which even now stands in act, that, for their souls,
Another of his fathom they have none
To lead their business; in which regard,
Though I do hate him as I do hell pains,
Yet, for necessity of present life,   155

158. *Sagittary* an inn or house with the sign of Sagittarius, the centaur. A centaur is a divided (half-man, half-horse) creature, so this hints at the split personalities of Othello and Iago, as well as humanity's internal struggle between its physical (animal) instincts versus rational (human) nature (see also line 112, *cover'd with a Barbary horse*).

166. *moe tapers* more candles.

171. *charms* wicked spells, love potions.
172. *property* true nature.
172. *maidhood* female youth (by implication, tender and vulnerable).

177. *apprehend* discover or find (the implication being they will be discovered doing something wrong).

I must show out a flag and sign of love,
Which is indeed but sign. That you shall surely find
   him,
Lead to the Sagittary the raised search;
And there will I be with him. So, farewell.

[Exit.]

[Enter below, BRABANTIO, in his night gown, and
Servants with torches.]

Brabantio
It is too true an evil. Gone she is;   160
And what's to come of my despised time
Is nought but bitterness. Now, Roderigo,
Where didst thou see her? – O unhappy girl! –
With the Moor, say'st thou? – Who would be a
   father? –
How didst thou know 'twas she? – O, thou deceivest
   me   165
Past thought! – What said she to you? – Get moe
   tapers;
Raise all my kindred. – Are they married think you?
Roderigo
Truly, I think they are.
Brabantio
O heaven! How got she out? O treason of the blood!
Fathers, from hence trust not your daughters' minds 170
By what you see them act. Is there not charms
By which the property of youth and maidhood
May be abus'd? Have you not read, Roderigo,
Of some such thing?
Roderigo
                Yes, sir, I have indeed.
Brabantio
Call up my brother. – O that you had had her! –   175
Some one way, some another. – Do you know
Where we may apprehend her and the Moor?

183. *deserve your pains* be worthy of and reward your efforts.

Roderigo

    I think I can discover him, if you please
    To get good guard, and go along with me.

Brabantio

    Pray lead me on. At every house I'll call;   180
    I may command at most. – Get weapons, ho!
    And raise some special officers of night. –
    On, good Roderigo; I'll deserve your pains.

[Exeunt]

SCENE 2

Othello's majestic entry dramatically reverses the unflattering impressions the audience has received from his enemies' descriptions in Scene 1. Unnamed and mis-described for the play's first 183 lines, we now see him for ourselves. (By contrast, in Shakespeare's tragedies – *King Lear*, *Macbeth* and *Hamlet* – the play's protagonist is named and reliably described by the end of the first scene.) Iago, posing as Othello's faithful servant, tries to stir up Othello's fear and anger towards his new father-in-law, but Othello is calm and secure in his marriage, noble rank and record of service to Venice. Cassio reports that war with the Turks is imminent and that the Senate has summoned Othello for his help. Iago tells Cassio of Othello's marriage, perhaps hoping to upset him. Brabantio attacks Othello with insults and physical threats and believes the Senate will support his racist and paranoid case against Othello.

2. *stuff* essence.
3. *contriv'd* premeditated; planned beforehand.
3–4. *I lack iniquity ... me service* Iago is shamelessly pretending to be too noble to kill (outside of war), even though he says he longs to serve Othello by doing so. As always, Iago delights in deceiving people and maligning them behind their backs (see also Act 1, Scene 1, line 66: *I am not what I am*).
5. *yerk'd* stabbed.

12. *magnifico* nobleman (Brabantio).
13–14. *a voice potential ... as the Duke's* Iago enjoys stirring up Othello's potential fear of Brabantio's influence, which is supposedly much greater than the Duke's. He fails to disturb Othello here, but will keep trying.

18. *signiory* the governors, the rulers of Venice.

21. *promulgate* make public.
22. *siege* rank.
22. *demerits* both merits and deficiencies.
23–4. *May speak unbonneted ... have reach'd* I am the equal of the family I have married into.

26–8. *I would not my unhoused free condition ... seas' worth* Only love of Desdemona could make Othello give up his sea-like independence and freedom.

SCENE 2

Venice. Another street.

[Enter OTHELLO, IAGO, and Attendants with torches.]

Iago

    Though in the trade of war I have slain men,
    Yet do I hold it very stuff o' th' conscience
    To do no contriv'd murder. I lack iniquity
    Sometime to do me service. Nine or ten times
    I had thought to have yerk'd him here under the ribs.   5

Othello

    'Tis better as it is.

Iago

              Nay, but he prated,
    And spoke such scurvy and provoking terms
    Against your honour
    That, with the little godliness I have,
    I did full hard forbear him. But I pray, sir,   10
    Are you fast married? For be assur'd of this,
    That the magnifico is much beloved,
    And hath in his effect a voice potential
    As double as the Duke's. He will divorce you,
    Or put upon you what restraint and grievance   15
    That law, with all his might to enforce it on,
    Will give him cable.

Othello

              Let him do his spite.
    My services which I have done the signiory
    Shall out-tongue his complaints. 'Tis yet to know –
    Which, when I know that boasting is an honour,   20
    I shall promulgate – I fetch my life and being
    From men of royal siege; and my demerits
    May speak unbonneted to as proud a fortune
    As this that I have reach'd. For know, Iago,
    But that I love the gentle Desdemona,   25
    I would not my unhoused free condition

27. *circumscription and confine* limitation and restriction.

31. *perfect soul* clear conscience.

33. *Janus* a two-faced Roman god, who looks both to the future and the past and represents duality. It is apt that the duplicitous Iago, who presents one 'face' to the world and hides his true intentions, swears by such a god.

38. *haste-post-haste* immediate.

41. *galleys* sailing ships used in warfare.
42. *sequent* successive, in sequence.

47. *several* separate.

Put into circumscription and confine
For the seas' worth.

[Enter CASSIO and Officers with torches.]

But look what lights come yonder.

Iago

Those are the raised father and his friends.
You were best go in.

Othello

Not I; I must be found.   30
My parts, my title, and my perfect soul
Shall manifest me rightly. Is it they?

Iago

By Janus, I think no.

Othello

The servants of the Duke and my lieutenant –
The goodness of the night upon you, friends!   35
What is the news?

Cassio

The Duke does greet you, General;
And he requires your haste-post-haste appearance
Even on the instant.

Othello

What is the matter, think you?

Cassio

Something from Cyprus, as I may divine.   40
It is a business of some heat: the galleys
Have sent a dozen sequent messengers
This very night at one another's heels;
And many of the consuls, rais'd and met,
Are at the Duke's already. You have been hotly call'd
    for;   45
When, being not at your lodging to be found,
The Senate hath sent about three several quests
To search you out.

Othello

'Tis well I am found by you.

50. *Ancient* Iago's rank (meaning Sergeant) is lower than Cassio's, who is also the 'Florentine' (Act 1, Scene 1, line 20) promoted to Lieutenant above him. For Iago this must be a prickly moment and a source of irritation.

51. *boarded a land carrack* to take a treasure ship like a pirate; the unpleasant suggestion here is that Othello's marriage is invasive and Desdemona is not a lawful 'prize' for him. The phrase also introduces Iago's misogynistic and relentlessly repeated view of marriage and women: wives are objects to be seized and controlled rather than honoured through marriage and loved.

54. *Marry* 'by Mary' – an oath to cover Iago's almost overheard malicious reference to Othello. This marks a key dramatic moment: if Othello had heard Iago's words before entering the tragedy might never have followed!

I will but spend a word here in the house,
And go with you. *[Exit.]*

Cassio
                    Ancient, what makes he here?   50

Iago
Faith, he to-night hath boarded a land carrack.
If it prove lawful prize, he's made for ever.

Cassio
I do not understand.

Iago
                    He's married.

Cassio
                                        To who?

[Re-enter OTHELLO.]

Iago
Marry, to – Come, Captain, will you go?

Othello
                                    Have with you.

*[Enter BRABANTIO, RODERIGO, and Officers with torches
and weapons.]*

Cassio
Here comes another troop to seek for you.   55

Iago
It is Brabantio. General, be advis'd;
He comes to bad intent.

Othello
                            Holla! stand there.

Roderigo
Signior, it is the Moor.

Brabantio
                                Down with him, thief.

[They draw on both sides.]

Iago
You, Roderigo; come, sir, I am for you.

60. *Keep up your bright swords ... rust them* Othello is impressively calm and strong, defusing this potential violence with a soldier's authority. The reference to 'bright swords' suggests their lack of use and perhaps warningly hints that they are little used to combat, unlike him.

63. *stow'd* stored or hidden away, as on a ship, but with the sense of stolen goods and the suggestion that Othello (*foul thief*) is a kind of pirate. The Barbary coast of Africa, with which 'the Moor' Othello is partly associated, was infamous for its pirates (see the Introduction, p.vii).

64. *thou* a disrespectful address, see line 78 below.

65. *I'll refer me to all things of sense* I'll present a sensible argument.

69. *curled darlings* fashionable (and rich) young gentlemen of Venice, often noblemen. Such dressy men wore artificial curls. Note the unconscious contrast with the 'valiant' Othello, a mighty warrior: there is nothing artificial or posing about Othello's manhood.

70. *general mock* public shame.

71. *guardage* (the first recorded use of this word) guardianship

71. *sooty bosom* (See note for Act 1, Scene 1, line 33.)

73. *gross in sense* obvious.

74. *practis'd on her with foul charms* used sinister tricks and spells, i.e. black magic.

75. *Abus'd her delicate youth* corrupted an innocent girl. Brabantio's accusation is that Othello has groomed (trained) Desdemona to be his sexual prey (see also line 79).

76. *motion* reason.

78. *attach* arrest.

78. *thee* a form of 'you' used here as to a social inferior, even though Othello has made clear to us (see lines 23–4) and presumably to Brabantio, during their friendship, his social equality (as a noble) – so this is an insulting pronoun ('thee' was also used to family members and friends but Brabantio is denying both here).

79. *abuser of the world* corrupter of Venetian society generally (repeating the abuse idea introduced in line 75).

80. *arts inhibited and out of warrant* forbidden and illegal actions, i.e. black magic.

Othello

    Keep up your bright swords, for the dew will rust
      them.   60
    Good signior, you shall more command with years
    Than with your weapons.

Brabantio

    O thou foul thief, where hast thou stow'd my
      daughter?
    Damn'd as thou art, thou hast enchanted her;
    For I'll refer me to all things of sense,   65
    If she in chains of magic were not bound,
    Whether a maid so tender, fair, and happy,
    So opposite to marriage that she shunn'd
    The wealthy curled darlings of our nation,
    Would ever have, to incur a general mock,   70
    Run from her guardage to the sooty bosom
    Of such a thing as thou – to fear, not to delight.
    Judge me the world, if 'tis not gross in sense
    That thou hast practis'd on her with foul charms,
    Abus'd her delicate youth with drugs or minerals   75
    That weakens motion. I'll have't disputed on;
    'Tis probable, and palpable to thinking.
    I therefore apprehend and do attach thee
    For an abuser of the world, a practiser
    Of arts inhibited and out of warrant.   80
    Lay hold upon him. If he do resist,
    Subdue him at his peril.

Othello

                    Hold your hands,
    Both you of my inclining and the rest.
    Were it my cue to fight, I should have known it
    Without a prompter. Where will you that I go   85
    To answer this your charge?

Brabantio

                    To prison; till fit time
    Of law and course of direct session
    Call thee to answer.

91. *present* urgent, immediate.

97. *brothers of the state* the other senators.

99–100. *For if such actions ... our statesmen be* Othello was once a slave, as we learn in the next scene (Act 1, Scene 3, line 138) and Brabantio's 'pagans' also suggests he was not or is not a Christian. The fear of social disorder, the chaotic reversal of norms, is a regular theme in Shakespeare's works (and a debated concern of Tudor times generally) reflecting the uncertainty and extreme social mobility of the age. Brabantio is giving alarmed expression to the conservative side of that debate: that adventurers and 'new men' of merit such as Othello threaten the established social order. The rhymed placing of this couplet at the scene's end gives it the added power of a slogan or a proverb.

Othello
                    What if I do obey?
How may the Duke be therewith satisfied,
Whose messengers are here about my side,   90
Upon some present business of the state,
To bring me to him.

Officer
                    'Tis true, most worthy signior;
The Duke's in council, and your noble self,
I am sure, is sent for.

Brabantio
                    How! The Duke in council!
In this time of the night! Bring him away.   95
Mine's not an idle cause. The Duke himself,
Or any of my brothers of the state,
Cannot but feel this wrong as 'twere their own;
For if such actions may have passage free,
Bond-slaves and pagans shall our statesmen be.   100

[Exeunt.]

SCENE 3

The Duke and Senators of Venice are debating rumours of a Turkish attack on their colony Cyprus and decide to act on these, rather than a pretended attack on Rhodes. They are interrupted by Brabantio's formal accusation of Othello as a seducer of his daughter. Othello sends Iago to fetch Desdemona to give her side of the story and, while they wait, gives a thrilling account of his life and adventures, including Desdemona, who dramatically arrives as he is describing her. Her father asks her to whom she owes duty and is told politely that she now owes it to her husband. Brabantio is broken by this. The Duke appoints Othello commander of Cyprus and it is agreed that Desdemona go there with him, Othello assuring the Senate this will not distract him from his duties as defender of the colony. 'Honest' Iago, appointed by Othello to look after Desdemona, reassures Roderigo that he will still get his chance to sleep with Desdemona when Othello tires of her and that he has a cunning plan to ruin their marriage and get revenge on Cassio (by making Othello believe he and Desdemona are lovers).

1. *composition* agreement.
2. *gives them credit* makes the account believable.
2. *disproportion'd* contradictory.
5. *jump* agree.
5. *just* exact.

9–12. *to judgment ... fearful sense* all things considered, just because the numbers disagree, I don't doubt the main point and fear it: the Turkish fleet is out to attack us.

SCENE 3

Venice. A council-chamber.

*[Enter DUKE and Senators, set at a table with lights; and
Attendants.]*

Duke
There is no composition in these news
That gives them credit.

1 Senator
                              Indeed, they are disproportion'd;
My letters say a hundred and seven galleys.

Duke
And mine a hundred and forty.

2 Senator
                              And mine two hundred.
But though they jump not on a just account –   5
As in these cases, where the aim reports,
'Tis oft with difference – yet do they all confirm
A Turkish fleet, and bearing up to Cyprus.

Duke
Nay, it is possible enough to judgment.
I do not so secure me in the error   10
But the main article I do approve
In fearful sense.

Sailor
[Within]   What, ho! what, ho! what, ho!

[Enter Sailor.]

Officer
A messenger from the galleys.

Duke
                              Now, what's the business?

Sailor
The Turkish preparation makes for Rhodes;
So was I bid report here to the state   15
By Signior Angelo.

18. *assay of reason* rational test, exercise of reasoning.
18. *a pageant* a pretence, trick, bluff.
19. *false gaze* looking in the wrong direction.

23. *more facile question bear it* make it (seem) a soft target.
24. *warlike brace* ready to defend itself.

30. *wake* be active.
30. *wage* risk.

33. *Ottomites* (Ottoman Empire) Turks.

35. *injointed* added to, reinforced.
35. *after* follow-up.

37. *restem* revert to.

40. *servitor* servant.
41. *free duty* limitless respect.
41. *recommends* informs.

Duke

    How say you by this change?

1 Senator

                    This cannot be,

    By no assay of reason. 'Tis a pageant

    To keep us in false gaze. When we consider

    The importancy of Cyprus to the Turk,   20

    And let ourselves again but understand

    That as it more concerns the Turk than Rhodes,

    So may he with more facile question bear it,

    For that it stands not in such warlike brace,

    But altogether lacks th' abilities   25

    That Rhodes is dress'd in – if we make thought of
        this,

    We must not think the Turk is so unskilful

    To leave that latest which concerns him first,

    Neglecting an attempt of ease and gain

    To wake and wage a danger profitless.   30

Duke

    Nay, in all confidence, he's not for Rhodes.

Officer

    Here is more news.

              [Enter a Messenger.]

Messenger

    The Ottomites, reverend and gracious,

    Steering with due course toward the isle of Rhodes,

    Have there injointed them with an after fleet.   35

1 Senator

    Ay, so I thought. How many, as you guess?

Messenger

    Of thirty sail; and now they do restem

    Their backward course, bearing with frank
        appearance

    Their purposes toward Cyprus. Signior Montano,

    Your trusty and most valiant servitor,   40

    With his free duty recommends you thus,

46. *post-post-haste dispatch* immediate sending. This was often written on letters to indicate their urgency (a variant of Act 1, Scene 2, line 38).

47–8. *valiant Moor ... Valiant Othello* Othello is identified honourably and named (at last, i.e. in the third scene of the play).

48. *straight* at once.
49. *general* universal. Note the contrast between Othello and Brabantio who, absorbed in private matters, has abdicated his public duty that evening. Othello, though just married, is ready to serve the public cause.

57. *engluts* eats.

And prays you to believe him.

Duke

'Tis certain, then, for Cyprus.
Marcus Lucchese, is not he in town?

1 Senator

He's now in Florence. 45

Duke

Write from us: wish him post-post-haste dispatch.

[*Enter* BRABANTIO, OTHELLO, IAGO, RODERIGO, *and Officers.*]

1 Senator

Here comes Brabantio and the valiant Moor.

Duke

Valiant Othello, we must straight employ you
Against the general enemy Ottoman.
[*To* BRABANTIO] I did not see you; welcome, gentle
     signior; 50
We lack'd your counsel and your help to-night.

Brabantio

So did I yours. Good your Grace, pardon me:
Neither my place, nor aught I heard of business,
Hath rais'd me from my bed; nor doth the general
     care
Take hold on me; for my particular grief 55
Is of so flood-gate and o'erbearing nature
That it engluts and swallows other sorrows,
And it is still itself.

Duke

                    Why, what's the matter?

Brabantio

My daughter! O, my daughter!

All

                              Dead?

Brabantio

                                   Ay, to me.
She is abus'd, stol'n from me, and corrupted, 60

33

61. *mountebanks* crooks, dishonest dealers.

64. *Sans* without (a French word with an English pronunciation).

66. *beguil'd your daughter of herself* groomed, deprived her of her own mind and self-possession.

69. *our* the royal 'we' of a Head of State.
69. *proper son* i.e. my own son.

77. *approv'd* tried and tested.
78. *ta'en* taken.
80–1. *The very head … this extent, no more* My only offence is (with a visual reference to his skin tone and facial features) to be Black – Othello is acknowledging the racial slur against him.
81–2. *Rude am I in my speech, And little blest with the soft phrase of peace* I am a plain-speaking soldier, more used to military language (commands, simple objectives, rules) and the language of war (interrogation, demands, negotiations) than the polite artful conversations used in civilian life. This is true up to a point: Othello is not a society gentleman/courtier like Cassio (or Cassio's parody, Roderigo); he is more like his fellow-soldier Iago in this. However, 'Honest' Iago hides a scheming deviousness beneath a similar blunt soldier's claim to be 'plain-speaking' and it may be asked whether Othello isn't hiding his own gift for romantic storytelling under a guise of 'plainness' here too.
83. *pith* strength.
84. *nine moons wasted* nine months gone.
85. *dearest* most important.
85. *tented field* a romantic description of a battlefield and of warriors gathered in their tents before battle.
87. *feats of broil and battle* heroic acts on the battlefield. In Shakespeare's time 'broil' combined the sense of furious fighting (the word's earliest meaning) with great heat (its modern meaning). Note the joy and energy in this description of fighting, conveyed in the punchy phrase/sounds, uplifting rhythm and the alliteration.

By spells and medicines bought of mountebanks;
For nature so preposterously to err,
Being not deficient, blind, or lame of sense,
Sans witchcraft could not.

Duke

Whoe'er he be that in this foul proceeding   65
Hath thus beguil'd your daughter of herself,
And you of her, the bloody book of law
You shall yourself read in the bitter letter
After your own sense; yea, though our proper son
Stood in your action.

Brabantio

              Humbly I thank your Grace.   70
Here is the man – this Moor whom now, it seems,
Your special mandate for the state affairs
Hath hither brought.

All

              We are very sorry for't.

Duke

[To OTHELLO*]* What, in your own part, can you say
    to this?

Brabantio

Nothing, but this is so.   75

Othello

Most potent, grave, and reverend signiors,
My very noble and approv'd good masters:
That I have ta'en away this old man's daughter,
It is most true; true, I have married her –
The very head and front of my offending   80
Hath this extent, no more. Rude am I in my speech,
And little blest with the soft phrase of peace;
For since these arms of mine had seven years' pith,
Till now some nine moons wasted, they have us'd
Their dearest action in the tented field;   85
And little of this great world can I speak
More than pertains to feats of broil and battle;
And therefore little shall I grace my cause

90. *round unvarnish'd* blunt and straightforward.

92. *conjuration* conjuring, spells.

95–6. *her motion/ Blush'd at herself* so shy she blushed at her own emotions. (Yet how well does Brabantio know his own daughter?)

104. *mixtures powerful o'er the blood* (wicked) love potions.
105. *dram* a small liquid measure used in medicines and spirits – or here, poison.

108. *habits* clothes (as disguise).
108–9. *thin habits ... modern seeming* The Duke is suggesting that Brabantio is indulging popular prejudices based on outward appearances rather than legally proving a case. A modern judge or lawyer might make the same point about assumptions of guilt based on race. By contrast, the play will explore what depths of villainy the *White* Venetian Iago hides behind his respectable appearance.

115–16. *Send for the lady ... before her father.* Note how calmly Othello responds to Brabantio's vicious accusations and the respect he affords Desdemona by allowing her to speak for herself. This shows a profound security and even a majesty of character that will lend a tragic stature to Othello's flaws as they unfold through the action: without his original 'greatness' his flaws would earn our scorn rather than our pity and terror.

In speaking for myself. Yet, by your gracious
   patience,
I will a round unvarnish'd tale deliver   90
Of my whole course of love – what drugs, what
   charms,
What conjuration, and what mighty magic,
For such proceedings am I charg'd withal,
I won his daughter.

Brabantio

             A maiden never bold,
Of spirit so still and quiet that her motion   95
Blush'd at herself; and she – in spite of nature,
Of years, of country, credit, every thing –
To fall in love with what she fear'd to look on!
It is a judgment maim'd and most imperfect
That will confess perfection so could err   100
Against all rules of nature, and must be driven
To find out practices of cunning hell,
Why this should be. I therefore vouch again
That with some mixtures powerful o'er the blood,
Or with some dram conjur'd to this effect,   105
He wrought upon her.

Duke

            To vouch this is no proof –
Without more wider and more overt test
Than these thin habits and poor likelihoods
Of modern seeming do prefer against him.

1 Senator

But, Othello, speak.   110
Did you by indirect and forced courses
Subdue and poison this young maid's affections?
Or came it by request, and such fair question
As soul to soul affordeth?

Othello

           I do beseech you,
Send for the lady to the Sagittary,   115
And let her speak of me before her father.

129. *Still* repeatedly.

135. *moving accidents* adventurous escapades.

136. *imminent* overhanging, ready to fall.

137–8. *taken by the insolent foe / And sold to slavery* Note the context of a slave trade; this could refer to the Atlantic slave trade (c. 1500–1800) that mostly enslaved West Africans and was conducted in Shakespeare's lifetime by the Portuguese and Spanish (and later by the British) or to an earlier slave trade beginning as Islam expanded in the 8th century, which originally focused on North and East Africa and was conducted by Muslim Arabs. Shakespeare's audiences would have known and feared this latter trade, as it had long since expanded and those kidnapped (often at sea) included Christians: Barbary pirates raided ships and coastal towns for slaves from Spain, Portugal, France, England, the Netherlands and as far as Iceland. Women and children were particular targets. The 'Barbary Coast' (modern-day Morocco, Algeria, Tunisia, Libya) maintained flourishing slave markets in Shakespeare's time and afterwards.

139. *portance in my travel's history* how I conducted myself through the journey of my life, with a possible pun on 'travailous': wearisome and full of trials ('travels' is rendered as 'travailous' in many editions of the play).

140. *antres* caves (from the Latin *antrum*).

144. *Anthropophagi* literally, 'man-eaters'.

If you do find me foul in her report,
The trust, the office, I do hold of you
Not only take away, but let your sentence
Even fall upon my life.

Duke

                         Fetch Desdemona hither.   120

Othello

Ancient, conduct them; you best know the place.
   [Exeunt IAGO *and* ATTENDANTS.*]*
And, till she come, as faithful as to heaven
I do confess the vices of my blood,
So justly to your grave ears I'll present
How I did thrive in this fair lady's love,   125
And she in mine.

Duke

Say it, Othello.

Othello

Her father lov'd me, oft invited me;
Still question'd me the story of my life
From year to year – the battles, sieges, fortunes,   130
That I have pass'd.
I ran it through, even from my boyish days
To th' very moment that he bade me tell it;
Wherein I spake of most disastrous chances,
Of moving accidents by flood and field;   135
Of hairbreadth scapes i' th' imminent deadly breach;
Of being taken by the insolent foe
And sold to slavery; of my redemption thence,
And portance in my travel's history;
Wherein of antres vast and deserts idle,   140
Rough quarries, rocks, and hills whose heads touch
   heaven,
It was my hint to speak – such was the process;
And of the Cannibals that each other eat,
The Anthropophagi, and men whose heads
Do grow beneath their shoulders. This to hear   145
Would Desdemona seriously incline;

153. *dilate* tell at length and in full detail.
155. *inventively* absorbed in every detail.

160. *passing* surpassing, beyond, more than.

171. *I think this tale would win my daughter too* The play is about the power of (conflicting) narratives. Here Othello's romantic tale completely wins over the Duke just as it won Desdemona's love. Iago's narratives, by contrast, weave doubt, despair and destruction and he frames people in the worst possible light.
173. *Take up this mangled matter at the best* make the best of a bad job.

But still the house affairs would draw her thence;
Which ever as she could with haste dispatch,
She'd come again, and with a greedy ear
Devour up my discourse. Which I observing,   150
Took once a pliant hour, and found good means
To draw from her a prayer of earnest heart
That I would all my pilgrimage dilate,
Whereof by parcels she had something heard,
But not intentively. I did consent,   155
And often did beguile her of her tears,
When I did speak of some distressful stroke
That my youth suffer'd. My story being done,
She gave me for my pains a world of sighs;
She swore, in faith, 'twas strange, 'twas passing
     strange;   160
'Twas pitiful, 'twas wondrous pitiful.
She wish'd she had not heard it; yet she wish'd
That heaven had made her such a man. She thank'd
     me;
And bade me, if I had a friend that lov'd her,
I should but teach him how to tell my story,   165
And that would woo her. Upon this hint I spake;
She lov'd me for the dangers I had pass'd;
And I lov'd her that she did pity them.
This only is the witchcraft I have us'd.
Here comes the lady; let her witness it.   170

[Enter DESDEMONA, IAGO, *and Attendants.]*

Duke
I think this tale would win my daughter too.
Good Brabantio,
Take up this mangled matter at the best.
Men do their broken weapons rather use
Than their bare hands.
Brabantio
                    I pray you hear her speak.   175
If she confess that she was half the wooer,

178. *Light* alight, fall.
178. *hither* here.

181. *I do perceive here a divided duty* Desdemona (and any daughter like her entering marriage in Venetian society) has a conflict of loyalties: loyalty to her father, her former 'lord', versus loyalty to her new lord, 'the Moor', by which she seems to mean – and this is crucial – loyalty to her own heart and its desires (*my husband*). The forensic clarity of her analysis of the social choice, and the feisty decisiveness of that choice in front of this potentially overwhelming patriarchal assembly, are two indications of her noble and attractive character.
182. *education* upbringing.
183. *learn me* teach me.

189. *God bu'y* Goodbye! ('God be with you' with the sense of 'good riddance.') Brabantio's irritable response lacks the maturity of his daughter's reasoning (see lines 186–8).
191. *get* beget, father.
195. *For your sake* because of you.
196–8. *I am glad at soul ... hang clogs on them* I am glad you are an only child because your escape from my liberal parenting regime would change me into the kind of father who excessively controls his children.

198. *clogs* wooden hobbles on a horse's legs.

199. *lay a sentence* give advice.
200. *grise* stairway.

203. *late on hopes depended* was hoping for a better outcome (now gone).

208. *The robb'd ... the thief* If the victim of a robbery is not upset by it, the robber is outwitted because the 'victim' refuses to *be* a victim. It's sage advice, but Brabantio refuses it; he insists on being the victim of Othello's 'robbery' of his daughter.

Destruction on my head if my bad blame
Light on the man! Come hither, gentle mistress.
Do you perceive in all this noble company
Where most you owe obedience?

Desdemona

My noble father,   180
I do perceive here a divided duty:
To you I am bound for life and education;
My life and education both do learn me
How to respect you; you are the lord of duty –
I am hitherto your daughter; but here's my husband,   185
And so much duty as my mother show'd
To you, preferring you before her father,
So much I challenge that I may profess
Due to the Moor, my lord.

Brabantio

God bu'y, I ha done.
Please it your Grace, on to the state affairs –   190
I had rather to adopt a child than get it.
Come hither, Moor:
I here do give thee that with all my heart
Which, but thou hast already, with all my heart
I would keep from thee. For your sake, jewel,   195
I am glad at soul I have no other child;
For thy escape would teach me tyranny,
To hang clogs on them. I have done, my lord.

Duke

Let me speak like yourself, and lay a sentence
Which, as a grise or step, may help these lovers   200
Into your favour.
When remedies are past, the griefs are ended
By seeing the worst, which late on hopes depended.
To mourn a mischief that is past and gone
Is the next way to draw new mischief on.   205
What cannot be preserv'd when fortune takes,
Patience her injury a mockery makes.
The robb'd that smiles steals something from the
    thief;

209. *bootless* pointless.

212. *He bears the sentence well that nothing bears* That's easy for you to say! You can advise me like this because you don't share the hurt I feel.

218–9. *I never yet did hear ... pierced through the ear* There are no words to heal a bruised heart.

221–8. Note that the Duke's discussion of state affairs is in prose. This marks the lowering of emotional temperature from the highly charged argument about Desdemona's marriage, which is in verse. In Shakespeare's tragedies, the convention is for comic scenes involving low-life characters to be in prose while Dukes and nobles, etc., speak in verse, so it is significant that high politics is 'lower' than the tragic personal drama here.

222. *fortitude* fortification, defences.

223. *substitute* regent, viceroy.

224. *of most allowed sufficiency* of generally well-regarded abilities.

224–5. *opinion, a sovereign ... safer voice on you* Opinion is a feminine word in Latin (*opinio*), which is why she is a 'sovereign mistress' here. Informed opinion in Venice is the ultimate decider of who should govern Cyprus in the current crisis. Note the continuation of the theme of how promotions are decided, about which Iago is so angry at the start: the same informed opinion that now chooses Othello over Montano also chose Cassio over Iago.

226. *slubber* smear.

227–8. *boisterous* rough, violent.

231. *thrice-driven bed of down* the very finest, softest feather bed.

231. *agnize* acknowledge, know (of myself).

232. *prompt alacrity* cheerful readiness (i.e. to resume the army life).

237. *exhibition* financial support, funding.

238. *besort* service (maids, servants, etc.) and companions.

239. *As levels with her breeding* as will keep her in the (comfortable) manner to which she is accustomed.

He robs himself that spends a bootless grief.

Brabantio

    So let the Turk of Cyprus us beguile: 210
    We lose it not so long as we can smile.
    He bears the sentence well that nothing bears
    But the free comfort which from thence he hears;
    But he bears both the sentence and the sorrow
    That to pay grief must of poor patience borrow.   215
    These sentences, to sugar or to gall,
    Being strong on both sides, are equivocal.
    But words are words: I never yet did hear
    That the bruis'd heart was pierced through the ear.
    I humbly beseech you proceed to th' affairs of state. 220

Duke

    The Turk with a most mighty preparation makes for
    Cyprus. Othello, the fortitude of the place is best
    known to you; and though we have there a substitute
    of most allowed sufficiency, yet opinion, a sovereign
    mistress of effects, throws a more safer voice on you. 225
    You must therefore be content to slubber the gloss of
    your new fortunes with this more stubborn and bois-
    terous expedition.

Othello

    The tyrant custom, most grave senators,
    Hath made the flinty and steel couch of war   230
    My thrice-driven bed of down. I do agnize
    A natural and prompt alacrity
    I find in hardness; and would undertake
    This present wars against the Ottomites.
    Most humbly, therefore, bending to your state,   235
    I crave fit disposition for my wife;
    Due reference of place and exhibition;
    With such accommodation and besort
    As levels with her breeding.

240. *her father's* The Duke's suggestion that Desdemona stay at her father's is just about the worst possible solution given all we've just heard, but a great cue line as the antagonists Brabantio and Othello unite in opposing it. However, it is capped by the daughter/wife's dramatic repetition and owning of Othello's *Nor I* (line 241). This provides a timely reminder to everyone (including the audience) of Desdemona's own existence and feelings about her fate. The Duke's next speech (line 247) accepts and acknowledges her self-empowerment.

244. *unfolding* explanation.
244. *prosperous* fruitful, sympathetic.
245. *charter* permission.

251. *Even to the very quality of my lord* I have become like my beloved (i.e. a soldier).
252. *visage* face, expression (character); Desdemona is saying that Othello's true nature is revealed in his face.
254. *my soul and fortunes consecrate* my life and very being pledged to him in a holy promise.
257. *The rites for why I love him are bereft me* my right to share my husband's life (and the risks that involves) is denied me ('rites' also implies the marriage ceremony).
260–74. Othello asks for the Senate to agree with Desdemona's suggestion that she go to Cyprus with him and develops her point that theirs is a love-relationship of two minds. 'Wanton' 'palate' (taste or liking) and 'appetite' (sexual desire) are all references to the physical aspect of love, which Othello asserts will not distract him from (or, as he suggests with his reference to Cupid, blind him to) his duties during the military campaign. The dramatic irony is that in fact he spends his entire time in Cyprus consumed by Desdemona's imagined infidelities.
260. *voice* agreement.
263. *heat* lust.
263. *affects* passions.
264. *proper satisfaction* consummation of the marriage, i.e. through sexual union. Note how Othello's respectful language here contrasts with Iago's crude reference to making 'the beast with two backs' in Act 1, Scene 1 (line 117).

Duke
                    If you please,
  Be't at her father's.
Brabantio
                    I'll not have it so.   240
Othello
  Nor I.
Desdemona
        Nor I. I would not there reside,
  To put my father in impatient thoughts
  By being in his eye. Most gracious Duke,
  To my unfolding lend your prosperous ear,
  And let me find a charter in your voice   245
  T' assist my simpleness.
Duke
  What would you, Desdemona?
Desdemona
  That I did love the Moor to live with him,
  My downright violence and storm of fortunes
  My trumpet to the world. My heart's subdu'd   250
  Even to the very quality of my lord:
  I saw Othello's visage in his mind;
  And to his honours and his valiant parts
  Did I my soul and fortunes consecrate.
  So that, dear lords, if I be left behind,   255
  A moth of peace, and he go to the war,
  The rites for why I love him are bereft me,
  And I a heavy interim shall support
  By his dear absence. Let me go with him.
Othello
  Let her have your voice.   260
  Vouch with me, heaven, I therefore beg it not
  To please the palate of my appetite;
  Nor to comply with heat – the young affects
  In me defunct – and proper satisfaction;
  But to be free and bounteous to her mind.   265
  And heaven defend your good souls that you think

47

OTHELLO

267. *scant* neglect.
268–9. *light-wing'd toys/ Of feather'd Cupid* the wings and arrows of Cupid, the god of sexual passion. In classical mythology, he was the blind son of the female god of Love, Venus, and the male god of War, Mars. Cupid shot people with an arrow from his bow and they fell in love, whether they wanted to or not. Cupid's blindness is also suggestive of Othello's lack of self-knowledge about the force of human sexual drives (which both he and Desdemona more or less deny here) and how Iago will use this lack of self-knowledge against him.
269. *seel* sew up.
269. *wanton dullness* an uncontrolled drowsiness, with the suggestion that it has been brought on by over-indulgence in sex.
270. *speculative and offic'd instuments* eyes (and mind).
271. *disports* sexual play.
272. *skillet* cooking pot.
273. *indign* undignified.
274. *Make head* form an army.
274. *estimation* reputation.

283–4. *So please your Grace, ... honesty and trust* Othello's description of Iago here is the height of dramatic irony.

289. *delighted* delightful.
290. *Your son-in-law is far more fair than black* Note the Duke's unquestioning distinction of 'black' connoting wicked along with 'fair' connoting honourable, alongside his assertion of Othello's goodness *despite* appearances. The Duke, unlike many of the play's characters, penetrates to the reality beneath the appearance, though he remains unaware of the racist assumptions in the language he uses.
290. The couple's happiness is at its height here and gradually destroyed from this point onwards. (For consideration of how well founded Othello and Desdemona's happiness is, see the section on structure on pp.xv–xvi of the Introduction.)

I will your serious and great business scant
For she is with me. No, when light-wing'd toys
Of feather'd Cupid seel with wanton dullness
My speculative and offic'd instruments,   270
That my disports corrupt and taint my business,
Let huswives make a skillet of my helm,
And all indign and base adversities
Make head against my estimation!

Duke

Be it as you shall privately determine,   275
Either for her stay or going. Th' affair cries haste,
And speed must answer it. You must away to-night.

Desdemona

To-night, my lord!

Duke

                    This night.

Othello

                              With all my heart.

Duke

At nine i' th' morning here we'll meet again.
Othello, leave some officer behind,   280
And he shall our commission bring to you;
With such things else of quality and respect
As doth import you.

Othello

                    So please your Grace, my ancient;
A man he is of honesty and trust.
To his conveyance I assign my wife,   285
With what else needful your good Grace shall
    think
To be sent after me.

Duke

                    Let it be so.
Good night to every one. *[To* BRABANTIO*]* And, noble
    signior,
If virtue no delighted beauty lack,
Your son-in-law is far more fair than black.   290

291. *use Desdemona well* take good care of Desdemona. This foreshadows the tragic downturn from the happy end of Act 1.

293. *She has deceiv'd her father, and may thee* Brabantio's accusation that his daughter will deceive Othello, just as she has deceived him, sows a doubt in Othello's mind that Iago will take advantage of later.

294. *Honest Iago* Othello's tragic flaw is his naivety (see Iago's lines 395–6), as Iago is the polar opposite of honest. Othello (mis)applies the attribute 'honest' sixteen times during the play, more even than Iago. He will fail to see that Desdemona really is 'honest' and that it is Iago who is 'dishonest'. His attachment of the phrase to the name effectively *names* Iago as 'Honesty'.
297. *advantage* opportunity.

305. *incontinently drown myself* a play on the sense of being extremely (i.e. 'incontinently') drunk such that one becomes incontinent (loses control, e.g. of one's bladder).

1 Senator
    Adieu, brave Moor; use Desdemona well.
Brabantio
    Look to her, Moor, if thou hast eyes to see:
    She has deceiv'd her father, and may thee.

    [Exeunt DUKE, SENATORS, OFFICERS etc.]

Othello
    My life upon her faith! – Honest Iago,
    My Desdemona must I leave to thee.   295
    I prithee let thy wife attend on her;
    And bring them after in the best advantage.
    Come, Desdemona, I have but an hour
    Of love, of worldly matter and direction,
    To spend with thee. We must obey the time.   300

    [Exeunt OTHELLO and DESDEMONA.]

Roderigo
    Iago!
Iago
    What say'st thou, noble heart?
Roderigo
    What will I do, thinkest thou?
Iago
    Why, go to bed and sleep.
Roderigo
    I will incontinently drown myself.   305
Iago
    Well, if thou dost, I shall never love thee after it. Why,
    thou silly gentleman!
Roderigo
    It is silliness to live when to live is torment; and then
    have we a prescription to die when death is our
    physician.   310
Iago
    O villainous! I ha look'd upon the world for four times
    seven years; and since I could distinguish betwixt a

318. *not in my virtue to amend it* my nature controls me; I do not have the strength (of will) to change.
319. *A fig!* What nonsense!

322. *hyssop ... thyme* fragrant herbs.
323. *gender* kind, type of.
323. *distract* vary.
325. *corrigible authority* corrective control.
327. *poise* balance.

329. *preposterous* deviant.
330. *carnal stings* lusts.
330. *unbitted* like a horse without a bit, unbridled. (The image of the horse here revisits that of the centaur from Act 1, Scene 1, line 159.)
331–2. *you call love to be a sect or scion* you (mistakenly) think lustful passions can be managed like we tend plants (*sect* – a cutting, *scion* – a shoot) in a garden.

338. *perdurable* endless, of eternal duration.
338. *stead* serve.
339. *Put money in thy purse* sell your assets to raise money. Iago repeats this over and over (lines 341–77) like an advertisement phrase or political slogan. As is well known in both advertising and politics (and poetry and songs) the hypnotic repetition of catchphrases is a key technique for controlling people's thoughts and actions. Iago hypnotises pretty much every character in the play to do his will one way or another, and this is an early example of his frightening power to do so.
340. *defeat thy favour with an usurp'd beard* make yourself appear less attractive by wearing a false beard.
345. *sequestration* end.

benefit and an injury, I never found a man that knew how to love himself. Ere I would say I would drown myself for the love of a guinea-hen, I would change 315 my humanity with a baboon.

Roderigo

What should I do? I confess it is my shame to be so fond, but it is not in my virtue to amend it.

Iago

Virtue? A fig! 'Tis in ourselves that we are thus or thus. Our bodies are our gardens to the which our wills are 320 gardeners; so that if we will plant nettles or sow lettuce, set hyssop and weed up thyme, supply it with one gender of herbs or distract it with many, either to have it sterile with idleness or manur'd with industry – why, the power and corrigible authority of this lies in our 325 wills. If the balance of our lives had not one scale of reason to poise another of sensuality, the blood and baseness of our natures would conduct us to most preposterous conclusions. But we have reason to cool our raging motions, our carnal stings, our unbitted 330 lusts; whereof I take this that you call love to be a sect or scion.

Roderigo

It cannot be.

Iago

It is merely a lust of the blood and a permission of the will. Come, be a man. Drown thyself? Drown cats 335 and blind puppies! I have profess'd me thy friend, and I confess me knit to thy deserving with cables of perdurable toughness. I could never better stead thee than now. Put money in thy purse; follow thou the wars; defeat thy favour with an usurp'd beard. I say, 340 put money in thy purse. It cannot be long that Desdemona should continue her love to the Moor – put money in thy purse – nor he his to her: it was a violent commencement in her, and thou shalt see an answerable sequestration – put but money in thy purse. These 345

347–50. *The food ... her choice* Note how cynical Iago is about everything: women, sex, men, love, life, the illusion of human happiness and all striving for it. This is the view of the world he will scheme to make true for everyone else.

348. *locusts* sweet fruit.

348. *acerbe* bitter.

348–9. *coloquintida* bitter apple-derived emetic (a substance that causes vomiting).

353. *sanctimony* sacred marriage.

358. *compassing* achieving.

360. *fast* true, loyal.

364. *hearted* heartfelt.

365. *conjunctive* joined, allied.

365–7. *If thou canst cuckold him ... me a sport* If you sleep with Desdemona (so making a 'cuckold' of Othello; see the detailed note on 'cuckold' lines 383–4), it will satisfy you (sexually) and I will take pleasure from knowing you have wronged him.

Moors are changeable in their wills – fill thy purse with
money. The food that to him now is as luscious as
locusts shall be to him shortly as acerbe as the coloquintida. She must change for youth; when she is sated
with his body, she will find the error of her choice. 350
Therefore put money in thy purse. If thou wilt needs
damn thyself, do it a more delicate way than drowning.
Make all the money thou canst. If sanctimony and a
frail vow betwixt an erring barbarian and a super-subtle
Venetian be not too hard for my wits and all the tribe 355
of hell, thou shalt enjoy her; therefore make money.
A pox a drowning thyself! 'Tis clean out of the way.
Seek thou rather to be hang'd in compassing thy joy
than to be drown'd and go without her.

Roderigo

Wilt thou be fast to my hopes, if I depend on the 360
issue?

Iago

Thou art sure of me – go make money. I have told
thee often, and I retell thee again and again I hate the
Moor. My cause is hearted: thine hath no less reason.
Let us be conjunctive in our revenge against him. If 365
thou canst cuckold him, thou dost thyself a pleasure,
me a sport. There are many events in the womb of
time which will be delivered. Traverse; go; provide thy
money. We will have more of this to-morrow. Adieu.

Roderigo

Where shall we meet i' th' morning?   370

Iago

At my lodging.

Roderigo

I'll be with thee betimes.

Iago

Go to; farewell. Do you hear, Roderigo?

Roderigo

What say you?

55

379–400. Iago's first soliloquy plainly reveals to the audience his cynical plan to exploit Roderigo. It also reveals with shocking clarity his feelings about Othello and the 'reason' for Iago's hatred: it is *rumoured* that Othello has cuckolded him (there is no evidence he has *actually* done so). But Iago is perhaps not so much revealing his reasoned motives as casting an evil spell on himself, willing himself to revenge an injury that hasn't even been done to him.

380. *gain'd knowledge* i.e. cynical street-wisdom of how the world works.

383–4. *'twixt my sheets ... my office* has cuckolded me (i.e. has slept with my wife). The cuckoo occupies the nest and eats the eggs of other birds and has been used as a symbol of an adulterer since Roman times; a 'cuckold' is the husband who has been betrayed in this way, his marriage bed (or 'nest') usurped by an intruder. For most husbands, an unfaithful wife would be a devastating challenge to their 'manhood', but for the notoriously prickly soldier Iago it is a challenge even when it hasn't happened. Likewise, for Othello, the mere *fear* of being a cuckold (again without evidence) will prove an intolerable one and elicit as much angst about the threat to rank – Cassio is his inferior officer – as the alleged straying of his wife, a hint that the obsession with female sexual purity is tied up with their notions of manhood and male honour.

388. *proper* good-looking.

389. *plume up my will* satisfy my ego, inflate my self-image and confidence (like a fighting cockerel).

393. *dispose* manner.

394. *fram'd* designed.

395–6. *a free and open nature ... but seem to be so* (see line 294).

399–400. *Hell and night ... world's light* The concluding (clinching) effect of the rhyme is like a spell being cast and suggests something being completed. (Iago exactly repeats the device and its effect at the end of Act 2.) For Iago the couplet marks the completion of his plot; for the audience it finalises the exposition, from which the play will now rise to its climax (see the Introduction, pp.xv–xvi).

Iago
  No more of drowning, do you hear?   375
Roderigo
  I am chang'd.
Iago
  Go to; farewell. Put money enough in your purse.
Roderigo
  I'll sell all my land. *[Exit* RODERIGO.*]*
Iago
  Thus do I ever make my fool my purse;
  For I mine own gain'd knowledge should profane   380
  If I would time expend with such a snipe
  But for my sport and profit. I hate the Moor;
  And it is thought abroad that 'twixt my sheets
  'Has done my office. I know not if't be true;
  Yet I, for mere suspicion in that kind,   385
  Will do as if for surety. He holds me well;
  The better shall my purpose work on him.
  Cassio's a proper man. Let me see now:
  To get his place, and to plume up my will
  In double knavery. How, how? Let's see: 390
  After some time to abuse Othello's ear
  That he is too familiar with his wife.
  He hath a person and a smooth dispose
  To be suspected – fram'd to make women false.
  The Moor is of a free and open nature   395
  That thinks men honest that but seem to be so;
  And will as tenderly be led by th' nose
  As asses are.
  I ha't – it is engender'd. Hell and night
  Must bring this monstrous birth to the world's light. 400
    [Exit.]

ACT 2 SCENE 1

Witnesses on the quay at Cyprus describe a terrible storm at sea, as first Cassio then Iago and Desdemona reach shore safely. The Turkish fleet is destroyed in the storm but Othello is still at sea. While they wait, Iago teases the worry-distracted Desdemona and Emilia with derogatory comments about wives and women. By contrast, Cassio innocently pays court to Desdemona, which Iago notes and will use against them. Othello finally arrives and the husband and wife rejoice in their reunion. Iago encourages Roderigo to read Cassio's attentions to Desdemona as her being tired of Othello and hatches his plan to provoke Cassio into a fight.

Stage direction: one of the Gentlemen stands on the upper stage, to act as lookout.

2. *high-wrought flood* a furiously stormy sea. Othello is associated with the sea and elemental forces, and the sea's fury foreshadows his own destructive anger later in the play.

4. *Descry* spy out, see.

7. *ha ruffian'd* has raged.

8. *ribs of oak* the ship's sides.

9. *hold the mortise* stay jointed on one piece (i.e. hold together).

10. *segregation* splitting up.

12. *chidden billow* hurled back waves.

13. *high and monstrous mane* the flaring mane of a monstrous beast (with a double pun on main meaning 'ocean' and 'strength').

14. *Bear* the constellation of Ursa Major, whose Latin name means Great She-Bear

15. *th' ever-fired pole* the light of the Pole star, a fixed point in the sky that sailors use for navigation

16. *never did like molestation view* never saw a disturbance such as this.

17. *enchafed* angry.

18. *embay'd* safe in a harbour.

ACT 2
SCENE 1

Cyprus. A sea-port.

[Enter MONTANO, *Governor of Cyprus, with two other Gentlemen.]*

Montano
What from the cape can you discern at sea?
1 Gentleman
Nothing at all; it is a high-wrought flood.
I cannot 'twixt the heaven and the main
Descry a sail.
Montano
Methinks the wind hath spoke aloud at land;   5
A fuller blast ne'er shook our battlements.
If it ha ruffian'd so upon the sea,
What ribs of oak, when mountains melt on them,
Can hold the mortise? What shall we hear of this?
2 Gentleman
A segregation of the Turkish fleet.   10
For do but stand upon the banning shore,
The chidden billow seems to pelt the clouds;
The wind-shak'd surge, with high and monstrous
     mane,
Seems to cast water on the burning Bear,
And quench the guards of th' ever-fired pole.   15
I never did like molestation view
On the enchafed flood.
Montano
                              If that the Turkish fleet
Be not enshelter'd and embay'd, they are drown'd:
It is impossible they bear it out.

[Enter a third Gentleman.]

22. *designment halts* plan has been stopped.
23. *sufferance* damage.

39. *main* ocean.
39. *th' aerial blue* the blue sky.
40. *indistinct regard* indistinguishable.

3 Gentleman

News, lads! Your wars are done. 20
The desperate tempest hath so bang'd the Turk
That their designment halts. A noble ship of Venice
Hath seen a grievous wreck and sufferance
On most part of their fleet.

Montano

How! Is this true?

3 Gentleman

              The ship is here put in, 25
A Veronesa; Michael Cassio,
Lieutenant to the warlike Moor Othello,
Is come ashore: the Moor himself at sea,
And is in full commission here for Cyprus.

Montano

I am glad on't; 'tis a worthy governor. 30

3 Gentleman

But this same Cassio, though he speak of comfort
Touching the Turkish loss, yet he looks sadly
And prays the Moor be safe; for they were parted
With foul and violent tempest.

Montano

              Pray heaven he be;
For I have serv'd him, and the man commands 35
Like a full soldier. Let's to the sea-side, ho!
As well to see the vessel that's come in
As to throw out our eyes for brave Othello,
Even till we make the main and th' aerial blue
An indistinct regard.

3 Gentleman

              Come, let's do so; 40
For every minute is expectancy
Of more arrivance.

[Enter CASSIO.]

Cassio

Thanks you, the valiant of this war-like isle,

44. *approve* honour.

48. *bark is stoutly timber'd* vessel (ship) is made from sturdy wood.
48. *pilot* ship's guide.
49. *approv'd allowance* tried and tested.
50. *surfeited to death* 'gorged to death', i.e. beyond expectation.
50. *Stand in bold cure* are likely to be restored.

59. *wiv'd* married.

61. *paragons* surpasses.
62. *quirks of blazoning pens* the skills of description.
63. *th' essential vesture of creation* the original perfection of the human form.
64. *tire the ingener* outdo the ability of a creative writer to describe.

That so approve the Moor. O, let the heavens
Give him defence against their elements,   45
For I have lost him on a dangerous sea!

Montano

Is he well shipp'd?

Cassio

His bark is stoutly timber'd, and his pilot
Of very expert and approv'd allowance;
Therefore my hopes, not surfeited to death, stand in
    bold cure.   50

        [Within: A sail, a sail, a sail!]

        [Enter a Messenger.]

Cassio

What noise?

Messenger

The town is empty; on the brow o' th' sea
Stand ranks of people, and they cry 'A sail!'

Cassio

My hopes do shape him for the Governor. *[A shot.]*

2 Gentleman

They do discharge the shot of courtesy: 55
Our friend at least.

Cassio

            I pray you, sir, go forth,
And give us truth who 'tis that is arriv'd.

2 Gentleman

I shall. *[Exit.]*

Montano

But, good Lieutenant, is your general wiv'd?

Cassio

Most fortunately: he hath achiev'd a maid   60
That paragons description and wild fame;
One that excels the quirks of blazoning pens,
And in th' essential vesture of creation
Does tire the ingener.

68. *gutter'd* submerged, i.e. under water.

68. *congregated* jagged, i.e. sandbanks.

69. *Traitors ensteep'd to enclog* the hidden rocks and sandbanks acting as treacherous underwater obstructions. Note the alliteration of 'en' working with the rhythm to suggest the impact of these 'traitors' and also Cassio's unconscious sense of threats below the surface in this new setting of Cyprus. Tragically, he does not see the human 'traitor' and threat (Iago) at work below the surface of this dialogue.

69. *guiltless keel* unsuspecting ship (a motif of the play, do not trust appearances under which dangers lurk).

75. *footing* landing ashore.

76. *s'ennight* a week ('seven nights').

76. *Great Jove* a conventional appeal to the classical Roman god Jupiter (Jovis pater, 'father of heaven') to protect someone in peril on Earth. The usage became so common in everyday life that it could express the slightest heightening of emotions, but in this (tragic, theatrical) context Cassio conveys genuine awe, the sense of being at the mercy of the gods on a wild island surrounded by a wild sea, and in a cosmos beyond human control.

77–9. *swell his sail ... bless this bay with his tall ship ... love's quick pants in Desdemona's arms* These words in Iago's mouth would be double entendres, but it would be out of character for the gentlemanly Cassio to talk of, or to, her in such a bawdy way. The effect is comic: here is someone who doesn't realise the vulgar double meanings of what he is saying. It shows Cassio's naïvety and unguarded innocence, just as Othello (directed by Iago's suspicious mind) will misinterpret Cassio's actions with Desdemona later (see, for example, Act 3, Scene 3, lines 34–36 and 338–46).

78. *tall* tall-masted.

79. *quick pants* fast (heavy) breathing.

83. *let her have your knees* kneel to her (Desdemona).

86. *Enwheel thee round* surround you.

[Re-enter second Gentleman.]

Now, who has put in?

2 Gentleman
'Tis one Iago, ancient to the General.   65

Cassio
'Has had most favourable and happy speed.
Tempests themselves, high seas, and howling winds,
The gutter'd rocks, and congregated sands,
Traitors ensteep'd to enclog the guiltless keel,
As having sense of beauty, do omit   70
Their mortal natures, letting go safely by
The divine Desdemona.

Montano
                            What is she?

Cassio
She that I spake of – our great Captain's Captain,
Left in the conduct of the bold Iago;
Whose footing here anticipates our thoughts   75
A se'nnight's speed. Great Jove, Othello guard,
And swell his sail with thine own powerful breath,
That he may bless this bay with his tall ship,
Make love's quick pants in Desdemona's arms,
Give renew'd fire to our extincted spirits,   80
And bring all Cyprus comfort!

*[Enter DESDEMONA, IAGO, EMILIA, RODERIGO, and
Attendants.]*

                            O, behold,
The riches of the ship is come ashore!
Ye men of Cyprus, let her have your knees.
Hail to thee, lady! and the grace of heaven,
Before, behind thee, and on every hand,   85
Enwheel thee round!

Desdemona
                    I thank you, valiant Cassio.
What tidings can you tell me of my lord?

97. *gall* irritate.
98. *extend* stretch.
98. *breeding* Cassio is a much more polished and courteous gentleman than the crude Iago, and he knows it.

101 *her tongue she oft bestows on me* she's always talking to (nagging) me.

104. *ha list* have need of.
105. *before your ladyship* in your presence.
106. *puts her tongue a little in her heart* keeps quiet, keeps her thoughts to herself.
107. *And chides with thinking* but even when she lets me sleep she still scolds me. The sense of Iago's whole speech is that even when he's asleep (and desperate for rest) his wife keeps nagging him.

Cassio

    He is not yet arriv'd; nor know I aught
    But that he's well, and will be shortly here.

Desdemona

    O, but I fear! How lost you company?   90

Cassio

    The great contention of the sea and skies
    Parted our fellowship.

               [Within: A sail, a sail!]

               But hark – 'A sail!' *[A shot.]*

2 Gentleman

    They give their greeting to the citadel:
    This likewise is a friend.

Cassio

              So speaks this voice.
    See for the news.   *[Exit Gentleman.]*   95
    Good ancient, you are welcome. *[To EMILIA]*
               Welcome, mistress.
    Let it not gall your patience, good Iago,
    That I extend my manners; 'tis my breeding
    That gives me this bold show of courtesy.

               [Kissing her.]

Iago

    Sir, would she give you so much of her lips   100
    As of her tongue she oft bestows on me,
    You'd have enough.

Desdemona

    Alas, she has no speech!

Iago

              I know too much
    I find it aye when I ha list to sleep.
    Marry, before your ladyship, I grant,   105
    She puts her tongue a little in her heart
    And chides with thinking.

109. *you* Iago's use of the plural 'you' cheekily includes Desdemona here and throughout the scandalous attacks on women's fidelity that follow.

109. *pictures* models of virtue, as in the expression 'she is a picture of innocence' but also as in 'painted', prettily made-up, false.

109. *bells* as noisy indoors as they are quiet (as pictures) outside, with a pun on the French word *belle*, meaning beautiful.

111. *players* actors (and pretence).

112. *huswifery* (or housewifery) domestic management, but with Iago's typical sexual grievance – economical in her favours to him, generous with them in bed with other men.

112. *huswifes* housewife, but with the additional suggestion of a 'hussy' – an unmarried and sexually available young woman. The double thinking behind this contradiction (the same word means both wife and unmarried flirt) is therefore embodied in the history of the word and reflects general attitudes to women; it is a particularly apt word for Iago to use.

114. *a Turk* the general enemy. See introduction p.viii for further information on the expansion of the Ottoman empire.

116. *You shall not write my praise.* i.e. that's not a fair description of me.

120. *assay* try.

122–3. *I do beguile / The thing I am by seeming otherwise* Desdemona's anxious thoughts are really with Othello on the sea. The (to her) meaningless banter with Iago is just to distract her.

126. *birdlime* a sticky substance smeared on trees to catch birds.

129. *fair* a light complexion.

Emilia

You ha little cause to say so.

Iago

Come on, come on; you are pictures out a-doors, bells
in your parlours, wildcats in your kitchens, saints in 110
your injuries, devils being offended, players in your
huswifery, and huswives in your beds.

Desdemona

O, fie upon thee, slanderer!

Iago

Nay, it is true, or else I am a Turk:
You rise to play, and go to bed to work.   115

Emilia

You shall not write my praise.

Iago

                          No, let me not.

Desdemona

What wouldst write of me if thou shouldst praise
    me?

Iago

O gentle lady, do not put me to't;
For I am nothing if not critical.

Desdemona

Come on, assay. – There's one gone to the harbour?   120

Iago

Ay, madam.

Desdemona

I am not merry; but I do beguile
The thing I am by seeming otherwise.
Come, how wouldst thou praise me?

Iago

I am about it; but, indeed, my invention comes from 125
my pate as birdlime does from frieze – it plucks out
brains and all. But my Muse labours, and thus she is
deliver'd:
If she be fair and wise – fairness and wit,
The one's for use, the other useth it.   130

131. *black* dark-haired.

133. *white* wight (creature or person).

133. *blackness hit* probably another sexual innuendo, i.e. touch her 'dark regions'. Note Iago's repeated (obsessive) references to black and white with reference to Othello and Desdemona's marriage.

137. *folly* foolishness, also sexual promiscuity.

141. *foul* ugly.

145–6. *one that, in the authority ... very malice itself* a woman so honest that even a person who hated her would have to approve of her.

154. *change the cod's head for the salmon's tail* to exchange something valuable for something of no value (with a misogynist pun on male versus female sexual organs).

Desdemona

Well prais'd. How if she be black and witty?

Iago

If she be black, and thereto have a wit,
She'll find a white that shall her blackness hit.

Desdemona

Worse and worse!

Emilia

How if fair and foolish? 135

Iago

She never yet was foolish that was fair;
For even her folly help'd her to an heir.

Desdemona

These are old fond paradoxes to make fools laugh i'
th' alehouse. What miserable praise hast thou for her
that's foul and foolish? 140

Iago

There's none so foul, and foolish thereunto,
But does foul pranks which fair and wise ones do.

Desdemona

O heavy ignorance! that praises the worst best. But
what praise couldst thou bestow on a deserving woman
indeed – one that, in the authority of her merits, did 145
justly put on the vouch of very malice itself?

Iago

She that was ever fair, and never proud;
Had tongue at will, and yet was never loud;
Never lack'd gold, and yet went never gay;
Fled from her wish, and yet said 'Now I may'; 150
She that, being ang'red, her revenge being nigh,
Bade her wrong stay and her displeasure fly;
She that in wisdom never was so frail
To change the cod's head for the salmon's tail;
She that could think, and ne'er disclose her
mind; 155
See suitors following, and not look behind:
She was a wight, if ever such wight were –

71

159. *suckle fools and chronicle small beer* breastfeeding and keeping household accounts, two 'female' occupations which Iago despises and trivialises.

162. *profane and liberal* coarse and immoral.

164. *speaks home* speaks plainly and to the point.

167. *well said* well done.

169. *gyve* trap.

173. *play the sir* act the fashionable polished gentleman (as despised by Iago).

175. *clyster-pipes* enema tubes, used in inject water into the rectum for medical purposes ('clyster' means injection).

177. *I know his trumpet* great men had their own fanfare.

Desdemona

To do what?

Iago

To suckle fools and chronicle small beer.

Desdemona

O most lame and impotent conclusion! Do not learn 160
of him, Emilia, though he be thy husband. How say
you, Cassio? Is he not a most profane and liberal
counsellor?

Cassio

He speaks home, madam. You may relish him more in
the soldier than in the scholar.   165

Iago

[Aside] He takes her by the palm.
Ay, well said, whisper. With as little a web as this will
I ensnare as great a fly as Cassio. Ay, smile upon her,
do; I will gyve thee in thine own courtship. You say
true; 'tis so, indeed. If such tricks as these strip you 170
out of your lieutenantry, it had been better you had
not kiss'd your three fingers so oft, which now again
you are most apt to play the sir in. Very good; well
kissed! and excellent courtesy! 'Tis so, indeed. Yet again
your fingers to your lips? Would they were clyster-pipes 175
for your sake!

[Trumpet within.]

The Moor! I know his trumpet.

Cassio

'Tis truly so.

Desdemona

Let's meet him, and receive him.

Cassio

Lo, where he comes!

[Enter OTHELLO and Attendants.]

Othello

O my fair warrior!

184. *labouring bark* i.e. wooden ship at sea.
185. *Olympus-high* as high as Olympus, abode of the Ancient Greek gods.
186–7. *If it were now to die … most happy* If I died now, I'd die the happiest I've ever been.

195. *discords* absence of harmony, disagreement.

197. *well tun'd* in harmony (like a musical instrument).
198. *set down the pegs* slacken the strings so that their music goes out of tune.

Desdemona
                    My dear Othello!
Othello
    It gives me wonder great as my content   180
    To see you here before me. O my soul's joy!
    If after every tempest come such calms,
    May the winds blow till they have waken'd death,
    And let the labouring bark climb hills of seas
    Olympus-high and duck again as low   185
    As hell's from heaven. If it were now to die,
    'Twere now to be most happy; for I fear
    My soul hath her content so absolute
    That not another comfort like to this
    Succeeds in unknown fate.
Desdemona
                        The heavens forbid   190
    But that our loves and comforts should increase
    Even as our days do grow!
Othello
                        Amen to that, sweet powers!
    I cannot speak enough of this content;
    It stops me here; it is too much of joy.
    And this, and this, the greatest discords be   195

                    [They kiss.]

    That e'er our hearts shall make!
Iago
    [Aside] O, you are well tun'd now!
    But I'll set down the pegs that make this music,
    As honest as I am.
Othello
                    Come, let us to the castle.
    News, friends: our wars are done; the Turks are
        drown'd.   200
    How do our old acquaintance of the isle?
    Honey, you shall be well desir'd in Cyprus;
    I have found great love amongst them. O my sweet,

204. *prattle out of fashion* speak wildly off the point.

206. *disembark my coffers* unload my luggage.
207. *Master* ship's captain.

215. *list* listen to.
215–16. *court of guard* guardhouse.
217. *directly* definitely.

222. *prating* idle chatter.

225. *act of sport* sexual intercourse.
226. *satiety* satisfied appetite.

230. *heave the gorge* to bring up the contents of one's stomach, i.e. to vomit, though Iago's tone is coarse here (i.e. 'puke up') and 'gorge' suggests over-eating.
230. *disrelish* enjoyed as food but not when it returns as vomit.
233. *pregnant and unforc'd* obvious.

235. *voluble* cunningly persuasive (a better description of Iago than Cassio!).

I prattle out of fashion, and I dote
In mine own comforts. I prithee, good Iago,   205
Go to the bay, and disembark my coffers;
Bring thou the Master to the Citadel;
He is a good one, and his worthiness
Does challenge much respect. Come, Desdemona,
Once more well met at Cyprus.   210

[Exeunt all but IAGO *and* RODERIGO.*]*

Iago

[To one leaving] Do thou meet me presently at the
harbour. *[To* RODERIGO*]* Come hither. If thou be'st
valiant – as they say base men being in love have then
a nobility in their natures more than is native to them
– list me. The Lieutenant to-night watches on the court   215
of guard. First, I must tell thee this: Desdemona is
directly in love with him.

Roderigo

With him! Why, 'tis not possible.

Iago

Lay thy finger thus, and let thy soul be instructed. Mark
me with what violence she first lov'd the Moor, but for   220
bragging and telling her fantastical lies. To love him
still for prating? – let not thy discreet heart think it.
Her eye must be fed; and what delight shall she have
to look on the devil? When the blood is made dull
with the act of sport, there should be – again to inflame 225
it, and to give satiety a fresh appetite – loveliness in
favour, sympathy in years, manners, and beauties – all
which the Moor is defective in. Now for want of these
requir'd conveniences, her delicate tenderness will find
itself abus'd, begin to heave the gorge, disrelish and   230
abhor the Moor; very nature will instruct her in it, and
compel her to some second choice. Now, sir, this
granted – as it is a most pregnant and unforc'd position
– who stands so eminent in the degree of this fortune
as Cassio does? A knave very voluble; no further   235

236. *conscionable* conscientious.
237. *compassing* accomplishing.
238. *salt* lecherous.
239. *slipper and subtle knave* slippery and crafty villain.

244. *green* immature.
244. *pestilent* deadly.

248. *Blest fig's end!* What nonsense! (See also Act 1, Scene 3, line 319.)

250. *paddle* sexual touching.

253. *index* preface.
253. *obscure* hidden.

257. *mutualities* intimacies.
257. *hard* close.
258. *main exercise* sexual sport.
258. *incorporate* bodily union.
259. *Pish* Ugh! (Iago is pretending disgust.)
259. *rul'd* guided.
261. *I'll lay't upon you* I'll leave it to you, on your head be it.

263. *tainting* scorning.

265. *minister* provide.

conscionable than in putting on the mere form of civil
and humane seeming, for the better compassing of his
salt and most hidden loose affection? Why, none; why,
none. A slipper and subtle knave; a finder-out of occasion; that has an eye can stamp and counterfeit 240
advantages, though true advantage never present itself;
a devilish knave! Besides, the knave is handsome,
young, and hath all those requisites in him that folly
and green minds look after; a pestilent complete knave,
and the woman hath found him already. 245

Roderigo

I cannot believe that in her; she's full of most blest
condition.

Iago

Blest fig's end! The wine she drinks is made of grapes.
If she had been blest, she would never have lov'd the
Moor. Blest pudding! Didst thou not see her paddle 250
with the palm of his hand? Didst not mark that?

Roderigo

Yes, that I did; but that was but courtesy.

Iago

Lechery, by this hand; an index and obscure prologue
to the history of lust and foul thoughts. They met so
near with their lips that their breaths embrac'd 255
together. Villainous thoughts, Roderigo! When these
mutualities so marshal the way, hard at hand comes
the master and main exercise, th' incorporate conclusion. Pish! But, sir, be you rul'd by me; I have brought
you from Venice. Watch you to-night; for your 260
command, I'll lay't upon you. Cassio knows you not;
I'll not be far from you. Do you find some occasion
to anger Cassio, either by speaking too loud, or tainting
his discipline, or from what other course you please,
which the time shall more favourably minister. 265

Roderigo

Well.

267. *choler* anger. Ancient classical scientists like Galen and Hippocrates believed that the four chief fluids of the body (choler, melancholy, phlegm and blood) determined a person's mental and physical being, moods and whims; an excess of any one would cause personality disorders such as anger or jealousy.

268. *truncheon* a short thick stick used as a weapon.

270. *qualification* pacification.

277. *warrant* guarantee, promise.

277. *thee* the change from 'you' marks agreement and renewed friendliness (equality of intimacy).

278. *necessaries* coffers.

278. *Farewell* fare (thee) well is spoken to an equal or intimate ('adieu' is a more formal way of saying goodbye).

280-306. Iago's second soliloquy provides a change of emphasis from his original anger at a missed promotion, with which the play begins, and shows him now plotting revenge on the basis of plain sexual jealousy.

288. *diet my revenge* feed with a sense of control – revenge needs a special diet.

289. *For that* however it may be.

290. *Hath leap'd into my seat* has had sex with my wife.

291. *like a poisonous mineral gnaw my inwards* eats away at my insides (innards), like gallstones or an ulcer. (See also Act 3, Scene 3, lines 168–9.)

296. *judgment cannot cure* irrational, cannot be reasoned away by good sense.

297. *poor trash of Venice* a worthless Venetian, i.e. Roderigo.

298. *quick hunting, stand the putting on* prevent Roderigo acting too hastily.

Iago

    Sir, he's rash, and very sudden in choler, and haply
    with his truncheon may strike at you; provoke him
    that he may; for even out of that will I cause these of
    Cyprus to mutiny, whose qualification shall come into   270
    no true taste again but by the displanting of Cassio.
    So shall you have a shorter journey to your desires by
    the means I shall then have to prefer them; and the
    impediment most profitably remov'd, without the
    which there were no expectation of our prosperity.   275

Roderigo

    I will do this, if you can bring it to any opportunity.

Iago

    I warrant thee. Meet me by and by at the citadel.
    I must fetch his necessaries ashore. Farewell.

Roderigo

    Adieu. *[Exit.]*

Iago

    That Cassio loves her, I do well believe it;   280
    That she loves him, 'tis apt and of great credit.
    The Moor, howbeit that I endure him not,
    Is of a constant, loving, noble nature;
    And I dare think he'll prove to Desdemona
    A most dear husband. Now I do love her too;   285
    Not out of absolute lust, though per-adventure
    I stand accountant for as great a sin,
    But partly led to diet my revenge,
    For that I do suspect the lustful Moor
    Hath leap'd into my seat; the thought whereof   290
    Doth like a poisonous mineral gnaw my inwards;
    And nothing can nor shall content my soul
    Till I am even'd with him, wife for wife;
    Or failing so, yet that I put the Moor
    At least into a jealousy so strong   295
    That judgment cannot cure. Which thing to do,
    If this poor trash of Venice, whom I trash
    For his quick hunting, stand the putting on,

299. *on the hip* at my mercy (a wrestling term).

300. *Abuse* discredit, slander.

300. *rank* lustful.

301. *with my night-cap* in bed with my wife.

303. *egregiously an ass* making a huge fool of him ('egregiously' meaning to an exaggerated degree).

305. *'Tis here, but yet confus'd* I have the initial idea but it's not clear (worked out) yet.

306. *plain* honest (heavily ironic).

I'll have our Michael Cassio on the hip,
Abuse him to the Moor in the rank garb – 300
For I fear Cassio with my night-cap too;
Make the Moor thank me, love me, and reward me,
For making him egregiously an ass,
And practising upon his peace and quiet
Even to madness. 'Tis here, but yet confus'd: 305
Knavery's plain face is never seen till us'd.

[Exit.]

SCENE 2

A herald announces a combined public celebration of the destruction of the Turkish fleet and of Othello's marriage. This point in the play marks the high point of the hero's fortunes.

2. *importing* reporting.
3. *mere perdition* total destruction.
4. *triumph* carnival.

6. *beneficial* good.
7. *his nuptial* Othello's marriage.
8. *offices* places to buy food.
9. *full liberty* unrestrained, excess.

SCENE 2

Cyprus. A street.

[Enter OTHELLO*'s Herald with a proclamation; People following.]*

Herald

It is Othello's pleasure, our noble and valiant general, that, upon certain tidings now arriv'd, importing the mere perdition of the Turkish fleet, every man put himself into triumph; some to dance, some to make bonfires, each man to what sport and revels his addic- 5 tion leads him; for, besides these beneficial news, it is the celebration of his nuptial. So much was his pleasure should be proclaimed. All offices are open; and there is full liberty of feasting from this present hour of five till the bell have told eleven. Heaven bless the isle of 10 Cyprus and our noble general Othello! *[Exeunt.]*

SCENE 3

Othello appoints Cassio to oversee Iago's guards and ensure that the all-night celebrations do not get out of hand, then goes to bed with Desdemona. Iago gets Cassio drunk and incapable at a wild victory party and, as Cassio goes on duty, sends Roderigo after him to pick a fight: a clever way to harm two 'superior' gentleman he hates. Iago explains to Montano that Cassio is a secret alcoholic and when the two men re-enter fighting, Montano steps in to stop them and is badly wounded. Othello, disturbed by the alarm, enters, makes enquiries of Iago, assumes Iago is protecting him when he won't say what happened and sacks his faithful and devastated lieutenant. Iago shares with Roderigo the next stage of his plan: to convince Othello that Cassio is having an affair with Desdemona.

2. *stop* restraint.
3. *outsport discretion* over-celebrate.

7. *with your earliest* as soon as possible, but more colloquial – closer to 'ASAP'.

9–10. *fruits are to ensue ... twixt me and you* Othello's words here suggest the marriage has not yet been consummated (i.e. completed through sexual union).

13–16. Iago switches to prose and thus a reduced formality. Cassio, his superior officer, should try to resist this but fails to (see lines 28–30).
15–16. *made wanton the night* had sex with.
16. *sport for Jove* Jupiter, king of the gods, was notoriously sex-driven; Iago is being vulgar here.

17. Cassio remains respectful in his description of Desdemona.

18. *full of game* expert in love-play (see line 16).

SCENE 3

Cyprus. The citadel.

[Enter OTHELLO, DESDEMONA, CASSIO, *and Attendants.]*

Othello
Good Michael, look you to the guard to-night.
Let's teach ourselves that honourable stop,
Not to outsport discretion.

Cassio
Iago hath direction what to do;
But, notwithstanding, with my personal eye   5
Will I look to't.

Othello
                    Iago is most honest.
Michael, good night. To-morrow with your earliest
Let me have speech with you. *[To* DESDEMONA*]*
                                Come, my dear love,
The purchase made, the fruits are to ensue;
That profit's yet to come twixt me and you. –   10
Good night. *[Exeunt* OTHELLO, DESDEMONA *and Attendants.]*

[Enter IAGO.*]*

Cassio
Welcome, Iago; we must to the watch.

Iago
Not this hour, Lieutenant; 'tis not yet ten o'the clock. Our
general cast us thus early for the love of his Desdemona;
who let us not therefore blame. He hath not yet made   15
wanton the night with her; and she is sport for Jove.

Cassio
She is a most exquisite lady.

Iago
And, I'll warrant her, full of game.

19. fresh ... delicate Cassio is once again too naïve to realise the way these respectful words can be heard (as Iago does) as lewd ones.

20. parley to provocation a military (or here, sexual) challenge; 'parley' is a trumpet call.

22. alarm call.

25. stoup a very large bottle or tankard.

25–6. a brace of Cyprus gallants 'a brace' refers to a pair of something – in this case young men ('gallants'), but Iago actually means a crowd here (he is lying to lure Cassio into the trap).

26. fain gladly.

26. have a measure to raise a glass (usually of wine) to toast/in honour of (Othello).

28–9. very poor and unhappy brains for drinking i.e. I cannot hold my alcohol/ it affects me strongly. It is naïve of Cassio to reveal this (dropping into prose shows the over-familiarity): the admission is made man to man rather than duty officer to lower rank.

34. innovation change, the effect of one drink on him (perhaps shown by Cassio physically staggering on stage).

37. What man! i.e. I don't believe this! Iago is over-familiar and pushy to a superior rank on duty; he should call Cassio 'Sir'.

Cassio
　Indeed, she is a most fresh and delicate creature.
Iago
　What an eye she has! Methinks it sounds a parley to
　　provocation.　　　　　　　　　　　　　　　　　　20
Cassio
　An inviting eye; and yet methinks right modest.
Iago
　And when she speaks, is it not an alarm to love?
Cassio
　She is indeed perfection.
Iago
　Well, happiness to their sheets! Come, Lieutenant, I
　have a stoup of wine; and here without are a brace of　25
　Cyprus gallants that would fain have a measure to the
　health of the black Othello.
Cassio
　Not to-night, good Iago. I have very poor and unhappy
　brains for drinking; I could well wish courtesy would
　invent some other custom of entertainment.　　　　30
Iago
　O, they are our friends – but one cup; I'll drink for
　you.
Cassio
　I have drunk but one cup to-night, and that was craftily
　qualified too, and behold what innovation it makes
　here. I am unfortunate in the infirmity, and dare not　35
　task my weakness with any more.
Iago
　What man! 'Tis a night of revels. The gallants desire
　it.
Cassio
　Where are they?
Iago
　Here at the door; I pray you call them in.　　　　40
Cassio
　I'll do't; but it dislikes me. *[Exit.]*

48. *Potations* alcoholic drinks.
48. *pottle deep* a half gallon tankard (4 pints).
49. *swelling* showing off.
50. *That hold their honours in a wary distance* that are quick to take offence (the offence referred to in line 43).
52. *fluster'd with flowing cups* got them drunk.
53. *watch* guards.

58. *a rouse already* more than enough alcohol (to get him drunk).

62. *canakin* a small drinking vessel.
62. *clink* the sound of drinking vessels clashed together.
62–74. Note all the 'c' (and 'k') sounds to help the actors convey the effects of heavy drinking on their shaping and expression of words. Shakespeare delights in such studies of drunkenness; *Twelfth Night* and *The Tempest* (among others) have similarly well-observed comic scenes.

Iago
    If I can fasten but one cup upon him,
    With that which he hath drunk to-night already,
    He'll be as full of quarrel and offence
    As my young mistress' dog. Now my sick fool
        Roderigo,   45
    Whom love hath turn'd almost the wrong side
        outward,
    To Desdemona hath to-night carous'd
    Potations pottle deep; and he's to watch.
    Three else of Cyprus – noble swelling spirits,
    That hold their honours in a wary distance,   50
    The very elements of this warlike isle –
    Have I to-night fluster'd with flowing cups,
    And they watch too. Now, 'mongst this flock of
        drunkards
    Am I to put our Cassio in some action
    That may offend the isle – but here they come.   55

    [Re-enter CASSIO with MONTANO, and Gentlemen,
        followed by Servant with wine.]

    If consequence do but approve my dream,
    My boat sails freely, both with wind and stream.
Cassio
    Fore God, they have given me a rouse already.
Montano
    Good faith, a little one; not past a pint, as I am a
    soldier.   60
Iago
    Some wine, ho!
    [Sings] And let me the canakin clink, clink;

        And let me the canakin clink.
        A soldier's a man;
        O, man's life's but a span;   65
        Why, then, let a soldier drink –

    Some wine, boys.

68–107. Note how a general undertone of menace gradually takes hold during this comic drinking scene, cloaked by good humour. Iago is manipulating Cassio for his own malicious ends: getting a successful promotion rival drunk in order to disgrace him. While the banter of drunken soldiers is entertaining there is always the danger that one comedy insult might go too far and escalate into the violence Iago eventually provokes Cassio to commit; see, for example, Iago's baiting repetition of 'Lieutenant' in lines 94 and 97 and Cassio's baited response in line 98).

70. *potent in potting* able to consume large quantities of alcohol (pots of ale). The English were (and are) famous for their drinking capacity.

71. *swag-bellied* fat, sagging ('beer') belly.

73. *expert* (and *exquisite* line 89) more opportunities for the actors to present comically slurred speech.

74–6. *your* repeated here, and through several speeches following, suggests the inappropriately matey drunken 'togetherness' Iago is creating.

75. *Almain* German.

78. *do you justice* match you drink for drink.

81. *crown* five shillings.

83. *lown* loon (crazy), rogue (dishonest).

87. *auld* old.

91–2. *I hold him … those things* Cassio expresses a vague (and drunken) awareness that he, a Lieutenant of the guard, should not be joining in with this drunken banter. Note how Iago gloatingly addresses Cassio by his official title of Lieutenant in his next two speeches (lines 94 and 97).

Cassio

Fore God, an excellent song!

Iago

I learn'd it in England, where indeed they are most
potent in potting: your Dane, your German, and your   70
swag-bellied Hollander – Drink, ho! – are nothing to
your English.

Cassio

Is your Englishman so expert in his drinking?

Iago

Why, he drinks you with facility your Dane dead drunk;
he sweats not to overthrow your Almain; he gives your   75
Hollander a vomit ere the next pottle can be fill'd.

Cassio

To the health of our General!

Montano

I am for it, Lieutenant; and I'll do you justice.

Iago

O sweet England! *[Sings.]*

> King Stephen was and a worthy peer,   80
> His breeches cost him but a crown;
> He held 'em sixpence all too dear,
> With that he call'd the tailor lown.
> He was a wight of high renown,
> And thou art but of low degree.   85
> 'Tis pride that pulls the country down;
> Then take thy auld cloak about thee –

Some wine, ho!

Cassio

Fore God, this is a more exquisite song than the other.

Iago

Will you hear't again?   90

Cassio

No; for I hold him to be unworthy of his place that does
those things. Well, God's above all; and there be souls
must be saved, and there be souls must not be saved.

95–6. *no offence … man of quality* not to be insulting to any man of high rank, i.e. though not Iago. The drink is making Cassio a bit irritable now.
96. *be saved* go to heaven.

98–9. *the Lieutenant … before the Ancient* Cassio is now pulling rank – rather late in the day – about going to heaven first (over the man he beat to promotion).
101–2. *Do not think … I am drunk* Cassio is too drunk to realise how drunk he is or how ridiculous he looks. This moment of high comedy also confirms that Iago has successfully manipulated Cassio into a position of great weakness and vulnerability.

108. *platform* artillery mount.
108. *set the watch* mount the guard. Cassio should be in overall charge of all this.

110. *fit to stand by Caesar* i.e. as good as a General (the highest rank in the army).
112. *a just equinox* i.e. in perfect balance (as are the length of night and day at the spring and autumn equinoxes). Iago is pretending to defend Cassio's *vice* (line 111) of drunkenness by calling it a balance to his *virtue* (line 112); in reality, of course, he is setting him up as unworthy of his office.

116. *shake* undermine (a reference to the shaking brought on by excessive alcohol).

117. *evermore* always and without fail.
118–9. *He'll watch the … rock not his cradle* He would stay awake all night if he didn't drink himself to sleep.
118. *horologue a double set* 24 hours, i.e. twice round the clock face.

Iago

  It's true, good Lieutenant.

Cassio

  For mine own part – no offence to the   95
  General, nor any man of quality – I hope to be
    saved.

Iago

  And so do I too, Lieutenant.

Cassio

  Ay, but, by your leave, not before me; the Lieutenant
  is to be saved before the Ancient. Let's have no more
  of this; let's to our affairs. God forgive us our sins. 100
  Gentlemen, let's look to our business. Do not think,
  gentlemen, I am drunk. This is my ancient; this is my
  right hand, and this is my left hand. I am not drunk
  now; I can stand well enough, and I speak well enough.

All

  Excellent well.   105

Cassio

  Why, very well, then. You must not think, then, that
  I am drunk. *[Exit.]*

Montano

  To the platform, masters; come, let's set the watch.

Iago

  You see this fellow that is gone before:
  He is a soldier fit to stand by Caesar   110
  And give direction; and do but see his vice;
  'Tis to his virtue a just equinox,
  The one as long as th' other. 'Tis pity of him.
  I fear the trust Othello puts him in,
  On some odd time of his infirmity,   115
  Will shake this island.

Montano

                But is he often thus?

Iago

  'Tis evermore the prologue to his sleep:
  He'll watch the horologe a double set,

119. *rock not his cradle* doesn't put him to sleep.

120. *put in mind* informed.

122. *Prizes* values.

127. *hazard* risk.

128. *ingraft infirmity* ingrained/inherited problem, i.e. alcoholism.

136–7. *beat the knave ... a twiggen bottle* beat him until he has a criss-cross of weals on his body (that look like the wicker-work on a bottle of wine). Note the alcohol-related metaphor; Cassio is now completely lost in drink-fuelled fury.

If drink rock not his cradle.

Montano

                              It were well
The General were put in mind of it.   120
Perhaps he sees it not, or his good nature
Prizes the virtue that appears in Cassio,
And looks not on his evils. Is not this true?

         [Enter RODERIGO.]

Iago

   [Aside to him] How, now, Roderigo!
I pray you, after the Lieutenant; go.   125

         [Exit RODERIGO.]

Montano

And 'tis great pity that the noble Moor
Should hazard such a place as his own second
With one of an ingraft infirmity:
It were an honest action to say
So to the Moor.

Iago

                Not I, for this fair island;   130
I do love Cassio well; and would do much
To cure him of this evil.

        [Within: Help, help!]

But hark, what noise?

    [Re-enter CASSIO, driving in RODERIGO.]

Cassio

Zounds, you rogue, you rascal!

Montano

What's the matter, Lieutenant?   135

Cassio

A knave teach me my duty! But I'll beat the knave into
a twiggen bottle.

139. *prate* boast – and note the use of *thou* (it was 'you' at line 134), the form of 'you' spoken to a social inferior. Cassio and Montana will address each other respectfully (*sir*, *you*) even as they fight.

141. *mazard* head.

142. *Come, come, you're drunk* Iago has primed Montano in advance how to read Cassio's drunkenness, i.e. as habitual/an addiction.

144. *cry a mutiny* alert others to this fight.

147. *goodly* good, but ironic here.

148. *Diablo* Shakespeare's only use of the Spanish word for the devil, echoing the Spanish name Iago ('James' in English).
149. *rise* revolt.

152. *He dies* I'll kill him!

Roderigo
  Beat me!
Cassio
  Dost thou prate, rogue? *[Strikes him.]*
Montano
  Nay, good Lieutenant; I pray you, sir, hold your hand. 140
Cassio
  Let me go, sir, or I'll knock you o'er the mazard.
Montano
  Come, come, you're drunk.
Cassio
  Drunk! *[They fight.]*
Iago
  [Aside to RODERIGO*]* Away, I say!
  Go out and cry a mutiny. *[Exit* RODERIGO*.]*
  Nay, good Lieutenant. God's will, gentlemen!   145
  Help, ho! – Lieutenant – sir – Montano – sir –
  Help, masters! Here's a goodly watch indeed!

        [A bell rung.]

  Who's that which rings the bell? Diablo, ho!
  The town will rise. God's will, Lieutenant, hold.
  You'll be asham'd for ever.   150

    [Re-enter OTHELLO and Gentlemen, with weapons.]

Othello
  What is the matter here?
Montano
  Zounds, I bleed still; I am hurt to the death – He dies.
Othello
  Hold, for your lives!
Iago
  Hold, ho! Lieutenant – sir – Montano – gentlemen –
  Have you forgot all sense of place and duty?   155
  Hold! The General speaks to you; hold, hold, for
    shame!

158. *turn'd Turks* In early modern English, this derogatory phrase meant to become barbarian or lose control. This was a supposed direct contrast to being Christian and English (or here Venetian). This focuses attention on Othello's ambiguous identity as both a 'Moor' and '*of* Venice'. 'Turn'd Turk' is ambiguous here depending on whether 'turn'd' is understood as a verb or an adjective; but Othello's whole situation is ambiguous. See introduction, p.viii.

161. *carve* cut (with a sword).

162. *Holds his soul ... dies upon the motion* He who doesn't value his life will lose it the moment he moves.

163. *dreadful* terrifying.

164. *propriety* peace, how things should be.

164. *masters* officials of rank (though not acting like it here).

166. *On thy love* by your loyalty to me (the audience will be aware of the heavy irony here).

168. *quarter* friendship.

172. *speak* explain.

173. *odds* at odds, quarrelling.

176. *you are thus forgot* you have forgotten yourself and your responsibility, let yourself down.

182. *mouths of wisest censure* in the opinion of wise judges.

182. *unlace your reputation* undo/lose your good name.

183. *rich opinion* worthy reputation.

Othello

    Why, how now, ho! From whence ariseth this?
    Are we turn'd Turks, and to ourselves do that
    Which Heaven hath forbid the Ottomites?
    For Christian shame, put by this barbarous brawl.   160
    He that stirs next to carve for his own rage
    Holds his soul light: he dies upon his motion.
    Silence that dreadful bell; it frights the isle
    From her propriety. What's the matter, masters?
    Honest Iago, that looks dead with grieving,   165
    Speak. Who began this? On thy love, I charge thee.

Iago

    I do not know. Friends all but now, even now,
    In quarter, and in terms, like bride and groom
    Divesting them for bed; and then, but now,
    As if some planet had unwitted men,   170
    Swords out, and tilting one at other's breast
    In opposition bloody. I cannot speak
    Any beginning to this peevish odds;
    And would in action glorious I had lost
    These legs that brought me to a part of it!   175

Othello

    How comes it, Michael, you are thus forgot?

Cassio

    I pray you, pardon me; I cannot speak.

Othello

    Worthy Montano, you were wont be civil;
    The gravity and stillness of your youth
    The world hath noted, and your name is great   180
    In mouths of wisest censure – what's the matter
    That you unlace your reputation thus,
    And spend your rich opinion for the name
    Of a night-brawler? Give me answer to't.

Montano

    Worthy Othello, I am hurt to danger;   185
    Your officer Iago can inform you,
    While I spare speech, which something now offends
      me,

190. *self-charity* self-defence.

193. *My blood begins my safer guides to rule* I'm starting to lose my temper.

194. *collied* blackened with dirt or grime as, for example, by coal dust, and used here as a metaphor for Othello's psychological state, but is perhaps also linked to his physical blackness. This metaphor marks a fleeting moment of self-insight into Othello's inner 'chaos' and his need to control it; all forgotten later as he allows Iago to provoke his jealousies and uncertainties as an outsider who lacks Venetian social graces and is the older husband of a young wife. Othello knows he acts too hastily when he is angry, but he continues to act anyway to dismiss Cassio. We might ask what this suggests about Othello's struggle to exercise good judgement when his emotions have been roused – meaning he acts prematurely and later regrets his actions. Iago takes advantage of this character flaw and it ultimately leads to Othello's downfall – so this is a pivotal moment in the play: Iago has found his means to destroy Othello and says as much in his next soliloquy (lines 321–47).

195. *Assays* tries.

198. *foul rout* ugly brawl.

199. *approv'd* found guilty.

206. *partially affin'd* partial, biased.

206. *leagu'd in office* afraid to speak out against a superior officer.

217. *entreats his pause* begs him to stop.

Of all that I do know; nor know I aught
By me that's said or done amiss this night,
Unless self-charity be sometimes a vice,   190
And to defend ourselves it be a sin
When violence assails us.

Othello

                  Now, by heaven,
My blood begins my safer guides to rule;
And passion, having my best judgment collied,
Assays to lead the way. Zounds if I stir   195
Or do but lift this arm, the best of you
Shall sink in my rebuke. Give me to know
How this foul rout began, who set it on;
And he that is approv'd in this offence,
Though he had twinn'd with me, both at a birth,   200
Shall lose me. What! in a town of war,
Yet wild, the people's hearts brim full of fear,
To manage private and domestic quarrel,
In night, and on the court and guard of safety!
'Tis monstrous. Iago, who began't?   205

Montano

If partially affin'd, or leagu'd in office,
Thou dost deliver more or less than truth,
Thou art no soldier.

Iago

                  Touch me not so near;
I had rather ha this tongue cut from my mouth
Than it should do offence to Michael Cassio;   210
Yet, I persuade myself, to speak the truth
Shall nothing wrong him. This it is, General.
Montano and myself being in speech,
There comes a fellow crying out for help,
And Cassio following him with determin'd sword   215
To execute upon him. Sir, this gentleman
Steps in to Cassio and entreats his pause;
Myself the crying fellow did pursue,
Lest by his clamour, as it so fell out,

233. *indignity* insult.

235. *mince* reduce, as with meat mixed with non-meat.

237. *never more be officer of mine* This will turn out to be true despite all Cassio and Desdemona's efforts (and Othello's evident private wishes) – but also to be less than the career disaster it appears at this point.

242. *Myself will be your surgeon* Othello takes personal responsibility for Montano's treatment.

244. *silence those … distracted* put an end to any gossip about this fight.

The town might fall in fright; he, swift of foot,   220
Outran my purpose, and I return'd the rather
For that I heard the clink and fall of swords,
And Cassio high in oath; which till to-night
I ne'er might see before. When I came back,
For this was brief, I found them close together   225
At blow and thrust, even as again they were
When you yourself did part them.
More of this matter can I not report;
But men are men; the best sometimes forget.
Though Cassio did some little wrong to him,   230
As men in rage strike those that wish them best,
Yet surely Cassio, I believe, receiv'd
From him that fled some strange indignity
Which patience could not pass.

Othello

                    I know, Iago,
Thy honesty and love doth mince this matter,   235
Making it light to Cassio. Cassio, I love thee;
But never more be officer of mine.

[Re-enter DESDEMONA, attended.]

Look if my gentle love be not rais'd up.
I'll make thee an example.

Desdemona

What is the matter, dear?

Othello

               All's well now, sweeting;   240
Come away to bed. *[To MONTANO]* Sir, for your hurts,
Myself will be your surgeon. Lead him off.

[MONTANO is led off.]

Iago, look with care about the town,
And silence those whom this vile brawl distracted.
Come, Desdemona; 'tis the soldiers' life   245
To have their balmy slumbers wak'd with strife.

[Exeunt all but IAGO and CASSIO.]

248. *past all surgery* more than physically.

249. *God forbid!* God willing, let it not be so; a pious expression spoken by a 'devil' – the cynical and duplicitous Iago.

252. *bestial* like an animal; corrupted.

256. *idle* pointless.
257. *imposition* forced on you by others.

259. *man!* an overfamiliar address, as to a social equal (see also line 37).

265. *sue* appeal.

267. *speak parrot* talk foolishly.
268. *discourse fustian* speak nonsense.

Iago

What, are you hurt, Lieutenant?

Cassio

Ay, past all surgery.

Iago

Marry, God forbid!

Cassio

Reputation, reputation, reputation! O, I have lost my 250
reputation! I have lost the immortal part of myself,
and what remains is bestial. My reputation, Iago, my
reputation!

Iago

As I am an honest man, I had thought you had receiv'd
some bodily wound; there is more sense in that than 255
in reputation. Reputation is an idle and most false
imposition; oft got without merit, and lost without
deserving. You have lost no reputation at all, unless
you repute yourself such a loser. What, man! there are
more ways to recover the General again; you are but 260
now cast in his mood, a punishment more in policy
than in malice; even so as one would beat his offence-
less dog to affright an imperious lion. Sue to him again,
and he's yours.

Cassio

I will rather sue to be despis'd than to deceive so good 265
a commander with so slight, so drunken, and so indiscreet an officer. Drunk! And speak parrot! And squabble,
swagger, swear! And discourse fustian with one's own
shadow! O thou invisible spirit of wine, if thou hast
no name to be known by, let us call thee devil! 270

Iago

What was he that you follow'd with your sword? What
had he done to you?

Cassio

I know not.

Iago

Is't possible?

282-3. It hath pleas'd the devil drunkenness ... devil wrath Shakespeare's audience would recognise this Bible reference to Ephesians 4.27: 'Be ye angry and sin not. Let not the sun go down on your wrath, neither give place to the devil' – meaning don't nurse your anger or let it lead you into evil deeds. Cassio's adaptation reveals his self-loathing and genuine remorse for his weakness. He knows anger is as much a sin that the devil can use as drunkenness.

283. wrath extreme anger. Cassio is angry now, not drunk.

290. Hydra the many-headed monster of Greek mythology; if you cut off one of its heads, two more grew in its place.

293. inordinate over the limit.
293. unblest cursed.

295. familiar creature a friend, but with a chilling pun (for Shakespeare's audience) on a witch's familiar: a demon or spirit in animal form, such as a cat or toad, that attends on a witch and helps her carry out evil schemes. This is one of the play's many references to Iago as a 'devil' involved in the dark arts.
298. approv'd evidenced.
300-1. Our General's wife is now the General Iago cynically suggests that Othello will now be influenced in all his professional decisions by his wife. He is being both honest and devious here. He is genuinely contemptuous of Othello's love for Desdemona (and of any man's love for a woman), which he believes is likely to weaken him. But it is also the foundation of Iago's plotting that Cassio should pursue Desdemona (in the hope of influencing her husband) and this suggestion advances that aim.
303. mark observation.
303. parts characteristics.

Cassio

I remember a mass of things, but nothing distinctly; 275
a quarrel, but nothing wherefore. O God, that men
should put an enemy in their mouths to steal away
their brains! That we should with joy, pleasance, revel
and applause, transform ourselves into beasts!

Iago

Why, but you are now well enough. How come you 280
thus recovered?

Cassio

It hath pleas'd the devil drunkenness to give place to
the devil wrath. One unperfectness shows me another,
to make me frankly despise myself.

Iago

Come, you are too severe a moraller. As the time, the 285
place, and the condition of this country stands, I could
heartily wish this had not so befall'n; but since it is
as it is, mend it for your own good.

Cassio

I will ask him for my place again: he shall tell me I
am a drunkard. Had I as many mouths as Hydra, such 290
an answer would stop them all. To be now a sensible
man, by and by a fool, and presently a beast! O strange!
Every inordinate cup is unblest, and the ingredience
is a devil.

Iago

Come, come, good wine is a good familiar creature if 295
it be well us'd; exclaim no more against it. And, good
Lieutenant, I think you think I love you.

Cassio

I have well approv'd it, sir. I drunk!

Iago

You or any man living may be drunk at a time, man.
I'll tell you what you shall do. Our General's wife is 300
now the General – I may say so in this respect, for
that he hath devoted and given up himself to the
contemplation, mark, and denotement, of her parts

304. *graces* virtues, attractions.

306. *blessed a disposition* good natured. This is more evidence of Iago's duplicity; compare how he described Desdemona in Act 2, Scene 1, lines 248–50.
309. *splinter* apply a splint to (a 'splint' is a strip of material used to support a broken bone, continuing the *broken joint* metaphor from line 309).
311. *grow stronger than it was before* a broken bone is stronger after it has healed.

316. *undertake for me* put forward my case (to Othello).

318. *You are in the right* I agree with you (and have justice on your side).

321–47. Iago's third soliloquy picks up where the second left off, but now he knows how to proceed in his scheme having witnessed Othello's loss of emotional control (see note to line 195).
322. *free* frank.
323. *Probal to thinking* i.e. supportive of reasoned argument, persuasive.

325. *inclining* lending a sympathetic ear, leaning towards (flirtatiously, in crude Iago's mind).

328–9. *To win the Moor ... redeemed sin* i.e. Desdemona has such a (sexual) hold over Othello, she could make him renounce his Christian baptism. (Ironically it is 'devil' Iago with whom Othello will 'renounce his baptism' in a murderous vow in Act 3 Scene 3 and the murder by which it is fulfilled.)
330. *enfetter'd* enslaved, under her power.
332–4. *How am I, then, a villain ... parallel course* Iago cheekily suggests that it is Desdemona who is the real villain by playing 'the god' with Othello's 'weak function' (poor reasoning because of his emotions).

and graces – confess yourself freely to her; importune
her help to put you in your place again: she is of so 305
free, so kind, so apt, so blessed a disposition, she holds
it a vice in her goodness not to do more than she is
requested. This broken joint between you and her
husband entreat her to splinter; and, my fortunes
against any lay worth naming, this crack of your love 310
shall grow stronger than it was before.

Cassio

You advise me well.

Iago

I protest, in the sincerity of love and honest
kindness.

Cassio

I think it freely; and betimes in the morning I will 315
beseech the virtuous Desdemona to undertake for me.
I am desperate of my fortunes if they check me here.

Iago

You are in the right. Good night, Lieutenant; I must
to the watch.

Cassio

Good night, honest Iago. *[Exit.]* 320

Iago

And what's he, then, that says I play the villain?
When this advice is free I give and honest,
Probal to thinking, and indeed the course
To win the Moor again? For 'tis most easy
The inclining Desdemona to subdue 325
In any honest suit: she's fram'd as fruitful
As the free elements. And then for her
To win the Moor – were't to renounce his baptism,
All seals and symbols of redeemed sin –
His soul is so enfetter'd to her love 330
That she may make, unmake, do what she list,
Even as her appetite shall play the god
With his weak function. How am I, then, a villain
To counsel Cassio to this parallel course,

335. *Divinity of hell!* Hell's religion. Iago might here be seen to directly address the Devil, as the character of Vice from the medieval morality plays would. Vice is the personification of evil who continuously attempts to corrupt mankind; he is not the Devil himself (although sometimes it's hard to tell the difference), but he is very much the Devil's agent in the world.

336. *devils* Iago includes himself in this reference.

341. *pestilence* corrupting evil, infection, poison.

342. *repeals him for her body's lust* advances Cassio's cause because she wants to sleep with him.

345. *turn her virtue into pitch* pitch (tar) is a sticky, thick black liquid. Iago is saying he will deliberately blacken (destroy) Desdemona's good name.

353. *wit* good judgment.

358. *dilatory* slow-moving.

360. *cashier'd Cassio* got Cassio sacked.

363. *By th' mass* a holy oath (referring to the Christian service).

363. *'tis morning!* This long scene takes about 20 minutes to act. Shakespeare made it clear in line 13 that the all-night party it represents began around 10 in the evening and (helped by the reference to the sun at line 361) that stage time has brought us all the way to dawn.

365. *billeted* housed.

Directly to his good? Divinity of hell!   335
When devils will their blackest sins put on,
They do suggest at first with heavenly shows,
As I do now; for whiles this honest fool
Plies Desdemona to repair his fortunes,
And she for him pleads strongly to the Moor,   340
I'll pour this pestilence into his ear –
That she repeals him for her body's lust;
And by how much she strives to do him good
She shall undo her credit with the Moor.
So will I turn her virtue into pitch;   345
And out of her own goodness make the net
That shall enmesh them all.

[Enter RODERIGO.]

How now, Roderigo!
Roderigo
I do follow here in the chase, not like a hound that
hunts, but one that fills up the cry. My money is almost
spent; I have been to-night exceedingly well cudgell'd;   350
and I think the issue will be – I shall have so much
experience for my pains as that comes to; and so, with
no money at all, and a little more wit, return again to
Venice.
Iago
How poor are they that have not patience!   355
What wound did ever heal but by degrees?
Thou know'st we work by wit, and not by
     witchcraft;
And wit depends on dilatory time.
Doesn't not go well? Cassio hath beaten thee,
And thou, by that small hurt, hast cashier'd Cassio.   360
Though other things grow fair against the sun,
Yet fruits that blossom first will first be ripe.
Content thyself awhile. By th' mass, 'tis morning!
Pleasure and action make the hours seem short.
Retire thee; go where thou art billeted.   365

372. *bring him jump* bring him exactly on time. Iago's schemes are brilliantly skillful and daring in their manipulation of time and persons but also require a fortuitous development of events (as here) that seems almost supernatural.
373. *Soliciting* In Shakespeare's time the word had opposite meanings: petitioning legally *or* inciting to lawlessness. This verbal slipperiness suits Iago's moral deviousness. (Today the word has the added meaning of petitioning for sexual business; Iago would be delighted.)
374. *device* cunning plan.

Away, I say; thou shalt know more here-after.
Nay, get thee gone. *[Exit* RODERIGO.*]*
Two things are to be done:
My wife must move for Cassio to her mistress;
I'll set her on;   370
Myself awhile to draw the Moor apart
And bring him jump when he may Cassio find
Soliciting his wife. Ay, that's the way;
Dull not device by coldness and delay. *[Exit.]*

ACT 3 SCENE 1

A musical entertainment hired by Cassio for the newlyweds, and heckled by a Clown, rapidly gives way to a conversation between Emilia, Iago's wife, about how Cassio can be restored into Othello's favour. Emilia reassures him that Othello is only making a temporary public example of him.

1. *content your pains* pay you for your trouble (musicians had to endure a clown's bawdy banter).
2. *Good morrow* a traditional greeting to a bride and groom emerging from their wedding night.

8. *thereby hangs a tail* if spelt 'tale' this would mean 'there's a story attached to that', but the pun ('tail') here means penis.

10. *a wind instrument* here, a (flatulent) anus.

13–15. *make no more noise … music that may not be heard* The music is literally a non-event and these twenty-eight lines are often cut in production but it foreshadows the fate of the marriage, which comes to nothing.

ACT 3
SCENE 1

Cyprus. Before the citadel.

[Enter CASSIO, *with Musicians.]*

Cassio

    Masters, play here; I will content your pains.
    Something that's brief; and bid 'Good morrow,
      General'. *[Music.]*

[Enter Clown.]

Clown

    Why masters, ha your instruments been in Naples, that
    they speak i' th' nose thus?

1 Musician

    How, sir, how?   5

Clown

    Are these, I pray, call'd wind instruments?

1 Musician

    Ay, marry, are they, sir.

Clown

    O, thereby hangs a tail.

1 Musician

    Whereby hangs a tale, sir?

Clown

    Marry, sir, by many a wind instrument that I know.   10
    But, masters, here's money for you; and the General
    so likes your music that he desires you, of all loves, to
    make no more noise with it.

1 Musician

    Well, sir, we will not.

Clown

    If you have any music that may not be heard, to't   15
    again; but, as they say, to hear music the General does

23. *quillets* word-play.

25. *stirring* awake.

27. *stirring* The Clown picks up on the alternative meaning of the word Cassio used in line 25: sexually arousing.

29. *happy* lucky, well met.

not greatly care.

1 Musician

We have none such, sir.

Clown

Then put up your pipes in your bag, for I'll away. Go;
vanish into air; away.   20

[Exeunt Musicians.]

Cassio

Dost thou hear, my honest friend?

Clown

No, I hear not your honest friend; I hear you.

Cassio

Prithee keep up thy quillets. There's a poor piece of
gold for thee. If the gentlewoman that attends the
General's wife be stirring, tell her there's one Cassio   25
entreats her a little favour of speech. Wilt thou do this?

Clown

She is stirring, sir; if she will stir hither, I shall seem
to notify unto her.

Cassio

Do, good my friend.   *[Exit Clown.]*

[Enter IAGO.]

In happy time, Iago.

Iago

You have not been abed, then?   30

Cassio

Why, no; the day had broke before we parted.
I have made bold, Iago,
To send in to your wife: my suit to her
Is that she will to virtuous Desdemona
Procure me some access.

Iago

I'll send her to you presently;   35
And I'll devise a mean to draw the Moor

119

39–40. *I never knew … more kind and honest* Iago is as honest and kind as friends Cassio has known in his home town of Florence (except he isn't).

44. *speaks for you stoutly* speaks highly of you.

46. *great affinity* a family of high rank.

49. *front* forelock.

55. *bosom* private thoughts and feelings.
55. *bound to* indebted to.

Out of the way, that your converse and business
May be more free.

Cassio

I humbly thank you for't. *[Exit IAGO]* I never knew
A Florentine more kind and honest.   40

[Enter EMILIA.]

Emilia

Good morrow, good Lieutenant. I am sorry
For your displeasure; but all will sure be well.
The General and his wife are talking of it;
And she speaks for you stoutly: the Moor replies
That he you hurt is of great fame in Cyprus   45
And great affinity, and that in wholesome wisdom
He might not but refuse you; but he protests he
          loves you,
And needs no other suitor but his likings
To take the safest occasion by the front
To bring you in again.

Cassio

                    Yet, I beseech you,   50
If you think fit, or that it may be done,
Give me advantage of some brief discourse
With Desdemona alone.

Emilia

                    Pray you come in.
I will bestow you where you shall have time
To speak your bosom freely.

Cassio

                         I am much bound to you.   55

[Exeunt.]

SCENE 2

This short scene, like Act 3 Scene 1, covers the passing of time. Shakespeare uses it to show us Othello as an impressive public official (most of the play is about his private life). Othello exits to inspect the fortifications.

4. *Repair* return.

SCENE 2

Cyprus. The citadel.

[Enter OTHELLO, IAGO, and Gentlemen.]

Othello
    These letters give, Iago, to the pilot;
    And by him do my duties to the Senate.
    That done, I will be walking on the works;
    Repair there to me.

Iago
                Well, my good lord, I'll do't.

Othello
    This fortification, gentlemen – shall we see't?   5

Gentleman
    We'll wait upon your lordship.

[Exeunt.]

SCENE 3

Desdemona, prompted by Emilia, meets with Cassio and readily agrees to be an advocate for him with her husband. Iago has set this situation up and directs Othello's attention to the intimacy between the two, encouraging Othello to see it as adulterous. He then cleverly fosters and directs Othello's growing jealousy and paranoia about Cassio while seeming to defend him. He then encourages Othello to view his new wife – and Venetian women in general – as routinely unfaithful and of loose morals. The more Othello trusts 'honest' Iago the less he trusts Desdemona. They make a solemn vow together as friends to avenge Othello's 'grievances' against Cassio and Desdemona.

11. *You have known him long* Othello has good reasons for trusting Cassio.

13. *politic distance* will have to seem distant to reassure the public.

23. *I'll watch him tame* Desdemona will keep Othello awake, and by this forced wakefulness make him obedient. Note the association of Othello with unconfined natural things (as previously the sea). He will return the compliment by comparing his marriage to her with hawk-taming (see lines 261–4). (See also p.xiv of the Introduction.)

SCENE 3

Cyprus. The garden of the citadel.

[Enter DESDEMONA, CASSIO, and EMILIA.]

Desdemona
Be thou assur'd, good Cassio, I will do
All my abilities in thy behalf.
Emilia
Good madam, do. I warrant it grieves my husband
As if the case were his.
Desdemona
O, that's an honest fellow. Do not doubt, Cassio,   5
But I will have my lord and you again
As friendly as you were.
Cassio
                                    Bounteous madam,
Whatever shall become of Michael Cassio,
He's never any thing but your true servant.
Desdemona
I know't – I thank you. You do love my lord;   10
You have known him long; and be you well assur'd
He shall in strangeness stand no farther off
Than in a politic distance.
Cassio
                                    Ay, but, lady,
That policy may either last so long,
Or feed upon such nice and waterish diet,   15
Or breed itself so out of circumstances,
That, I being absent, and my place supplied,
My general will forget my love and service.
Desdemona
Do not doubt that; before Emilia here
I give thee warrant of thy place. Assure thee,   20
If I do vow a friendship, I'll perform it
To the last article. My lord shall never rest;
I'll watch him tame, and talk him out of patience;

125

24. *shrift* the confessional box in church.

28. *give thy cause away* give up on your case.

34. *your discretion* as you think fit.

42. *I have been talking with a suitor here* Desdemona's honest directness and clear conscience undoes Iago's first attempt to implicate her and Cassio (see his use of *sneak* and *guilty-like* to describe their behaviour in line 39). This unassuming honesty and trust increases the tragic impact later.

His bed shall seem a school, his board a shrift;
I'll intermingle everything he does   25
With Cassio's suit. Therefore be merry, Cassio;
For thy solicitor shall rather die
Than give thy cause away.

[Enter OTHELLO and IAGO.]

Emilia
Madam, here comes my lord.
Cassio
Madam, I'll take my leave.   30
Desdemona
Why, stay, and hear me speak.
Cassio
Madam, not now. I am very ill at ease,
Unfit for mine own purposes.
Desdemona
Well, do your discretion.

[Exit CASSIO.]

Iago
Ha! I like not that.
Othello
                          What dost thou say?   35
Iago
Nothing, my lord; or if – I know not what.
Othello
Was not that Cassio parted from my wife?
Iago
Cassio, my lord! No, sure, I cannot think it,
That he would sneak away so guilty-like,
Seeing your coming.
Othello
                          I do believe 'twas he.   40
Desdemona
How now, my lord!
I have been talking with a suitor here,

47. *reconciliation* restoration into favour.

50. *I have no judgement in an honest face* i.e. 'If Cassio doesn't loyally love you, then I'm no judge of an honest man.' He does, and she is, but Othello will adopt Iago's paranoid view of both instead.
51. *prithee* I pray thee.

58. *dinner* the midday meal.

60–3. Ridley suggests that Desdemona is like a persistent child here that 'would try a patience considerably more placid that Othello's' (footnote to lines 61–62 of *Othello*, Arden edition, 1958, p.96). But there is another way of looking at this: she is attempting to persuade him to hear her reasoning. For example, she reminds him of how well Cassio has treated him previously. However, he refuses to hear her plea. This raises the question of women's power and how Desdemona is disempowered by marriage: what power can she have as an 'obedient wife'? Perhaps in this moment she is beginning to learn the limits of her power and that Othello is not listening to her good reason and kindness.

A man that languishes in your displeasure.
Othello
Who is't you mean?
Desdemona
Why, your lieutenant, Cassio. Good my lord,   45
If I have any grace or power to move you,
His present reconciliation take;
For if he be not one that truly loves you,
That errs in ignorance, and not in cunning,
I have no judgment in an honest face.   50
I prithee call him back.
Othello
                    Went he hence now?
Desdemona
Yes, faith; so humbled
That he hath left part of his grief with me
To suffer with him. Good love, call him back.
Othello
Not now, sweet Desdemona; some other time.   55
Desdemona
But shall't be shortly?
Othello
                  The sooner, sweet, for you.
Desdemona
Shall't be to-night at supper?
Othello
                      No, not to-night.
Desdemona
To-morrow dinner, then?
Othello
                  I shall not dine at home;
I meet the captains at the citadel.
Desdemona
Why, then, to-morrow night, or Tuesday morn,   60
On Tuesday noon or night, on Wednesday morn.
I prithee name the time; but let it not
Exceed three days. I'faith, he's penitent;

64. *our common reason* the general view.

70. *mamm'ring on* delaying, perhaps stammering.

72. *dispraisingly/ Hath ta'en your part* pretending to be critical so that Cassio would praise him.

74. *By'r Lady* By Our Lady (i.e. the Virgin Mary) – a mild swear word.

76. *I will deny thee nothing* I cannot keep refusing you.
76. *boon* favour.

81. *touch* test.
82. *full of poise and difficult weight* difficult to weigh up, to decide.

85. *leave me but a little to myself* allow me a little time to myself; an ominous statement for the future of a marriage.

87. *straight* straightaway.

89. *Whate'er you be, I am obedient* I am a good wife whether you, Othello, are a good husband or not. Note the respectful 'you'. He calls her 'thou', as to an intimate or an inferior. These are subtle clues as to how Desdemona is now constrained to 'obedience' by marriage and cannot question him, and how Othello reinforces this.

And yet his trespass, in our common reason –
Save that, they say, the wars must make example   65
Out of her best – is not almost a fault
T' incur a private check. When shall he come?
Tell me, Othello – I wonder in my soul
What you would ask me that I should deny,
Or stand so mamm'ring on. What! Michael Cassio,   70
That came a-wooing with you, and so many a time,
When I have spoke of you dispraisingly,
Hath ta'en your part – to have so much to do
To bring him in! By'r Lady, I could do much –

Othello

Prithee, no more; let him come when he will;   75
I will deny thee nothing.

Desdemona

                Why, this is not a boon;
'Tis as I should entreat you wear your gloves,
Or feed on nourishing dishes, or keep you warm,
Or sue to you to do a peculiar profit
To your own person. Nay, when I have a suit   80
Wherein I mean to touch your love indeed,
It shall be full of poise and difficult weight,
And fearful to be granted.

Othello

             I will deny thee nothing.
Whereon I do beseech thee grant me this,
To leave me but a little to myself.   85

Desdemona

Shall I deny you? No; farewell, my lord.

Othello

Farewell, my Desdemona. I'll come to thee straight.

Desdemona

Emilia, come. – Be as your fancies teach you;
Whate'er you be, I am obedient.

[Exeunt DESDEMONA *and* EMILIA.*]*

90-2. This famous brief speech as Othello begins to doubt his marriage approaches the linguistic intensity of the metaphysical love poet John Donne. The ominous oxymoron *Excellent wretch* yokes praise with ambiguity ('wretch' as a term of both affection and the abuse the general will soon be hurling at his new wife). The grammar here is illogical, representing Othello's mental chaos. *Perdition*, the damnation of his soul, joins with *But I do love thee*, and this paradox is compounded by the addition of (*and*) its absence or opposite (*I love thee not*) via the modifying adverb *when*. When love is gone, *Chaos is come again* – so love (not Chaos) and Chaos (not love) exist simultaneously. Language is cracking under the strain, and so is Othello!

92. *Chaos* Love was the first god to emerge from Chaos in Greek Mythology.

94-5. *Did Michael Cassio ... Know of your love?* Iago's great temptation starts here. He is more than incredibly skilled, using supremely varied in tactics. Here he plants questions in Othello's mind while *seemingly* reluctant to have them answered. He would have made a superb prosecuting attorney. Note the poignant reminder of close friendship in Othello by using Cassio's first name.

97. *satisfaction* proof.

100. *went between us* i.e. as a messenger.

102. *aught in that?* anything odd in that?

103-4. *Is he not honest? ... Ay, honest* This key word/idea is introduced early in Act 3 by the Clown and Cassio and repeated seventeen times during it, fourteen times in this third scene. Othello uses the word seven times in this Act and nineteen times in the play as a whole, like a refrain; Iago says the word four times in Act 3, once as 'honesty', and sixteen times in the play. Here Iago uses a kind of reverse psychology, planting the question of Cassio's honesty in Othello's mind then planting the answer that Cassio is not honest while seeming to say that he is.

Othello

    Excellent wretch! Perdition catch my soul   90
    But I do love thee; and when I love thee not
    Chaos is come again.

Iago

    My noble lord!

Othello

              What dost thou say, Iago?

Iago

    Did Michael Cassio, when you woo'd my lady,
    Know of your love?   95

Othello

    He did, from first to last. Why dost thou ask?

Iago

    But for a satisfaction of my thought – No further
    harm.

Othello

        Why of thy thought, Iago?

Iago

    I did not think he had been acquainted with her.

Othello

    O, yes; and went between us very often.   100

Iago

    Indeed!

Othello

    Indeed? Ay, indeed. Discern'st thou aught in that?
    Is he not honest?

Iago

              Honest, my lord?

Othello

    Honest? Ay, honest.

Iago

             My lord, for aught I know.

Othello

    What dost thou think?

Iago

             Think, my lord?   105

111. *of my counsel* in my confidence.

115. *conceit* idea.

120. *stops* pauses (in conversation).

123. *close delations* secret accusations (with a possible pun on 'dilations', the valves of the heart pumping out blood).
123. *working from the heart* expressions of true, heartfelt thoughts.

125. *dare presume* assume, but with a cunning suggestion of doubt.

126. *Men should be what they seem* a person should be what they *appear* to be. While Othello is (to a tragic fault) the speaker (Iago) is certainly not. Pretending to be something while actually being something else is a key theme of the play. This is a supremely ironic line, spoken by a man who is anything but what he seems, then repeated – put into the mouth of – Othello (line 128), the very man duped by the pretence. The duplicity might provide comic amusement to an audience if the resulting consequences weren't so tragic.

Othello

Think, my lord! By-heaven, he echoes me,
As if there were some monster in his thought
Too hideous to be shown. Thou dost mean
    something:
I heard thee say but now thou lik'st not that,
When Cassio left my wife. What didst not like?   110
And when I told thee he was of my counsel
In my whole course of wooing, thou criedst
    'Indeed!'
And didst contract and purse thy brow together,
As if thou then hadst shut up in thy brain
Some horrible conceit. If thou dost love me,   115
Show me thy thought.

Iago

My lord, you know I love you.

Othello

                        I think thou dost;
And for I know thou art full of love and honesty,
And weigh'st thy words before thou giv'st them
    breath,
Therefore these stops of thine affright me the more;   120
For such things in a false disloyal knave
Are tricks of custom; but in a man that's just
They are close delations, working from the heart
That passion cannot rule.

Iago

                        For Michael Cassio,
I dare presume I think that he is honest.   125

Othello

I think so too.

Iago

                Men should be that they seem;
Or those that be not, would they might seem none!

Othello

Certain, men should be what they seem.

129. *Why then, I think Cassio's an honest man* Iago sows doubt with both these qualifying words and the comma-marked pause.

132. *ruminate* think it over.

135. *that* that which.

139. *apprehensions* ideas.
140. *leets and law-days* special local courts, legal sessions.

144–50. Iago never makes the sinister meaning of this sentence quite clear (great deceptions are often built on half-truths). His deliberately confused and confusing sentence checks back on itself through qualifying words (*though, as, perchance, would, if*), two parentheses on top of each other and further subordinated clauses. It is no surprise that Othello answers it with *Zounds! What dost thou mean?* (line 155). Othello's language too will also start to break down into meaningless soon. Disintegration of meaning is deliberately calculated in Iago, but a genuine mental chaos and failure of reason in Othello.
145. *vicious* faulty.
146. *my nature's plague* the fault in my nature.
147. *my jealousy* protectiveness of Othello (more irony).
149. *conjects* conjectures, imaginings.
151. *observance* observation.

Iago

    Why then, I think Cassio's an honest man.

Othello

    Nay, yet there's more in this.   130

    I prithee speak to me as to thy thinkings,

    As thou dost ruminate; and give thy worst of

        thoughts

    The worst of words.

Iago

                Good my lord, pardon me.

    Though I am bound to every act of duty,

    I am not bound to that all slaves are free to –   135

    Utter my thoughts. Why, say they are vile and false,

    As where's that palace whereinto foul things

    Sometimes intrude not? Who has that breast so pure

    But some uncleanly apprehensions

    Keep leets and law-days, and in sessions sit   140

    With meditations lawful?

Othello

    Thou dost conspire against thy friend, Iago,

    If thou but think'st him wrong'd, and mak'st his ear

    A stranger to thy thoughts.

Iago

                I do beseech you,

    Though I perchance am vicious in my guess,   145

    As, I confess, it is my nature's plague

    To spy into abuses, and oft my jealousy

    Shapes faults that are not – that your wisdom

    From one that so imperfectly conjects,

    Would take no notice; nor build yourself a trouble.   150

    Out of his scattering and unsure observance.

    It were not for your quiet nor your good,

    Nor for my manhood, honesty, or wisdom,

    To let you know my thoughts.

Othello

    Zounds! What dost thou mean?   155

160. *filches* takes, steals.

166. *beware, my lord, of Jealousy* Iago uses reverse psychology here: he is planting the very jealousy he pretends to warn against!

166–71. This famous speech encapsulates the play's central themes of jealousy, betrayal (real and imagined), male sexual paranoia and deception. It is also a blueprint of Iago's (and Shakespeare's) entire plot and the brutal manipulations by which that plot will destroy the two principals. In this way, the speech foreshadows the tragedy. 'Honest' Iago will drive Othello mad with jealousy by means of (and through) the wreckage of all he holds dear while – with supreme irony – appearing to be Othello's one trustworthy friend. The irony extends to the audience who can see what is happening (while Othello cannot) and so feels implicated in the deception.

167. *green-ey'd monster* In Renaissance times, emotions were linked with colours and the colour chosen for envy and jealousy – green – has endured and become a proverb for it. Green is traditionally associated with the pallor of ill-health or with foods that have gone bad; Iago's speech memorably links the colour with the vicious emotion, adding the frightful idea of a monster that sickens itself by feeding on itself.

167–8. *mock/ The meat it feeds on* the 'meat' is the victim's heart, which is 'mocked' (laughed at) as it is consumed.

168. *cuckold* (See note for Act 1, Scene 3, lines 383–4.)

170. *tells* counts.

171. *dotes* to be silly or weak-minded, especially in old age ('dotage') including in one's emotional attachments. Iago is perhaps deliberately touching a nerve with the word here (while pretending to counsel against such thoughts): alluding to the older Othello's relationship with Desdemona.

174. *fineless* boundless, infinite.

179. *follow still the changes of the moon* to change constantly (like the moon).

Iago

Good name in man and woman, dear my lord,
Is the immediate jewel of their souls:
Who steals my purse steals trash; 'tis something,
nothing;
'Twas mine, 'tis his, and has been slave to
thousands;
But he that filches from me my good name   160
Robs me of that which not enriches him
And makes me poor indeed.

Othello

By heaven, I'll know thy thoughts.

Iago

You cannot, if my heart were in your hand;
Nor shall not, whilst 'tis in my custody.   165

Othello

Ha!

Iago

O, beware, my lord, of jealousy;
It is the green-ey'd monster which doth mock
The meat it feeds on. That cuckold lives in bli
Who, certain of his fate, loves not his wronger,
But, O, what damned minutes tells he o'er   170
Who dotes, yet doubts, suspects, yet strongly loves!

Othello

O misery!

Iago

Poor and content is rich, and rich enough;
But riches fineless is as poor as winter
To him that ever fears he shall be poor.   175
Good God, the souls of all my tribe defend
From jealousy!

Othello

Why, why is this?
Think'st thou I'd make a life of jealousy,
To follow still the changes of the moon
With fresh suspicions? No; to be once in doubt   180

181. *goat* a horned animal legendary for its lust and associated with the devil because of it. (Note also the ominous hint of the sacrificial victim of Tragedy, which means, literally, 'goat song' in the original Greek. See Introduction, p.x.)

183. *exsufflicate and blown surmises* literally ideas swollen and fed on by flies, but meaning 'suspicions sordidly inflated beyond probability'.

200–1. *free and noble nature/ Out of self-bounty* a trusting and honest person, and so mistakenly assuming the same goodness in others.

202. *country disposition* (and see line 238) Iago's suggestion is that Desdemona as a Venetian woman will have loose morals and secret extra-marital affairs. This exploits Othello's weakness as an outsider who is unsure of the ways of Venice.

207. *She did deceive her father, marrying you* A reminder of Brabantio's warning at the end of Act 1, Scene 3, line 293. Iago is fiendishly encouraging doubt the father-in-law's warning may have planted in Othello's now much less secure mind.

208–9. *And when she seem'd ... lov'd them most* Iago alleges Desdemona's two-facedness, i.e. her love for Othello concealed from her father beneath a show of demure fear of Othello's manliness. This resonates with Othello, as he immediately responds *And so she did* (line 209). Iago therefore succeeds in twisting Desdemona's awed appreciation of the mighty warrior come into the protective world of her father's house, painting a paranoid revision of her genuine excited feelings, love mingled with fear and awakening into womanhood.

209. *Why, go to then!* 'well then, what more proof do you need?'

Is once to be resolv'd. Exchange me for a goat
When I shall turn the business of my soul
To such exsufflicate and blown surmises
Matching thy inference. 'Tis not to make me jealous
To say my wife is fair, feeds well, loves company,   185
Is free of speech, sings, plays, and dances well;
Where virtue is, these are more virtuous.
Nor from mine own weak merits will I draw
The smallest fear or doubt of her revolt;
For she had eyes, and chose me. No, Iago;   190
I'll see before I doubt; when I doubt, prove;
And, on the proof, there is no more but this –
Away at once with love or jealousy!

Iago

I am glad of this; for now I shall have reason
To show the love and duty that I bear you   195
With franker spirit. Therefore, as I am bound,
Receive it from me. I speak not yet of proof.
Look to your wife; observe her well with Cassio;
Wear your eyes thus, not jealous nor secure.
I would not have your free and noble nature   200
Out of self-bounty be abus'd; look to't.
I know our country disposition well:
In Venice they do let God see the pranks
They dare not show their husbands; their best
    conscience
Is not to leave't undone, but keep't unknown.   205

Othello

Dost thou say so?

Iago

She did deceive her father, marrying you;
And when she seem'd to shake and fear your looks,
She lov'd them most.

Othello

                  And so she did.

Iago

                      Why, go to then!

211. *seel her father's eyes up close as oak* shut her father's eyes (like a close-fitting oak door) to her real character.

216. *Not a jot* not at all.

219–20. *not to strain my speech/ To grosser issues* don't take my words to more than I says, with a sense of 'gross' sexual behaviour.

228. *nature erring from itself* Othello himself feeds Iago his next destructive idea.

230. *affect* look favourably upon.
231. *clime, complexion and degree* country, colour (white) and social rank.

She that, so young, could give out such a seeming,   210
To seel her father's eyes up close as oak –
He thought 'twas witchcraft. But I am much to blame;
I humbly do beseech you of your pardon
For too much loving you.

Othello

                        I am bound to thee for ever.

Iago

I see this hath a little dash'd your spirits.   215

Othello

Not a jot, not a jot.

Iago

                I'faith, I fear it has.
I hope you will consider what is spoke
Comes from my love; but I do see you are mov'd.
I am to pray you not to strain my speech
To grosser issues nor to larger reach   220
Than to suspicion.

Othello

I will not.

Iago

           Should you do so, my lord,
My speech should fall into such vile success
Which my thoughts aim'd not. Cassio's my worthy
    friend –
My lord, I see you are mov'd.

Othello

                   No, not much mov'd.   225
I do not think but Desdemona's honest.

Iago

Long live she so! and long live you to think so!

Othello

And yet, how nature erring from itself –

Iago

Ay, there's the point: as – to be bold with you –
Not to affect many proposed matches   230
Of her own clime, complexion, and degree,

233. *smell* suspect.
234. *disproportion* lack of moderation.

237. *recoiling* giving way to.
238. *forms* the outward appearance of the body; *country forms* the fashions or style of beauty associated with Desdemona's own country, Venice. Venice was famous for its fashionable and alluring women and for their sexual sophistication. Iago plays on Othello's insecurities about this. Given Iago's vulgar mind and low opinion of women he is also probably using *country* as a sort of code-word for sexual abandon, because the countryside was associated with animals and uncontrolled appetites.

243. *Why did I marry?* a stock question of the wronged husband in marriage comedies.
244. *unfolds* reveals.

251. *strain his entertainment* insist on Cassio's reinstatement.
252. *vehement importunity* powerful pleading.

256. *hold her free* believe her innocent (until proven guilty).

257. *Fear not my government* Don't worry, I am in control of my self (an ironic comment, in view of what happens later).

Whereto we see in all things nature tends –
Foh! one may smell in such a will most rank,
Foul disproportion, thoughts unnatural.
But pardon me – I do not in position   235
Distinctly speak of her; though I may fear
Her will, recoiling to her better judgment,
May fall to match you with her country forms,
And happily repent.

Othello

              Farewell, farewell.
If more thou dost perceive, let me know more;   240
Set on thy wife to observe. Leave me, Iago.

Iago

My lord, I take my leave. *[Going.]*

Othello

Why did I marry? This honest creature doubtless
Sees and knows more – much more than he unfolds.

Iago

[Returning] My lord, I would I might entreat your
    honour   245
To scan this thing no further; leave it to time.
Although 'tis fit that Cassio have his place,
For, sure, he fills it up with great ability,
Yet if you please to hold him off awhile,
You shall by that perceive him and his means.   250
Note if your lady strain his entertainment
With any strong or vehement importunity;
Much will be seen in that. In the mean time
Let me be thought too busy in my fears –
As worthy cause I have to fear I am –   255
And hold her free, I do beseech your honour.

Othello

Fear not my government.

Iago

I once more take my leave. *[Exit.]*

Othello

This fellow's of exceeding honesty,

260–1. knows all qualities ... human dealing has studied and understands human nature (rather like his creator, Shakespeare, and certainly more than the speaker, Othello).

261. haggard an untamed female hawk, with ruffled plumage.

262. jesses a hawk's leg straps, by which the bird is held.

263–4. whistle her off ... prey at fortune a hawk was 'whistled off' into the wind to hunt. If Desdemona's untameable, he will cut her loose to 'go down the wind' to ruin, the prey of fortune. Iago has suggested to Othello that his wife is not under his control and never will be. Othello seems to be accepting this and that, like the hawk, she will never fly back. So he will abandon her to her fate. (He has no plan to kill her at this point.)

264. Haply, for perhaps because.

266–7. declin'd / Into the vale of years old (i.e. nearer the valley of the shadow of Death).

268. abus'd wronged. Note Othello's decision to believe Iago's rumours without speaking to Desdemona or having witnessed any direct evidence of her alleged affair with Cassio.

270. call these delicate creatures ours upper-class wives were considered the legal 'property' of their husbands and called them 'my lord'.

273–4. keep a corner ... others' uses 'She's mine; I don't want other men to be able to use my wife sexually.' Othello's possessiveness is paranoid and immature, but we must remember the marital context for the landed upper classes in Shakespeare's time. Our modern belief in marriage by choice and for love (rather than as a feudal property arrangement and for the begetting of heirs) did exist: it was always the official belief of the Christian Church and its marriage service, favoured among the middle classes and frequently argued for in Shakespeare's plays. However, Othello and Desdemona's (upper) class did not necessarily expect love within marriage and often pursued it outside.

275. Prerogativ'd Privileged.

277. forked plague horned; signed as a cuckold.

285. pain upon my forehead a subtle reference to the cuckold's horns.

286. watching over-work.

287. bind it hard Note Desdemona's first use of the famous handkerchief – here as a nursing object – and her role as domestic comforter (nurse-guardian of Othello's work–life balance.) The handkerchief is established as a symbol of this 'wifely' role.

And knows all qualities, with a learned spirit,   260
Of human dealing. If I do prove her haggard,
Though that her jesses were my dear heart-strings,
I'd whistle her off and let her down the wind
To prey at fortune. Haply, for I am black
And have not those soft parts of conversation   265
That chamberers have, or for I am declin'd
Into the vale of years – yet that's not much –
She's gone; I am abus'd; and my relief
Must be to loathe her. O curse of marriage,
That we can call these delicate creatures ours,   270
And not their appetites! I had rather be a toad,
And live upon the vapour of a dungeon,
Than keep a corner in the thing I love
For others' uses. Yet 'tis the plague of great ones;
Prerogativ'd are they less than the base;   275
'Tis destiny unshunnable, like death:
Even then this forked plague is fated to us
When we do quicken. Look where she comes.

[Re-enter DESDEMONA *and* EMILIA.*]*

If she be false, O, then heaven mocks itself!
I'll not believe it.
Desdemona

          How now, my dear Othello?   280
Your dinner, and the generous islanders
By you invited, do attend your presence.
Othello
I am to blame.
Desdemona

          Why do you speak so faintly?
Are you not well?
Othello
I have a pain upon my forehead here.   285
Desdemona
Faith, that's with watching; 'twill away again.
Let me but bind it hard, within this hour

288–90. Note the stage direction. The handkerchief is rejected (*too little*) and so the rejected carer drops it.

294. *Woo'd* persuaded (with a hint of Iago's scheming pillow talk).

295. *conjur'd her* made her promise.

297. *work* embroidery or needlework; *ta'en out* copied. Emilia, conditioned to serve Iago's cravings, will have the handkerchief *copied* for him. Iago will seize the original instead (line 317 and stage direction) and have it dropped in Cassio's lodgings.

298–300. *What he'll do ... please his fantasy* Note Emilia's role here as subservient wife; her existence is defined by serving Iago not her mistress. Her first 'I' is the object of these verbs yet the second becomes the subject – of 'please his fantasy'.

304. *a common thing* no big deal. Iago automatically belittles his wife and her service to him (echoing Othello's 'too little' in line 288).

It will be well.

[He puts the handkerchief from him, and she drops it.]

Othello

           Your napkin is too little.
Let it alone. Come, I'll go in with you.

Desdemona

  I am very sorry that you are not well.   290

[Exeunt OTHELLO and DESDEMONA.]

Emilia

  I am glad I have found this napkin.
This was her first remembrance from the Moor.
My wayward husband hath a hundred times
Woo'd me to steal it; but she so loves the token –
For he conjur'd her she should ever keep it –   295
That she reserves it evermore about her
To kiss and talk to. I'll ha the work ta'en out,
And give't Iago. What he'll do with it
Heaven knows, not I;
I nothing but to please his fantasy.   300

[Re-enter IAGO.]

Iago

  How now! What do you here alone?

Emilia

  Do not you chide; I have a thing for you,

Iago

  You have a thing for me?
It is a common thing!

Emilia

  Ha!   305

Iago

  To have a foolish wife.

Emilia

  O, is that all? What will you give me now
For that same handkerchief?

311. *which so often you did bid me steal* Why did Iago covet the handkerchief and urge his wife to get it for him? Is it his desire for Desdemona, whom he has said he 'loves' (Act 2, Scene 1, line 285) or a sign of Othello and Desdemona's marriage, which he envies and hates? Either way, the handkerchief will become increasingly important in signifying Desdemona. For Othello, it will represent his ownership of her and her favour given (he believes) to Cassio.

314. *to the advantage* by lucky chance. The most astonishing luck attends all of Iago's schemes; if he makes his own luck, an evil fate supports him. Some critics, including Coleridge and Alvin Kernan, have suggested that Iago is to some extent a version of the Vice character from medieval morality plays and that the play is therefore partly an allegory of good (Desdemona) versus evil (Iago). On this reading, Iago's luck can be read as the Devil's own: the force of evil is with him. Other critics, such as Ridley and Empson, depart from the allegorical view: Ridley sees Iago as a 'superbly skilful and opportunist tactician', motivated by power rather than evil (Ridley, M.R. (ed.) 'Introduction', *Othello*, Arden, 1958, p. ixx); Empson views him as an agent of truth who bluntly exposes the romantic nonsense on which Othello's marriage is based and hopes to be loved for doing so.

318. *import* importance.
319–20. Note Emilia's concern for Desdemona.

321. *Be not acknown on't* keep quiet about it.
322. *Go, leave me* Iago's instructions to Emilia here echo Othello's words to Desdemona (line 85).

326. *holy writ* religious texts, i.e. the Bible.
328. *conceits* fantasies.

Iago

What handkerchief?

Emilia

What handkerchief!
Why that the Moor first gave to Desdemona;   310
That which so often you did bid me steal.

Iago

Hast stole it from her?

Emilia

No, faith; she let it drop by negligence,
And to the advantage, I, being here, took't up.
Look, here it is.

Iago

A good wench! Give it me.   315

Emilia

What will you do with't, that you have been so
       earnest
To have me filch it?

Iago

Why, what's that to you?

[Snatching it.]

Emilia

If it be not for some purpose of import,
Give me't again. Poor lady, she'll run mad
When she shall lack it.   320

Iago

Be not acknown on't; I have use for it.
Go, leave me.

[Exit EMILIA.]

I will in Cassio's lodging lose this napkin,
And let him find it. Trifles light as air
Are to the jealous confirmations strong   325
As proofs of holy writ; this may do something.
The Moor already changes with my poison.
Dangerous conceits are in their natures poisons

151

331. *Burn like the mines of sulphur* fires that are incredibly hard to put out.

332. *poppy* opium.
332. *mandragora* a soporific, a drug to induce sleep.

334. *medicine* used as verb; i.e. act as a medicine.
335. *owed'st* had.

337. *how now?* What's the matter? (As if he didn't know!)

338. *Avaunt!* Away!

341. *What sense … of lust?* Othello has convinced himself of Desdemona's infidelity by *imagining* her in bed with other soldiers.
343. *free* carefree.

348. *the general camp* the whole army.
349. *Pioneers* the lowest rank of soldier.
352. *plumed* feathered.
352–60. The 'farewell speech' – here to army life – was a set piece of classical poetry and drama much imitated by Shakespeare's contemporaries and successors. This fine example tragically re-invokes the grand Othello of Act 1. His majestic farewell to *plumed troops, and the big wars* (line 352) appears at first to be just an epic emotional gesture: saying that his loss of Desdemona and of his reputation in (imagined) cuckoldry means he no longer has any interest in his professional life. But it will turn out to be his actual farewell to arms (the events set in train by Iago will deprive Othello of both his army command and his life).

Which at the first are scarce found to distaste
But, with a little act upon the blood,   330
Burn like the mines of sulphur.

[Re-enter OTHELLO.]

                    I did say so.
Look where he comes! Not poppy, nor mandragora,
Nor all the drowsy syrups of the world,
Shall ever medicine thee to that sweet sleep
Which thou owed'st yesterday.   335

Othello

Ha! ha! false to me, to me?

Iago

Why, how now, General? No more of that.

Othello

Avaunt! be gone! Thou hast set me on the rack.
I swear 'tis better to be much abus'd
Than but to know 't a little.

Iago

                    How now, my lord!   340

Othello

What sense had I in her stol'n hours of lust?
I saw 't not, thought it not, it harm'd not me.
I slept the next night well, fed well, was free and
    merry;
I found not Cassio's kisses on her lips.
He that is robb'd, not wanting what is stol'n,   345
Let him not know't, and he's not robb'd at all.

Iago

I am sorry to hear this.

Othello

I had been happy if the general camp,
Pioneers and all, had tasted her sweet body,
So I had nothing known. O, now for ever   350
Farewell the tranquil mind! farewell content!
Farewell the plumed troops, and the big wars
That makes ambition virtue! O, farewell!

357. *Pride, pomp, and circumstance, of glorious war!* all seen as positives, of a wonderful former life now lost to him (and it's true, his army days are over, line 360).

358. *mortal engines* deadly artillery.

359. *immortal Jove's dread clamours* thunder.

360. *occupation's gone* no more fulfilling work.

[Taking him by the throat.] It has become a custom in the theatre for the actor to seize Iago by the throat here or at line 367, thus this stage direction added to Shakespeare's text. It signifies a moment of passion from Othello, a reminder to the audience of the titanic forces contained within him and the enormity of what is at stake. The play pivots around this: Othello *could* be about to seize back his marriage, happiness and optimistic world-view from the abyss Iago is engineering for him. It is also a critical moment for Iago: he could easily have lost his nerve and his plot could have unravelled in the face of such fury. This is one of those moments of agonised engagement, of an audience wanting to shout out advice, for which the play is famous.

366. *Is't come to this?* Are you serious?

367–9. *Make me to see't … or woe upon thy life!* Give me proof (***probation***) of her infidelity – or else! Othello is a man of action, a soldier hero whose thinking breaks down under pressure of Iago's clever manipulations into howls of agony and meaninglessness. He is out-thought from start to finish by his subtle antagonist Iago.

372. *remorse* repentance.

373. *accumulate* pile up.

376–9. *O heaven forgive me! … thine honesty a vice!* Forgive me for daring to be so honest. Iago is being cheekily and fiendishly devious here, but as Shakespeare himself wrote in *The Merchant of Venice*, his other play set in Venice, 'The devil can cite Scripture for his purpose'.

378. *God buy you* if that's your attitude, I'll be off! I'll resign as your ensign and friend.

378. *wretched fool* Iago addresses himself here (disingenuously).

Farewell the neighing steed and the shrill trump,
The spirit-stirring drum, th' ear-piercing fife,   355
The royal banner, and all quality,
Pride, pomp, and circumstance, of glorious war!
And O ye mortal engines whose rude throats
Th' immortal Jove's dread clamours counterfeit,
Farewell! Othello's occupation's gone.   360

Iago

Is't possible, my lord?

Othello

Villain, be sure thou prove my love a whore –
   [Taking him by the throat.]
Be sure of it; give me the ocular proof;
Or, by the worth of man's eternal soul,
Thou hadst been better have been born a dog   365
Than answer my wak'd wrath.

Iago

                  Is't come to this?

Othello

Make me to see't; or, at the least, so prove it
That the probation bear no hinge nor loop
To hang a doubt on; or woe upon thy life!

Iago

My noble lord –   370

Othello

If thou dost slander her and torture me,
Never pray more; abandon all remorse;
On horror's head horrors accumulate;
Do deeds to make heaven weep, all earth amaz'd;
For nothing canst thou to damnation add   375
Greater than that.

Iago

            O grace! O heaven forgive me!
Are you a man? Have you a soul or sense? –
God buy you; take mine office. O wretched fool,
That liv'st to make thine honesty a vice!
O monstrous world! Take note, take note, O world,   380

382. *profit* lesson.
383. *sith love breeds such offence* since my friendship causes you such distress.

386. *that* what.

390. *Dian's* Diana the goddess of virginity.
390–1. *begrim'd and black / As mine own face* Note how Othello accepts the negative (racist) associations of his physical appearance. (See also the Introduction, p.vi.)
393. *satisfied* certain (of the truth of Iago's allegations).

399. *topp'd* mounted (by a man).

401. *bring them to that prospect* where you could see them.
402. *see them bolster* share the same pillow, i.e. have sex.

406. *prime as goats, as hot as monkeys* Under the guise of a close and tender friendship between men, or 'bromance', Iago tortures Othello with disgusting images of Desdemona's supposed infidelity while pretending to protect him from them.

To be direct and honest is not safe.
I thank you for this profit; and from hence
I'll love no friend, sith love breeds such offence.

Othello

Nay, stay. Thou shouldst be honest.

Iago

I should be wise; for honesty's a fool,   385
And loses that it works for.

Othello

                              By the world,
I think my wife be honest, and think she is not;
I think that thou art just, and think thou art not.
I'll have some proof. Her name, that was as fresh
As Dian's visage, is now begrim'd and black   390
As mine own face. If there be cords or knives,
Poison, or fire, or suffocating streams,
I'll not endure it. Would I were satisfied!

Iago

I see, sir, you are eaten up with passion;
I do repent me that I put it to you.   395
You would be satisfied?

Othello

                      Would! Nay, and I will.

Iago

And may; but how – how satisfied, my lord?
Would you, the supervisor, grossly gape on –
Behold her topp'd?

Othello

                Death and damnation! O!

Iago

It were a tedious difficulty, I think,   400
To bring them to that prospect. Damn them, then,
If ever mortal eyes do see them bolster
More than their own! What then? How then?
What shall I say? Where's satisfaction?
It is impossible you should see this,   405
Were they as prime as goats, as hot as monkeys,

407. *As salt as wolves in pride* as lustful as wolves in sexual heat.
409. *imputation and strong circumstances* circumstantial evidence.

415. *Prick'd to't* spurred on to it.
416–29. Critics have wondered whether Iago's sympathetic friendship with Othello is based on an unrequited sexual attraction, as some productions have explored. In which case does Iago's comically vivid description of sleeping with Cassio inform this? Or are Iago's words here simply a ploy to convey the sleeping Cassio's supposed indiscretions with Desdemona?
419. *loose* indiscreet.

432. *foregone conclusion* a previous fact (more logical than the way we now use this phrase).

434. *a shrewd doubt* a sharp guess.
434–5. *thicken other proofs / That do demonstrate thinly* provide more support for weak (insubstantial) evidence.
436. *I'll tear her all to pieces* Note the extent of Othello's rage now. At line 263 he planned simply to abandon her; it has taken Iago just half a scene to work Othello's mood up from resigned abandonment to savagery, a dehumanized intent to murder.

As salt as wolves in pride, and fools as gross
As ignorance made drunk. But yet, I say,
If imputation and strong circumstances
Which lead directly to the door of truth   410
Will give you satisfaction, you might have't.

Othello

Give me a living reason she's disloyal.

Iago

I do not like the office;
But, sith I am enter'd in this cause so far,
Prick'd to't by foolish honesty and love,   415
I will go on. I lay with Cassio lately,
And, being troubled with a raging tooth,
I could not sleep.
There are a kind of men so loose of soul
That in their sleeps will mutter their affairs: 420
One of this kind is Cassio.
In sleep I heard him say 'Sweet Desdemona,
Let us be wary, let us hide our loves',
And then, sir, would he gripe and wring my hand,
Cry 'O sweet creature!' then kiss me hard,   425
As if he pluck'd up kisses by the roots,
That grew upon my lips – then laid his leg
Over my thigh – and sigh'd, and kiss'd, and then
Cried 'Cursed fate that gave thee to the Moor!'

Othello

O Monstrous! Monstrous!   430

Iago

Nay, this was but his dream.

Othello

But this denoted a foregone conclusion.

Iago

'Tis a shrewd doubt, though it be but a dream,
And this may help to thicken other proofs
That do demonstrate thinly.   435

Othello

I'll tear her all to pieces.

440. *Spotted with strawberries* stained with strawberry juice. Iago's choice of the word 'spotted' hints at female sin or dirtiness: this 'spotted' handkerchief also 'symbolizes in miniature the wedding bedsheets which should be displayed with hymenial blood' (to prove that the bride was a virgin) (Thompson, A. ed. 'Introduction', *Othello*, Arden, 2017, p. 51). This was a cultural tradition of the time in both Africa and Europe yet based on a number of misconceptions about women's bodies. As Desdemona is later murdered in these sheets, we might ask if the red spots foreshadow her death.

440. *your wife* Iago's nagging refrain, repeated at line 443, suggests Othello's possession of Desdemona as a way of casting doubt upon it, linking this fear to Cassio (see next note).

442–4. *such a handkerchief ... wipe his beard with* Iago is setting up the next stage in his opportunity-seizing plot: Othello seeing Cassio in possession of Desdemona's handkerchief (currently in Iago's pocket!). Note how Desdemona is becoming identified with the handkerchief – an object passed around that men compete for and want to own; which Iago cunningly manipulates to settle male-on-male scores and which Othello will finally use to justify her murder.

447–9. *O that the slave ... see 'tis true* Othello's heightened anger and distress cause him to think the allegations must be true. He uses the language of deductive reason but he is driven by emotion not logic.

452. *black vengeance* (See note on lines 390–1 and the Introduction, pp.vi–vii.)

454. *fraught* cargo.

455. *aspics' tongues* the forked tongue of the asp, an Egyptian cobra and a venomous snake. In Shakespeare's tragedy *Antony and Cleopatra*, Cleopatra famously commits suicide by allowing an asp to bite her.

456. *blood, blood, blood* (see also line 440) Is Othello thinking of Desdemona's murder or his fury here? Note how in his charged emotional state he has lost the ability to speak (see also note on lines 144–50).

458. *Pontic sea* The Black Sea. Othello's overwhelming masculinity, his titanic force-of-nature, is repeatedly suggested by the sea.

461. *Propontic and the Hellespont* the seas of Marmara and the Dardanelles.

Iago

    Nay, but be wise; yet we see nothing done;
    She may be honest yet. Tell me but this:
    Have you not sometimes seen a handkerchief
    Spotted with strawberries in your wife's hand?   440

Othello

    I gave her such a one; 'twas my first gift.

Iago

    I know not that; but such a handkerchief –
    I am sure it was your wife's – did I to-day
    See Cassio wipe his beard with.

Othello

                       If it be that –

Iago

    If it be that, or any that was hers,   445
    It speaks against her with the other proofs.

Othello

    O that the slave had forty thousand lives!
    One is too poor, too weak for my revenge.
    Now do I see 'tis true. Look here, Iago –
    All my fond love thus do I blow to heaven.   450
    'Tis gone.
    Arise, black vengeance, from the hollow hell.
    Yield up, O love, thy crown and hearted throne
    To tyrannous hate! Swell, bosom, with thy fraught,
    For 'tis of aspics' tongues.

Iago

                       Yet be content.   455

Othello

    O, blood, blood, blood!

Iago

    Patience, I say; your mind perhaps may change.

Othello

    Never, Iago. Like to the Pontic sea,
    Whose icy current and compulsive course
    Ne'er feels retiring ebb, but keeps due on   460
    To the Propontic and the Hellespont;

464. *capable* comprehensive.
465. *marble* stone that is hard and pure (as is Othello and this vow of revenge). (See also Act 4, Scene 1, lines 181–2.)

468. *ever-burning lights above* the heavens.
469. *elements* heavenly powers. These 'heavenly' words turn this vow into a sort of conjuration of evil, a reversal of holiness while appearing to be holy.
469. *clip us round about* encircle us.

473. *remorse* charity, repentance.
474. *What bloody business ever* however bad it is.

475. *acceptance bounteous* rich reward.

477–9. *Within these three days ... 'Tis done at your request* This is the crucial point where Othello instructs Iago to murder Cassio and Iago agrees, all based on Iago's account and with no supporting evidence! If the climax of a play is the point of no return, the point from which the tragic conclusion is inevitable, these lines are part of that climax.
479. *let her live* Iago plants the idea of killing Desdemona by seeming to say the opposite.

483. *Now art thou my lieutenant* Both parts of Iago's original 'double knavery' (Act 1, Scene 3, line 390) are now achieved: Iago has undone the plot (Cassio's promotion over himself) that set the play going and, in its place, substituted his own.
484. *your own for ever* your faithful lieutenant always! The audience might shudder at a diabolical level to this vow, a kind of contract with a devil. Think of the 'daily beauty' Othello (like Cassio; see Act 5, Scene 1, line 19) had in his life before he 'sold his soul' to Iago's world of hatred, jealously and murder. (Shakespeare's audience would have been familiar with the famous contemporary play by Christopher Marlowe, *Dr Faustus*, in which the cheated hero sells his soul to the devil, losing everything for nothing.)

Even so my bloody thoughts, with violent pace,
Shall ne'er look back, ne'er ebb to humble love,
Till that a capable and wide revenge
Swallow them up. *[He kneels]* Now, by yond marble
   heaven,   465
In the due reverence of a sacred vow
I here engage my words.

Iago

                    [Kneeling] Do not rise yet.
Witness, you ever-burning lights above,
You elements that clip us round about,
Witness that here Iago doth give up   470
The execution of his wit, hands, heart,
To wrong'd Othello's service! Let him command,
And to obey shall be in me remorse,
What bloody business ever. *[They rise.]*

Othello

                    I greet thy love,
Not with vain thanks, but with acceptance
   bounteous,   475
And will upon the instant put thee to't.
Within these three days let me hear thee say
That Cassio's not alive.

Iago

                My friend is dead;
'Tis done at your request. But let her live.

Othello

Damn her, lewd minx! O, damn her, damn her!   480
Come, go with me apart; I will withdraw
To furnish me with some swift means of death
For the fair devil. Now art thou my lieutenant.

Iago

I am your own for ever. *[Exeunt.]*

SCENE 4

After a very brief comic turn with the Clown over the location of Cassio's lodgings, Desdemona confides to Emilia that she lost the handkerchief. Othello asks her for the handkerchief to put her on the spot, pretending he has a cold. He explains the magical origins and properties of the handkerchief to frighten her about its loss. Everything he says now is double-edged, with an innocent surface and a malicious depth. The 'free and open nature / That thinks men honest that but seem so' (Act 1, Scene 3, lines 395–6) has gone. Iago brings Cassio to her just as Othello exits. She explains that it's not a good time for her to put his case to Othello, as the latter is not himself and she seems out of favour. Cassio asks Bianca to make him a copy of the handkerchief, which she fears is another woman's love token.

1. *sirrah* 'sir', used to one of lower rank (hey, mister!).
1. *Lieutenant* actually ex-Lieutenant, as Cassio has been dismissed, so a show of defiance from Desdemona here.
2. *lies* lives.

8. *To tell you … where I lie* i.e. I don't know where he 'lies' so I'd be lying if I told you. This brief Clown episode (which holds up the action) is often cut and the quality of the clowning dismissed. Shakespeare may have needed its 'interruption' for staging purposes. It is worth considering whether the first nineteen lines of this scene have a function in a play that speeds to its conclusion without a sub-plot and, if so, what it is.

13. *edified* informed.

14. *catechize* a question and answer instruction device used in the Christian religion.

18. *compass* extent.

SCENE 4

Cyprus. Before the citadel.

[*Enter* DESDEMONA, EMILIA, *and Clown.*]

Desdemona
Do you know, sirrah, where the Lieutenant Cassio
lies?
Clown
I dare not say he lies anywhere.
Desdemona
Why, man?
Clown
He's a soldier; and for one to say a soldier lies, 'tis   5
stabbing.
Desdemona
Go to. Where lodges he?
Clown
To tell you where he lodges is to tell you where I lie.
Desdemona
Can anything be made of this?
Clown
I know not where he lodges; and for me to devise a   10
lodging, and say he lies here or he lies there, were to
lie in mine own throat.
Desdemona
Can you inquire him out, and be edified by report?
Clown
I will catechize the world for him; that is, make ques-
tions, and by them answer.   15
Desdemona
Seek him; bid him come hither: tell him I have mov'd
my lord on his behalf, and hope all will be well.
Clown
To do this is within the compass of man's wit; and
therefore I will attempt the doing it. [*Exit.*]

20. *should I lose* could I have lost.

23. *crusadoes* cross-bearing Portuguese coins, not referenced in any other Shakespeare play. The 'crusader' is a reminder perhaps of the historic tension between Christian Venice and Muslim states, which remained an active threat. The wreck of the Turkish fleet described in Act 1, Scene 3, was based on an attack by Turks on Cyprus in 1570, so *Othello* is an unusually 'contemporary' tale for Shakespeare's audiences.

26. *Is he not jealous?* a warning to Desdemona (and an ironic moment for the audience).

28. *humours* moods, whims. Desdemona's assertion that jealousy is not in Othello's nature is tragic irony.

31. *hardness to dissemble* either hard to hide his true feelings (his nature is very new to deceit) or how hardened she is in doing so (in his Iago-warped view).

33. *moist* supposed to indicate a lustful nature (see line 36).

36. *hot, hot, and moist* sexually excited.
37. *sequester* isolation.
38. *castigation* correction.

Desdemona
　　Where should I lose the handkerchief, Emilia?　　　　20
Emilia
　　I know not, madam.
Desdemona
　　Believe me, I had rather lose my purse
　　Full of crusadoes; and but my noble Moor
　　Is true of mind, and made of no such baseness
　　As jealous creatures are, it were enough　　　　25
　　To put him to ill thinking.
Emilia
　　　　　　　　　　Is he not jealous?

Desdemona
　　Who, he? I think the sun where he was born
　　Drew all such humours from him.

　　　　　[Enter OTHELLO.]

Emilia
　　　　　　　　　　Look where he comes.
Desdemona
　　I will not leave him now till Cassio
　　Be call'd to him. How is't with you, my lord?　　　30
Othello
　　Well, my good lady. *[Aside]* O,
　　　　hardness to dissemble! –
　　How do you, Desdemona?
Desdemona
　　　　　　　　　　Well, my good lord.
Othello
　　Give me your hand. This hand is moist, my lady.
Desdemona
　　It yet hath felt no age nor known no sorrow.
Othello
　　This argues fruitfulness and liberal heart:　　　　35
　　Hot, hot, and moist. This hand of yours requires
　　A sequester from liberty, fasting and prayer,
　　Much castigation, exercise devout;

39. *sweating devil* hot for hell. The implication is that Desdemona's moist hand reveals a lecherous nature that makes her ripe for hell and damnation (see line 33).

41. *frank* free and open (i.e. immoral). Othello is now incapable of 'honest' speech. Everything is an innuendo, normal on the surface, accusing Desdemona of infidelity underneath.

47. *chuck* dear.

49. *salt and sorry rheum* a miserable streaming cold.

54. *Egyptian* often misunderstood as 'gipsy', but Othello would have met real Egyptians, who were romantic faraway figures to Shakespeare's audiences (see also line 72).

55. *charmer* witch.

57. *amiable* lovely.

58–60. *if she lost it … hold her loathely* Othello may be threatening Desdemona here or informing her that this has already happened.

For here's a young and sweating devil here
That commonly rebels. 'Tis a good hand,   40
A frank one.

Desdemona

You may indeed say so;
For 'twas that hand that gave away my heart.

Othello

A liberal hand. The hearts of old gave hands;
But our new heraldry is hands, not hearts.   45

Desdemona

I cannot speak of this. Come now, your promise.

Othello

What promise, chuck?

Desdemona

I have sent to bid Cassio come speak with you.

Othello

I have a salt and sorry rheum offends me;
Lend me thy handkerchief.

Desdemona

                             Here, my lord.   50

Othello

That which I gave you.

Desdemona

                       I have it not about me.

Othello

Not?

Desdemona

      No, faith, my lord.

Othello

That's a fault. That handkerchief
Did an Egyptian to my mother give.
She was a charmer, and could almost read   55
The thoughts of people; she told her, while she kept
   it,
'Twould make her amiable, and subdue my father
Entirely to her love; but if she lost it,
Or made a gift of it, my father's eye

60. *loathley* loathsome, repulsive.

63. *take heed on't* keep it safe.

65. *perdition* ruin.

67. *web* weave.
68. *sibyl* prophetess.
69. *The sun to course two hundred compasses* 200 years old (the age of the sibyl).
70. *sew'd* i.e. the embroidery on the handkerchief.
71. *worms* silkworms.
71. *hallowed* holy.
72. *mummy* a liquid extracted from mummified bodies.
73. *Conserv'd of maidens' hearts* made of preserved virgins' blood.
73. *Is't true?* A good question! Othello tells quite a story here, and he gives a very different account of the handkerchief's origins later (see Act 5, Scene 2, lines 224–5). Othello's storytelling is now used to intimidate. Do we assume his romantic life story wasn't true either? Or has Iago corrupted Othello's previously honest telling?
74. *veritable* true, accurate.
74. *look to't well* keep it safe.
75. *would to God that I had never seen't!* a feisty response and a furious quarrel will follow.
76. *Wherefore?* Why?
77. *startlingly and rash* with such a sudden sense of urgency.

81. *It is not lost; but what an if it were?* Desdemona is so frightened by the consequences of losing the handkerchief that, betraying her honest and open nature, she lies about it here.

Should hold her loathely, and his spirits should
    hunt   60
After new fancies. She, dying, gave it me,
And bid me, when my fate would have me wive,
To give it her. I did so; and take heed on't;
Make it a darling like your precious eye;
To lose't or give't away were such perdition   65
As nothing else could match.

Desdemona
                          Is't possible?

Othello
'Tis true. There's magic in the web of it.
A sibyl that had numb'red in the world
The sun to course two hundred compasses
In her prophetic fury sew'd the work;   70
The worms were hallowed that did breed the silk;
And it was dy'd in mummy which the skilful
Conserv'd of maidens' hearts.

Desdemona
                    I'faith! Is't true?

Othello
Most veritable; therefore look to't well.

Desdemona
Then would to God that I had never seen't!   75

Othello
Ha! Wherefore?

Desdemona
Why do you speak so startingly and rash?

Othello
Is't lost? Is't gone? Speak. Is 't out o' th' way?

Desdemona
Heaven bless us!

Othello
Say you?   80

Desdemona
It is not lost; but what an if it were?

85. *suit* purpose.

94. *to blame* wrong.

95. *Zounds!* God's wounds; quite a strong swear word, which was once considered so objectionable that it had to be replaced with 'Away!' in versions of the play. But a passionate man who believes himself cuckolded is unlikely to use mild language.

96. *Is not this man jealous?* Emilia repeats the idea from line 26. In the wake of Othello's classic demonstration of jealous rage, the delivery of the line would be funny if the situation weren't so tragic.

98. *wonder* magic. Is Desdemona wondering if the Egyptian's prophecy has come true? (And note the complete fusion of two meanings in the one pun: 'wonder' as noun, a marvellous thing, and verb, speculation or pondering.)

Othello
  How!
Desdemona
  I say it is not lost.
Othello
                Fetch't, let me see't.
Desdemona
  Why, so I can, sir, but I will not now.
  This is a trick to put me from my suit: 85
  Pray you let Cassio be receiv'd again.
Othello
  Fetch me the handkerchief: my mind misgives.
Desdemona
  Come, come;
  You'll never meet a more sufficient man.
Othello
  The handkerchief!
Desdemona
            I pray talk me of Cassio.   90
Othello
  The handkerchief!
Desdemona
          A man that all his time
  Hath founded his good fortunes on your love,
  Shar'd dangers with you –
Othello
              The handkerchief!
Desdemona
  I'faith, you are to blame.
Othello
  Zounds! *[Exit* OTHELLO.*]*   95
Emilia
  Is not this man jealous?
Desdemona
  I ne'er saw this before.
  Sure there's some wonder in this handkerchief;
  I am most unhappy in the loss of it.

100. *'Tis not a year or two shows us a man* It's hardly any time before a man's true nature reveals itself.

101. *stomachs* appetites.

102. *eat us hungerly* devour us.

103. *belch* vomit. Emilia espouses a grim view of men in these lines (evidently based on her experience as Iago's wife). How well does it describe the other male characters? Desdemona would surely be thinking how it applies to Othello, and possibly also Cassio.

105. *happiness* lucky chance (as always with Iago's plots and the evil fate he seems to embody).

105. *importune* ask.

108–9. *I may again / Exist* i.e. as Lieutenant Cassio. This develops the idea of a person's 'real' identity proposed in line 100, echoed by Desdemona in line 121.

110. *office* loyal duty.

119. *thrice-gentle Cassio* an unusually lavish compliment. But Cassio represents the height of Italian Renaissance manners and civility in Cyprus. Desdemona, a Venetian lady, hasn't seen much civility lately.

120. *advocation is not now in tune* it's not a good time for me to put forward your case.

121. *My lord is not my lord* Othello isn't himself at the moment (a denial of Emilia's view in line 100).

122. *favour* appearance.

122. *humour* mood.

123. *So help me every spirit sanctified* So help me God!

125. *blank* the bull's eye on a target.

Emilia

'Tis not a year or two shows us a man. 100
They are all but stomachs, and we all but food;
They eat us hungerly, and when they are full,
They belch us.

[*Enter* CASSIO *and* IAGO.]

Look you, Cassio and my husband.

Iago

There is no other way; 'tis she must do 't.
And, lo, the happiness! Go and importune her. 105

Desdemona

How now, good Cassio, what's the news with you?

Cassio

Madam, my former suit. I do beseech you
That by your virtuous means I may again
Exist, and be a member of his love
Whom I, with all the office of my heart, 110
Entirely honour. I would not be delay'd.
If my offence be of such mortal kind
That nor my service past, nor present sorrows,
Nor purpos'd merit in futurity,
Can ransom me into his love again, 115
But to know so must be my benefit;
So shall I clothe me in a forc'd content,
And shut myself up in some other course,
To fortune's alms.

Desdemona

Alas, thrice-gentle Cassio!
My advocation is not now in tune; 120
My lord is not my lord; nor should I know him,
Were he in favour as in humour alter'd.
So help me every spirit sanctified,
As I have spoken for you all my best,
And stood within the blank of his displeasure 125
For my free speech! You must awhile be patient.
What I can do I will; and more I will
Than for myself I dare; let that suffice you.

131–4. *Can he be angry? ... is he angry?* Iago points out how momentous it is to see Othello losing his self-control. Iago has seen him under cannon fire, which blew away the ranks he stood in, including Othello's brother, without emotion. Iago clearly admired this in Othello and seems staggered at his own achievement in causing such a change. (In this scene we hear of Othello's mother and father, the Egyptian – and now a brother. Do these details make him seem less a force of Nature and more everyday, more human?)
135. *moment* momentous.

138. *sure of state* work-related.
139. *some unhatch'd practice* some business in prospect.

141. *puddled his clear spirit* confused his usually clear mind.
142–3. *Men's natures wrangle ... their object* displace their worry about greater matters (of state) to more trivial concerns. Note how she counts herself and their domestic marriage concerns as 'inferior'.
144. *endues* leads.
145. *members* limbs.

148. *As fits the bridal* as befits the wedding night.

150. *Arraigning* accusing unkindness, unnatural behaviour.
151. *suborn'd the witness* corrupted herself.

154. *toy* a trivial fancy.

Iago
    Is my lord angry?
Emilia
                                He went hence but now,
    And certainly in strange unquietness.   130
Iago
    Can he be angry? I have seen the cannon
    When it hath blown his ranks into the air,
    And, like the devil, from his very arm
    Puff'd his own brother – and is he angry?
    Something of moment, then. I will go meet him.   135
    There's matter in't indeed, if he be angry.
Desdemona
    I prithee do so. *[Exit* IAGO.*]*
    Something sure of state
    Either from Venice, or some unhatch'd practice
    Made demonstrable here in Cyprus to him,   140
    Hath puddled his clear spirit; and in such cases
    Men's natures wrangle with inferior things,
    Though great ones are their object. 'Tis even so;
    For let our finger ache, and it endues
    Our other healthful members even to a sense   145
    Of pain. Nay, we must think, men are not gods,
    Nor of them look for such observancy
    As fits the bridal. Beshrew me much, Emilia,
    I was – unhandsome warrior as I am –
    Arraigning his unkindness with my soul;   150
    But now I find I had suborn'd the witness,
    And he's indicted falsely.
Emilia
    Pray heaven it be state matters, as you think,
    And no conception nor no jealous toy
    Concerning you.   155
Desdemona
    Alas the day, I never gave him cause!
Emilia
    But jealous souls will not be answer'd so;
    They are not ever jealous for the cause,

159–60. jealous … born on it self a description of jealousy as a self-bred monster; see also Iago's description of the 'green-ey'd monster' (Act 3, Scene 3, line 167).
161–2. Heaven keep that monster … amen A Jacobean audience might shudder at the evident failure of such prayers, knowing that the monster (jealousy) already possesses Othello.

163. walk hereabout Desdemona moves Cassio from a 'private' space (Othello and Desdemona's, perhaps upstage) to a 'public' one (possibly downstage). Notice the extreme respect he shows her as she leaves (line 166).

Stage direction: [Enter BIANCA.] How should the courtesan Bianca look? Dressing her in red-petticoats would be unlikely in a play that questions and challenges the way men view women as sexual objects. Her costume should probably challenge the sex-object stereotype as well. Her profession is a 'female escort' but her love relationship with Cassio is not as a sex worker, at least as far as she is concerned. (See also the note for lines 192–3 and the Index, p.293.)
167. Save you God save you, i.e. good morning.

173. dial clock.

175. with leaden thoughts been press'd I've had a lot on my mind.
176. continuate uninterrupted.

Stage direction: Note the plot function served by the handkerchief being given to Bianca. The audience can readily imagine how Iago might use this lucky chance.
178. Take me this work out Cassio wants Bianca to make a copy of the handkerchief.

But jealous for they are jealous. 'Tis a monster
Begot upon it self, born on it self.   160

Desdemona

Heaven keep that monster from Othello's mind!

Emilia

Lady, amen.

Desdemona

I will go seek him. Cassio, walk hereabout.
If I do find him fit, I'll move your suit,
And seek to effect it to my uttermost.   165

Cassio

I humbly thank your ladyship.

[Exeunt DESDEMONA and EMILIA.]

[Enter BIANCA.]

Bianca

Save you, friend Cassio!

Cassio

                           What make you from home?
How is it with you, my most fair Bianca?
I' faith, sweet love, I was coming to your house.

Bianca

And I was going to your lodging, Cassio.   170
What, keep a week away? seven days and nights?
Eightscore eight hours? and lovers' absent hours,
More tedious than the dial eight score times?
O weary reckoning!

Cassio

                    Pardon me, Bianca.
I have this while with leaden thoughts been press'd;   175
But I shall in a more continuate time
Strike off this score of absence. Sweet Bianca,

[Giving her DESDEMONA's handkerchief.]

Take me this work out.

178. *whence came this?* Bianca's words here echo Emilia's (Act 3, Scene 3, lines 298–9). To Bianca, the handkerchief signifies a rival woman's love. It will now be used by Iago to signify (to Othello) Cassio's supposed adultery with Desdemona. Cassio is innocent of that, though we note his wish for *this* particular handkerchief to be copied and what this suggests about his feelings for Desdemona. Consider also how the handkerchief (another woman's, which she is asked to copy) represents Bianca's relationship with Cassio and how this would make her feel (a cheap substitute for another more desired woman).

180. *felt absence now I feel a cause* now I know why you've been avoiding me. Note Bianca's insecurity and jealousy, key themes of the play.

192–3. *think it no addition ... see me woman'd* It won't help my cause for him to see me with a woman (because Bianca is a courtesan, a sex-companion for the upper classes, but also because, in the man's world of this play, 'woman' is an insult). (See also the Introduction, p.iv and viii–ix, and the Index, p.296.)

196. *soon at night* tonight.

199. *I must be circumstanc'd* I'll have to make do with that, then. Note the extreme insecurity of Bianca's position with Cassio, which reflects Desdemona's vulnerability with Othello and Emilia's with Iago. This is the only Act ending without a 'clinching' couplet, which might reflect Bianca's uncertain position and also the general precariousness of the 'falling action' as we move from the crisis towards the denouement.

Bianca

　　　　　　　　O Cassio, whence came this?
This is some token from a newer friend:
To the felt absence now I feel a cause.　　　　　　180
Is't come to this? Well, well.

Cassio

　　　　　　　　Go to, woman!
Throw your vile guesses in the devil's teeth,
From whence you have them. You are jealous now
That this is from some mistress, some remembrance.
No, by my faith, Bianca.

Bianca

　　　　　　　　Why, whose is it?　　　185

Cassio

I know not neither; I found it in my chamber.
I like the work well; ere it be demanded –
As like enough it will – I would have it copied.
Take it, and do't; and leave me for this time.

Bianca

Leave you! Wherefore?　　　　　　190

Cassio

I do attend here on the General;
And think it no addition, nor my wish,
To have him see me woman'd.

Bianca

　　　　　　　　Why, I pray you?

Cassio

Not that I love you not.

Bianca

　　　　　　　　But that you do not love me.
I pray you bring me on the way a little;　　　195
And say if I shall see you soon at night.

Cassio

'Tis but a little way that I can bring you,
For I attend here; but I'll see you soon.

Bianca

'Tis very good; I must be circumstanc'd.

[Exeunt.]

ACT 4 SCENE 1

Iago tortures Othello with sordid fantasies of Desdemona's supposed infidelities. Othello is overcome with emotion and suffers a seizure. Iago sets up Cassio so that he appears to be boasting of sex with Desdemona, and to be sharing his handkerchief with his 'strumpet' (line 99), further torturing Othello. Othello (deviously guided by Iago) determines to kill Cassio and strangle Desdemona in their bed. Lodovico brings orders from Venice ordering Othello to Mauritania and replacing him with Cassio. Othello publicly and shockingly strikes Desdemona. Iago tells Lodovico this is only a minor example of Othello's recent behaviour.

1. *Think so, Iago?* The Act opens mid-conversation, as did the play. Iago and Othello's roles in Act 3, Scene 3 are now reversed: Iago leads (torturing Othello with images of Desdemona being unfaithful) and Othello follows, echoing his words, completing his lines.
2. *unauthoriz'd kiss* Some kissing was allowed in polite Venetian society, but see Iago's response to this in Act 2, Scene 1, lines 98–102.

8. *they tempt heaven* i.e. to punish their sin.

9. *a venial slip* a minor, pardonable, offence.
10. *But if I give my wife a handkerchief* Iago will now carefully work Othello up into a fit about 'Desdemona's handkerchief'. The phrase has become famous, outside of the play, to describe a symbol discussed so much it no longer means anything! – but it means plenty to Othello here.

14. *her honour* Othello adds Desdemona's chastity to all the things the handkerchief can represent.

ACT 4
SCENE 1

Cyprus. Before the citadel.

[Enter OTHELLO and IAGO.]

Iago
  Will you think so?
Othello
           Think so, Iago?
Iago
                    What,
  To kiss in private?
Othello
           An unauthoriz'd kiss.
Iago
  Or to be naked with her friend abed
  An hour or more, not meaning any harm?
Othello
  Naked abed, Iago, and not mean harm!   5
  It is hypocrisy against the devil.
  They that mean virtuously and yet do so,
  The devil their virtue tempts, and they tempt
      heaven.
Iago
  So they do nothing, 'tis a venial slip;
  But if I give my wife a handkerchief –   10
Othello
  What then?
Iago
  Why, then 'tis hers, my lord; and, being hers,
  She may, I think, bestow't on any man.
Othello
  She is protectress of her honour too:
  May she give that?   15

16. *essence* her very self.
17. **They have it … have it not** Women are often reputed for an honour they do not have (the exact reverse of Desdemona's case).

19. **I would most gladly have forgot it.** Iago makes sure he doesn't.
21. *raven* This large black bird was seen as a herald of death and associated with witchcraft.
21. *infected* plague-stricken.
22. *Boding* acting as a bad omen.

26. *importunate suit* smooth-talking for a sexual purpose.
27. *voluntary dotage* self-inflicted infatuation.
28. *Convinced or supplied* seduced.
29. *blab* brag (about it).

34. *Lie* This pun references the two meanings of 'dishonesty' as directed at a woman, i.e. telling a lie and lying (down to have sex) with a man who isn't her husband. Note also how Iago pauses to allow Othello to draw (the worst possible) conclusions.

Iago

    Her honour is an essence that's not seen;
    They have it very oft that have it not.
    But, for the handkerchief –

Othello

    By heaven, I would most gladly have forgot it.
    Thou said'st – O, it comes o'er my memory   20
    As doth the raven o'er the infected house,
    Boding to all – he had my handkerchief.

Iago

    Ay, what of that?

Othello

                    That's not so good now.

Iago

                            What
    If I had said I had seen him do you wrong?
    Or heard him say – as knaves be such abroad,   25
    Who having, by their own importunate suit,
    Or voluntary dotage of some mistress,
    Convinced or supplied them, cannot choose
    But they must blab –

Othello

                 Hath he said anything?

Iago

    He hath, my lord; but be you well assur'd,   30
    No more than he'll unswear.

Othello

                    What hath he said?

Iago

    Faith, that he did – I know not what he did.

Othello

    What? what?

Iago

    Lie –

Othello

    With her?

35. *what you will* Iago's implication here is that other men have done *anything* Othello can imagine – or that Iago can make him imagine – with his wife.

36–44. This speech marks Othello's breaking point and ends in barely connected exclamations.

37. *belie* slander.

37. *fulsome* foul.

40–2. *Nature … instruction* my mind would not become so darkened if there weren't truth in this accusation (an illogical statement). He made the same error in Act 3 Scene 3, lines 447–9.

43. *noses, ears, and lips* In his disturbed mental state, Othello is thinking of male and female sexual organs and using these words to stand for them. When Iago talks of leading Othello by the nose at the end of Act 1 (Scene 3, line 397) he is presumably planning to exploit Othello's sexual insecurity and also mentions the ear (line 391) in this context. Othello's feverish surrogate naming of a sexual organ seems to continue in line 143 below ('nose').

43–4. *Confess! Handkerchief! O devil!* Othello and his language breaks down, goaded beyond endurance by Iago's hints and the powerful sexual symbol he makes of the handkerchief. The unrecognised 'devil' gleefully responds, *Work on, / My medicine, work* (lines 45–6). The breaking point into chaos Othello foresees in Act 3, Scene 3, lines 90–2, is confirmed in the disconnected and incoherent language of Act 4.

52. *epilepsy* a disorder that causes brain seizures, also known as the falling sickness.

55. *lethargy* unconsciousness.

57. *savage madness* Iago's suggestion of Othello's 'savagery' could be a racist slur in this description; it wouldn't be the first Iago applies, when safely out of hearing, to Othello.

58. *Do you withdraw yourself* Once again, Iago is moving a character (here Cassio) into position and into role for his audience (here Othello), having established the context (Desdemona's infidelity with Cassio) in which it will be misread.

Iago

                    With her, on her; what you will.   35

Othello

    Lie with her – lie on her? We say lie on her when they
    belie her. Lie with her. Zounds, that's fulsome.
    Handkerchief – confessions – handkerchief! To confess,
    and be hang'd for his labour – first, to be hang'd, and
    then to confess. I tremble at it. Nature would not invest 40
    herself in such shadowing passion without some
    instruction. It is not words that shakes me thus – pish!
    – noses, ears, and lips. Is't possible? Confess!
    Handkerchief! O devil!

[Falls in a trance.]

Iago

    Work on,   45
    My medicine, work. Thus credulous fools are caught;
    And many worthy and chaste dames even thus,
    All guiltless, meet reproach. What, ho! my lord!
    My lord, I say! Othello!

[Enter CASSIO.]

    How now, Cassio!   50

Cassio

    What's the matter?

Iago

    My lord is fall'n into an epilepsy.
    This is his second fit; he had one yesterday.

Cassio

    Rub him about the temples.

Iago

                      No, forbear.
    The lethargy must have his quiet course;   55
    If not, he foams at mouth, and by and by
    Breaks out to savage madness. Look, he stirs.
    Do you withdraw yourself a little while;
    He will recover straight; when he is gone,

61. *Have you not hurt your head?* i.e. by falling, but Othello takes it as a reference to a cuckold's horns (see Act 3, Scene 3, line 168 and note).

63. *Would* I wish.

64. *A horned man's a monster and a beast* Othello's focus on the cuckold's horns emphasises how savage and dangerous a cuckolded husband can be. (Othello first hinted at the violence beneath his surface in Act 3, Scene 3, lines 194–5).

65–6. *There's many a beast ... civil monster* Iago cynical suggestion is that every city is full of monstrous savagery hidden behind a civilised surface: that civilisation itself is a veneer, a false appearance under which humanity disguises its bestial drives and actions. This idea was later explored in 19th-century texts such as Stevenson's *Strange Case of Dr Jekyll and Mr Hyde* (1886) and anticipates Sigmund Freud's psychology, which has influenced the production of Shakespeare's plays since the early 20th century. The idea is also central to Ancient Greek tragedy. The god of Greek theatre, Dionysus, is also the god of wild nature including our *own* inner wild nature as *released*, for example, by dance, music, theatre and intoxication (see also the Introduction, p.xii).

67. *be a man* i.e. don't be a wimp. Iago spoke to (and manipulated) Roderigo just as disrespectfully as this in Act 1.

68. *bearded fellow* a reference to Cassio (who is bearded).

68. *yok'd* harnessed, like an ox, which has horns. An ox is a beast of burden and the implication here is that marriage is a burden, tying a man down.

69. *draw* pull.

70–1. *unproper* i.e. not theirs; *peculiar* theirs. Married men sleep with wives who seem to be faithful but who are not and so, in that sense, do not belong to them.

73. *lip a wanton* kiss a lecherous person (he means Desdemona) obscenely.

77. *Stand you awhile apart* (more stage-managing) i.e. stand over here while I set up a scene (using Cassio and Bianca) in which you will 'overhear' exactly what I have arranged for you to hear.

81. *shifted him away* (more stage managing) got rid of him.

84. *encave yourself* conceal yourself (perhaps in the curtained area upstage).

85. *fleers* mocking.

I would on great occasion speak with you.   60

[Exit CASSIO.]

How is it, General? Have you not hurt your head?
Othello
  Dost thou mock me?
Iago
              I mock you? No, by heaven!
Would you would bear your fortune like a man!
Othello
  A horned man's a monster and a beast.
Iago
  There's many a beast then in a populous city,   65
  And many a civil monster.
Othello
  Did he confess it?
Iago
           Good sir, be a man;
  Think every bearded fellow that's but yok'd
  May draw with you; there's millions now alive
  That nightly lie in those unproper beds   70
  Which they dare swear peculiar: your case is better.
  O, 'tis the spite of hell, the fiend's arch-mock,
  To lip a wanton in a secure couch,
  And to suppose her chaste! No, let me know;
  And knowing what I am, I know what she shall be.   75
Othello
  O, thou art wise; 'tis certain.
Iago
  Stand you awhile apart.
  Confine yourself but in a patient list.
  Whilst you were here o'erwhelmed with your grief –
  A passion most unsuiting such a man –   80
  Cassio came hither; I shifted him away,
  And laid good 'scuse upon your ecstasy;
  Bade him anon return, and here speak with me;
  The which he promis'd. Do but encave yourself,
  And mark the fleers, the gibes, and notable scorns,   85

89. *cope* have sex with (with the brutal and obscene sense of 'poke' or thrust).

91. *all in all in spleen* overwhelmed with a furious sorrow.

95. *But yet keep time* all in good time.

97. *huswife* housewife/hussy. The word itself blurs the distinction but Iago uses its hybrid of 'keeping house' and 'sex worker' of his own wife (and of all women); see also Act 2, Scene 1, line 112.
99–100. *strumpet's plague ... beguil'd by one* to make many men fall in love with her (using her professional pretence of love) but to suffer for it by really falling in love with someone who is unavailable to her.

104. *unbookish* ignorant; but Iago has little respect for books and book-readers, especially Cassio as described in Act 1, Scene 1, line 23.
104. *construe* interpret.
105. *light* facetious; being trivial or humorous where one should be serious.
106. *in the wrong* mistakenly.
106. *Lieutenant* No doubt Iago enjoys 'innocently' taunting Cassio by the title he has now taken from him.
107. *addition* title.
108. *want* lack.
110. *dower* from endow, to give; a reference to the sum of money given as a wedding gift (by a bride's family) to the husband when she marries. Iago is suggesting that Cassio will be marrying Bianca.
111. *speed* succeed.

That dwell in every region of his face;
For I will make him tell the tale anew –
Where, how, how oft, how long ago, and when,
He hath, and is again to cope your wife.
I say, but mark his gesture. Marry, patience;   90
Or I shall say you are all in all in spleen,
And nothing of a man.

Othello

             Dost thou hear, Iago?
I will be found most cunning in my patience;
But – dost thou hear? – most bloody.

Iago

                That's not amiss;
But yet keep time in all. Will you withdraw?   95

[OTHELLO withdraws.]

Now will I question Cassio of Bianca,
A huswife that by selling her desires
Buys herself bread and clothes; it is a creature
That dotes on Cassio, as 'tis the strumpet's plague
To beguile many and be beguil'd by one.   100
He, when he hears of her, cannot restrain
From the excess of laughter.

[Re-enter CASSIO.]

             Here he comes.
As he shall smile Othello shall go mad;
And his unbookish jealousy must construe
Poor Cassio's smiles, gestures, and light behaviours,   105
Quite in the wrong. How do you now, Lieutenant?

Cassio

The worser that you give me the addition
Whose want even kills me.

Iago

Ply Desdemona well, and you are sure on't.
Now, if this suit lay in Bianca's dower,   110
How quickly should you speed!

111. *caitiff* wretch; does Cassio pity Bianca for being in love with him?

114. *rogue* this *could* be a term of affection, i.e. poor dear.
115. *faintly* without much conviction.

116. *importunes* urges.
117. *tell it o'er* say it again.

120. *Ha, ha, ha!* a cue for the actor to laugh a long time (and for Othello to think that Cassio is laughing at cuckolding him).
121. *triumph, Roman?* Do you parade your victory like a Roman general?
122. *customer* the reference here could be to a sex worker (Bianca) or her client (Cassio).
122–3. *bear some charity to my wit* give me some credit!
123. *unwholesome* faulty.

125. *they laugh that wins* let's see who has the last laugh.

126. *cry* rumour.

128. *I am a very villain else* If it's not true then I am a villain (says 'honest Iago', but he *is* a villain and nothing he says is true).
129. *scor'd* wounded (as in fencing).

Cassio
                    Alas, poor caitiff!
Othello
  Look how he laughs already!
Iago
  I never knew a woman love man so.
Cassio
  Alas, poor rogue! I think, i' faith, she loves me.
Othello
  Now he denies it faintly, and laughs it out.   115
Iago
  Do you hear, Cassio?
Othello
                    Now he importunes him
  To tell it o'er. Go to; well said, well said.
Iago
  She gives it out that you shall marry her.
  Do you intend it?
Cassio
  Ha, ha, ha!   120
Othello
  Do you triumph, Roman? Do you triumph?
Cassio
  I marry her! What, a customer! I prithee bear some
  charity to my wit; do not think it so unwholesome.
  Ha, ha, ha!
Othello
  So, so, so, so – they laugh that wins.   125
Iago
  Faith, the cry goes that you marry her.
Cassio
  Prithee say true.
Iago
  I am a very villain else.
Othello
  Ha you scor'd me? Well.

130. *monkey's own giving out* childish.
131. *out of her own love and flattery* she's flattering herself!

135. *sea-bank* shore.
136. *the bauble* the airhead (Bianca).

140. *lolls* dangles.
140. *hales* shakes.

142. *chamber* bedroom
143. *nose* (see note to line 43).
143–4. *not that dog I shall throw't to* I will be throwing your 'nose' to the dogs (Othello is barely controlling his violence at this point).
145. *must leave her company* must break up with her.

147. *fitchew* a polecat, famous for its stink and thought to have an extremely strong sex drive.
147. *perfum'd* drenched in cheap perfume like a tart, but also the 'perfume' of a polecat.
149. *dam* mother.

152. *a likely piece of work* a likely story! i.e. your account is probably untrue.

Cassio

This is the monkey's own giving out: she is persuaded 130
I will marry her, out of her own love and flattery, not
out of my promise.

Othello

Iago beckons me; now he begins the story.

Cassio

She was here even now; she haunts me in every place.
I was t'other day talking on the sea-bank with certain 135
Venetians, and thither comes the bauble – by this hand,
she falls me thus about my neck.

Othello

Crying 'O dear Cassio!' as it were: his gesture imports
it.

Cassio

So hangs, and lolls, and weeps upon me; so hales, and 140
pulls me. Ha, ha, ha!

Othello

Now he tells how she pluck'd him to my chamber.
O, I see that nose of yours, but not that dog I shall
throw't to.

Cassio

Well, I must leave her company. 145

[Enter BIANCA.]

Iago

Before me! Look where she comes.

Cassio

'Tis such another fitchew! marry, a perfum'd one. What
do you mean by this haunting of me?

Bianca

Let the devil and his dam haunt you. What did you
mean by that same handkerchief you gave me even 150
now? I was a fine fool to take it. I must take out the
whole work – a likely piece of work that you should
find it in your chamber and know not who left it there!
This is some minx's token, and I must take out the

155. *hobby-horse* Another degrading image of a woman and of sexual union, i.e. likened to riding an animal. Bianca is herself depersonalising women by this metaphor but under considerable emotional provocation (and most likely using a term that others use to depersonalise her).

156. *on't* out of it.

158. *By heaven, that should be my handkerchief!* Bianco angrily returns the handkerchief to Cassio, refusing to copy it. (The audience doubtless sympathises with her reluctance to copy another woman's 'token of love' for him.) Othello, primed by Iago, interprets this as Cassio giving his romantic gift to Desdemona to a sex worker. Iago has also successfully implicated Cassio as an adulterer with Othello's wife, and Bianca's exit is the perfect chance to get Cassio out of the way (if Othello had challenged Cassio directly here, Iago's entire scheme would have unravelled).

160. *when you are next prepar'd for* i.e. never.

162. *rail* shout; *else* otherwise.

165. *fain* gladly.

169. *How shall I murder him Iago?* It's been suggested that Othello loses grandeur at this point and acts like a comic villain, his passion veering between tragedy and farce. Note how the shift into prose for the first time between Othello and Iago contributes to this loss of grandeur. Also note during this passage how Iago deprives Othello's potentially noble responses – for example, 'gentle' (line 192) and 'pity' (line 195) – of their dignity.

172. *And did you see the handkerchief?* Note how important the handkerchief is to both men. It is vital to Iago's plot, so he continually draws Othello's attention to it.

173. *Was that mine?* The actor could be directed to try to list and sum up *all* that the handkerchief represents for him as he says this.

174. *prizes* values.

work? There – give it your hobby-horse. Wheresoever 155
you had it, I'll take out no work on't.

Cassio

How now, my sweet Bianca! how now! how now!

Othello

By heaven, that should be my handkerchief!

Bianca

An you'll come to supper to-night, you may; an you
will not, come when you are next prepar'd for. *[Exit.]* 160

Iago

After her, after her.

Cassio

Faith, I must; she'll rail i' th' street else.

Iago

Will you sup there?

Cassio

Faith, I intend so.

Iago

Well, I may chance to see you; for I would very fain 165
speak with you.

Cassio

Prithee come; will you?

Iago

Go to; say no more. *[Exit CASSIO.]*

Othello

[Coming forward] How shall I murder him, Iago?

Iago

Did you perceive how he laugh'd at his vice?   170

Othello

O Iago!

Iago

And did you see the handkerchief?

Othello

Was that mine?

Iago

Yours, by this hand. And to see how he prizes the
foolish woman your wife! She gave it him, and he hath 175
giv'n it his whore.

178. *A fine woman! a fair woman! a sweet woman!* Othello bemoans the loss of the Desdemona he loved, something Iago has persuaded him was a fantasy. The agony of this loss is tragic, not least because the loss is but imagined in his (Iago-corrupted) mind. The real fantasy is Iago's immoral version of Desdemona, which Othello believes without a shred of evidence.

180–2. The shift of sentiment from Othello's eulogy of the Desdemona he has lost (line 178) to this angry, stony-hearted rage and vengefulness after Iago's short rebuke (line 179) confirms how demeaned Othello is by believing Iago's lies.

185. *Nay, that's not your way* Iago directs his characters again.

188. *high* superior.

192. *gentle* both socially (a lady by birth) and in temperament.

193. *Ay, too gentle* too yielding and of easy virtue. Iago turns Othello's compliment immediately sour.

196–7. *patent to offend* licence to betray you. Iago expertly turns Othello's heartrending refrain *the pity of it* (line 195) into a reminder of Desdemona's wrongdoing.

198. *chop her into messes* cut her up into mincemeat, i.e. destroy her utterly.

Othello

    I would have him nine years a-killing.
    A fine woman! a fair woman! a sweet woman!

Iago

    Nay, you must forget that.

Othello

    Ay, let her rot, and perish, and be damn'd to-night; 180
    for she shall not live. No, my heart is turn'd to stone;
    I strike it, and it hurts my hand. O, the world hath
    not a sweeter creature; she might lie by an emperor's
    side and command him tasks.

Iago

    Nay, that's not your way. 185

Othello

    Hang her! I do but say what she is: so delicate with
    her needle, an admirable musician – O, she will sing
    the savageness out of a bear! – of so high and plenteous
    wit and invention.

Iago

    She's the worse for all this. 190

Othello

    O, a thousand, a thousand times – and then of so
    gentle a condition.

Iago

    Ay, too gentle.

Othello

    Nay, that's certain. But yet the pity of it, Iago! O, Iago,
    the pity of it, Iago! 195

Iago

    If you be so fond over her iniquity, give her patent to
    offend; for, if it touch not you, it comes near nobody.

Othello

    I will chop her into messes. Cuckold me!

Iago

    O, 'tis foul in her.

200. *With my officer!* not just infidelity but with my lieutenant!

203. *expostulate* reason.
204. *unprovide* disarm.

205–6. *Do it not with poison... hath contaminated* Iago even directs Othello in the murder of his wife!
207. *Good, good* a repeated answer to a deeply evil suggestion (*strangle her in her bed*, line 205) and Othello repeats the word twice more (lines 207 and 210). There is something hypnotic about Iago's evil.

208. *let me be his undertaker* let me deal with him (with a pun on undertaker, i.e. I will send him to his funeral).

211. (and Stage direction) Othello is suddenly back on duty and in Desdemona's presence too. Consider whether his answers to Lodovico here are focused or distracted.

216. *instrument* a formal document of command.

Othello

With mine officer! 200

Iago

That's fouler.

Othello

Get me some poison, Iago – this night.
I'll not expostulate with her, lest her body and beauty
unprovide my mind again – this night, Iago.

Iago

Do it not with poison; strangle her in her bed, even 205
the bed she hath contaminated.

Othello

Good, good; the justice of it pleases; very good.

Iago

And for Cassio – let me be his undertaker.
You shall hear more by midnight.

Othello

Excellent good. *[A trumpet.]*

What trumpet is that same? 210

Iago

I warrant, something from Venice.

[Enter LODOVICO, DESDEMONA, and Attendants.]

'Tis Lodovico – this comes from the Duke.
See, your wife's with him.

Lodovico

God save thee, worthy General!

Othello

With all my heart, sir.

Lodovico

The Duke and Senators of Venice greet you. 215
[Gives him a packet.]

Othello

I kiss the instrument of their pleasures.

[Opens the packet and reads.]

223. *unkind breach* a quarrel.

227. *in the paper* reading the document.

229. *unhappy* unfortunate.
230. *atone them* bring them back together.
231. *Fire and brimstone!* a Bible reference to Almighty anger. Othello's reaction is not surprising to the audience, given how he will have understood Desdemona's words (lines 229–30).

233. *wise* sane.

236. *Deputing Cassio* replacing Othello (as General) with Cassio.

Desdemona

  – And what's the news, good cousin Lodovico?

Iago

    I am very glad to see you, signior;

    Welcome to Cyprus.

Lodovico

    I thank you. How does Lieutenant Cassio?   220

Iago

    Lives, sir.

Desdemona

    Cousin, there's fall'n between him and my lord

    An unkind breach; but you shall make all well.

Othello

    Are you sure of that?

Desdemona

    My lord?   225

Othello

    [Reads] 'This fail you not to do as you will' –

Lodovico

    He did not call; he's busy in the paper.

    Is there division 'twixt thy lord and Cassio?

Desdemona

    A most unhappy one. I would do much

    T' atone them, for the love I bear to Cassio.   230

Othello

    Fire and brimstone!

Desdemona

    My lord?

Othello

    Are you wise?

Desdemona

    What, is he angry?

Lodovico

              May be the letter mov'd him;

    For, as I think, they do command him home,   235

    Deputing Cassio in his government.

238. *Indeed!* Othello repeats this word of Iago's almost as if hypnotised by him (see also Act 3, Scene 3, lines 101–2).

240. *mad* foolish (and unpleasantly reverses her 'glad' in line 237).

242. *I have not deserv'd this* Desdemona has just been struck by her soldier husband. Her response is unusual and thought provoking; it could be read/ seen (and played by the actress) as passive or defiant, or perhaps even both at once. It is possibly also the reaction of someone in shock. (Compare this with Desdemona's 'half-asleep' responses later, notably in Act 4, Scene 3, lines 6 and 9, and Act 5, Scene 2, lines 26–50.)

244. *very much* too much!

246. *teem with* give birth to, overflow with.

246–7. *woman's tears ... prove a crocodile* Othello claims Desdemona's tears are as false as a crocodile's are supposed to be. Like many a domestic abuser, he presents as the victim, blaming Desdemona for making him angry and therefore seeing his violence towards her as justified. He has no sympathy for her distress (unlike Lodovico).

251. *Mistress!* Used to address a sex worker not a wife.

252. *My lord?* This address is repeated like a refrain in the following lines. This 'refrain' has a subtly different meaning when Desdemona's male cousin Lodovico says it to Othello (as his superior officer) than when Desdemona says it to him as her husband (four times since line 225). The repetition by the two cousins has a twinned/contrasted crescendo effect, tracing the escalation in tension. But it also links two shocked people who can't believe what is happening. The shocked refrain repeatedly emphasises Othello's position of authority over those calling him 'my lord' *and* questions (for them and for the audience) his right to such authority when behaving like this. Emilia will take up the address as a refrain in the next scene, and will in due course go on to challenge its application to the general.

Desdemona
    By my troth, I am glad on't.
Othello
    Indeed!
Desdemona
    My lord?
Othello
    I am glad to see you mad.
Desdemona

                        Why, sweet Othello?   240

Othello
    Devil! *[Striking her.]*
Desdemona
    I have not deserv'd this.
Lodovico
    My lord, this would not be believ'd in Venice,
    Though I should swear I saw't. 'Tis very much.
    Make her amends; she weeps.
Othello

                        O devil, devil!   245

    If that the earth could teem with woman's tears,
    Each drop she falls would prove a crocodile.
    Out of my sight!
Desdemona

                I will not stay to offend you.

                        [Going.]

Lodovico
    Truly, an obedient lady.
    I do beseech your lordship, call her back.   250
Othello
    Mistress!
Desdemona
    My lord?
Othello
    What would you with her, sir?
Lodovico

                        Who, I, my lord?

205

254. *turn* Othello is suggesting that Desdemona has a fickle and promiscuous nature.

257. *obedient* would perform any sexual act she was invited or instructed to; Othello twists Lodovico's conventional admiration (line 249) into a degrading insult.

261. *mandate* command.
262. *avaunt* get out!

263. *Cassio shall have my place* i.e. as General of Cyprus, but also as Desdemona's sexual partner. Othello was once so honest and straightforward; now so much of what he says has an underlying nastier meaning, like the two-faced Iago.
265. *Goats and monkeys!* a repetition of Iago's lewd suggestion from Act 3, Scene 3, line 406.

267. *all in all sufficient* all-round skilled, competent.
267–8. *the nature / Whom passion could not shake* Othello's *hamartia* (fatal flaw) seems genuinely tragic here as Lodovico reminds us of his former grandeur and self-control. It is the scale of Othello's fall from his former greatness and calm self-control to this paranoid aggression that is tragic; if he had never had majestic self-control and dignity we would not feel its loss so sharply. The Greek philosopher Aristotle said tragedy must deal with great men, people of high social rank and personal nobility, falling into misfortune because of a *hamartia* or error of judgment. (See also pp.x–xi of the Introduction.)
269. *The shot of accident nor dart of chance* whatever fate threw at him. According to Aristotle (see note to lines 267–8 above), a tragic plot must also feature one or more *peripetea* (surprising downturns of fortune) and an *anagnorisis* (a final recognition of some unwelcome truth).
271. *Are his wits safe?* Is he of sane mind; has he lost his reason?
272. *breathe my censure* hint at my criticism, blame.

275. *yet would I knew* if only that (stroke) were the worst thing he's done.

276. *use* usual behaviour.

Othello

    Ay; you did wish that I would make her turn.
    Sir, she can turn, and turn, and yet go on,   255
    And turn again; and she can weep, sir, weep;
    And she's obedient, as you say, obedient,
    Very obedient. – Proceed you in your tears. –
    Concerning this, sir, – O, well-painted passion! –
    I am commanded home. – Get you away;   260
    I'll send for you anon. – Sir, I obey the mandate,
    And will return to Venice. – Hence, avaunt!

[Exit DESDEMONA.*]*

    Cassio shall have my place. And, sir, to-night,
    I do entreat that we may sup together.
    You are welcome, sir, to Cyprus. – Goats and
        monkeys! *[Exit.]*   265

Lodovico

    Is this the noble Moor whom our full Senate
    Call all in all sufficient? Is this the nature
    Whom passion could not shake, whose solid virtue
    The shot of accident nor dart of chance
    Could neither graze nor pierce?

Iago

                         He is much chang'd.   270

Lodovico

    Are his wits safe? Is he not light of brain?

Iago

    He's that he is. I may not breathe my censure.
    What he might be, if what he might he is not,
    I would to heaven he were!

Lodovico

                      What, strike his wife!

Iago

    Faith, that was not so well; yet would I knew   275
    That stroke would prove the worst!

Lodovico

                          Is it his use?

277. *blood* passion.

281. *his own courses* characteristic behaviour.
281. *denote* show.

284. *deceiv'd in him* got him so wrong, misjudged his character.

Or did the letters work upon his blood,
And new-create this fault?

Iago

                              Alas, alas!
It is not honesty in me to speak
What I have seen and known. You shall observe
     him;   280
And his own courses will denote him so
That I may save my speech. Do but go after,
And mark how he continues.

Lodovico

I am sorry that I am deceiv'd in him.

[Exeunt.]

SCENE 2

Othello quizzes Emilia about Desdemona's fidelity but dismisses Emilia's assurances. He insults both women, addressing them as if they are sex workers in a brothel, calling his wife a 'whore' to her face. Desdemona thinks work stress is warping his judgement. Emilia (perceptively) suspects some plot by a villain seeking promotion but (unperceptively) doesn't connect this with Iago, whom she reminds wrongly suspected her of infidelity with Othello. Desdemona professes undying love for Othello. They leave for dinner with the Venetian guests. Roderigo threatens Iago for not coming good on his promises and is once again duped (by cunning and flattery) into a plan to kill Cassio as he leaves Bianca's house.

1–23. The audience is invited to question its response to Othello's situation in these lines. Consider whether Shakespeare intends for us to blame or pity his Iago-warped perceptions.
1–11. Othello's responses during have a jumpy, skittish rhythm. They interrupt the confident verse as Emilia tries to reassure him. The verse then stabilises into iambic pentameter as Emilia testifies to Desdemona's noble character in lines 12–19.

12. *durst* dare.
16. *serpent's curse* a reference to the Book of Genesis, 3.14, when God curses the serpent in whose form Satan appeared to work the fall of humanity. Emilia is saying the crime of slandering Desdemona is worthy of Satan himself. This would make her an unfallen (uncorrupted) Eve, sexually innocent and falsely blamed; it's Othello who has been corrupted by Iago's 'poison'.
17–19. *For if she be not ... foul as slander* Emilia is defending the potential for a 'daily beauty' in human lives – ***honest, chaste and true*** – which her 'ugly' husband can only hate and destroy. Emilia's remark can also be read as a poetic way of saying, 'If Desdemona isn't faithful, no one is.'

SCENE 2

Cyprus. The citadel.

[Enter OTHELLO and EMILIA.]

Othello
  You have seen nothing, then?
Emilia
  Nor ever heard, nor ever did suspect.
Othello
  Yes, you have seen Cassio and she together.
Emilia
  But then I saw no harm, and then I heard
  Each syllable that breath made up between them.   5
Othello
  What, did they never whisper?
Emilia
  Never, my lord.
Othello
                    Nor send you out o'th' way?
Emilia
  Never.
Othello
  To fetch her fan, her gloves, her mask, nor nothing?
Emilia
  Never, my lord.   10
Othello
  That's strange.
Emilia
  I durst, my lord, to wager she is honest,
  Lay down my soul at stake. If you think other,
  Remove your thought – it doth abuse your bosom.
  If any wretch have put this in your head,   15
  Let heaven requite it with the serpent's curse;
  For if she be not honest, chaste, and true,
  There's no man happy; the purest of their wives
  Is foul as slander.

211

20. *bawd* a Madam, a brothel keeper.

22–3. *closet lock-and-key ... kneel and pray* hiding hideous secrets under a holy appearance. Note that it is in fact Othello, not his wife, who is anxious about appearances and covering up domestic secrets at line 31.

29. *Some of your function, mistress* Get on with your job as brothel keeper.

30. *procreants* those wishing to 'make the beast with two backs'! We have noticed before Othello's inexperience in marriage (aggravated by interruptions of its consummation: the posting to Cyprus; the street fight involving Cassio and Montano). This confrontation with his new wife's actual physical sexuality might partly explain his all too easily convinced, shocking mistrust (and miscasting) of her: he is identifying their roles here as furtive client and sex worker.

31. *cry hem* clear the throat.

32. *Your mystery* your (Emilia's) trade.

32. *dispatch* get on with it!

33. *Upon my knees* Desdemona kneels to him like a conventionally submissive, Christian wife. But he has already pre-empted her ability to make a *show* of holiness (line 23).

34–5. *I understand a fury in your words, / But not the words* This genuine heartfelt plea from Desdemona is heart-rending to witness, especially as we know she is innocent. As Emilia's lines 17–19 poetically implied: if Desdemona isn't innocent, no one is.

Othello

                Bid her come hither. Go.

[Exit EMILIA.]

She says enough; yet she's a simple bawd   20
That cannot say as much. This is a subtle whore,
A closet-lock-and-key of villainous secrets;
And yet she'll kneel and pray; I have seen her do't.

[Re-enter EMILIA with DESDEMONA.]

Desdemona
My lord, what is your will?
Othello
Pray you chuck, come hither.   25
Desdemona
What is your pleasure?
Othello
Let me see your eyes; look in my face.
Desdemona
What horrible fancy's this?
Othello
[To EMILIA] Some of your function, mistress:
Leave procreants alone, and shut the door;   30
Cough, or cry hem, if any body come.
Your mystery, your mystery; nay, dispatch.

[Exit EMILIA.]

Desdemona
Upon my knees, what doth your speech import?
I understand a fury in your words,
But not the words.   35
Othello
Why, what art thou?
Desdemona
Your wife, my lord; your true and loyal wife.
Othello
Come, swear it, damn thyself; lest, being like one of

40. *honest* chaste (but only when used of a woman).

48. *If haply you my father do suspect* Desdemona is surely clutching at straws here, trying and failing to imagine what can have made Othello so angry.

50. *have lost him* lost his favour and friendship.

51. *I have lost him too* A reminder that Desdemona has no other protection but Othello, whom she has trusted with her life.

52–5. *try me with affliction ... utmost hopes* this alludes to the Bible story of Job from the Old Testament. Job was a devout and prosperous patriarch deprived of all his possessions and subjected to undeserved afflictions by God as a test of faith. Job is a grand and all-representing figure, so the comparison is worthy of a tragic hero. But Job's undeserved suffering was a test of faith set by God. Does Othello make himself rather ridiculous and inflated by the comparison?

58–9. *The fixed figure ...O, O!* I am the very image of scorn in this time; the proverbial laughing stock. Anyone similarly humiliated by his wife will be called an Othello, he fears, and this ignoble reputation appals him. Othello's being an outsider of course increases his extreme sensitivity about his reputation; he is completely dependent on that reputation for acceptance by Venetian/Christian society.

61. *garner'd up my heart* stored up my love.

63. *fountain* source.

63. *current* river.

65. *cistern for foul toads* a water tank for toads – a reptile associated with poison, evil and witchcraft.

66. *knot and gender in* writhe together (snake-like) and copulate.

66. *Turn* The actor playing Othello might twist Desdemona's face towards his here.

67. *cherubin* a child-angel, symbol of absolute innocence.

heaven, the devils themselves should fear to seize thee;
therefore be double-damn'd – swear thou art honest.   40

Desdemona

Heaven doth truly know it.

Othello

Heaven truly knows that thou art false as hell.

Desdemona

To whom, my lord? With whom?
How am I false?

Othello

Ah, Desdemona! away! away! away!   45

Desdemona

Alas the heavy day! Why do you weep?
Am I the motive of these tears, my lord?
If haply you my father do suspect
An instrument of this your calling back,
Lay not your blame on me: If you have lost him,   50
Why, I have lost him too.

Othello

                Had it pleas'd heaven
To try me with affliction; had they rain'd
All kind of sores and shames on my bare head,
Steep'd me in poverty to the very lips,
Given to captivity me and my utmost hopes,   55
I should have found in some place of my soul
A drop of patience; but, alas, to make me
The fixed figure for the time of scorn
To point his slow unmoving finger at! – O, O!
Yet could I bear that too; well, very well;   60
But there, where I have garner'd up my heart,
Where either I must live or bear no life,
The fountain from the which my current runs,
Or else dries up – to be discarded thence!
Or keep it as a cistern for foul toads   65
To knot and gender in! Turn thy complexion there,
Patience, thou young and rose-lipp'd cherubin –
Ay, here, look grim as hell.

70. *the shambles* an open air butcher's market (the blood attracting a carpet of flies).
71. *quicken even with blowing* the maggots hatching out as soon as the flies' eggs are laid.

75. *ignorant* unwitting.
75. *committed* carried out, done. However, this is an unfortunate word choice: Desdemona is unaware of what it suggests to Othello (i.e. commit adultery); he seizes on it and repeats it in an obsessive refrain (lines 77–8, 81 and 85).

78. *public commoner* 'common whore', a derogatory term for a woman who is thought to be promiscuous.

82. *stops the nose* holds its nose (against the stink).
82. *the moon winks* the moon (a symbol of chastity) shuts her eyes to the sin.

84. *hollow mine of earth* caverns below the ground.

88. *vessel* (her) body.

91. *as I shall be sav'd* God save me. Desdemona's oath of chastity is the more powerfully made because of her sincerety.

Desdemona
I hope my noble lord esteems me honest.
Othello
O, ay; as summer flies are in the shambles,   70
That quicken even with blowing. O thou weed
Who art so lovely fair and smell'st so sweet
That the sense aches at thee!
Would thou had'st never been born!
Desdemona
Alas, what ignorant sin have I committed?   75
Othello
Was this fair paper, this most goodly book,
Made to write 'whore' upon? What committed!
Committed! O thou public commoner!
I should make very forges of my cheeks
That would to cinders burn up modesty,   80
Did I but speak thy deeds. What committed!
Heaven stops the nose at it, and the moon winks;
The bawdy wind, that kisses all it meets,
Is hush'd within the hollow mine of earth
And will not hear it. What committed!   85
Impudent strumpet!
Desdemona
                By heaven, you do me wrong.
Othello
Are not you a strumpet?
Desdemona
                 No, as I am a Christian.
If to preserve this vessel for my lord
From any other foul unlawful touch
Be not to be a strumpet, I am none.   90
Othello
What, not a whore?
Desdemona
                No, as I shall be sav'd.
Othello
Is't possible?

93. *cry you mercy* ask your pardon.
94. *took* mistook.
96. *Saint Peter* keeper of the Gate of Heaven.

99. *course* literally 'fought our battle', but the phrase also means 'had sex'.
99. *there's money for your pains* Othello makes a dramatic show of paying Desdemona for sex, as if she's a sex worker.
100. *pray you turn the key, and keep our counsel* keep everything hidden and secret, like a shameful act.

101. *conceive* imagine, with a sexual innuendo.

103. *half asleep* stunned, shocked. From this point on Desdemona changes: she is less a social being, more a dream-figure (the 'wronged woman') in a sad folk tale or song. The 'dream' of her marriage is shattered and she is lost in grief for her lost 'love'. This is not only an intense personal tragedy for Desdemona but reflects a folk tradition of marital disappointment for so many women before (and after) her. We may ask why doesn't she challenge Othello's account more forcefully; tell Emilia what is happening and ask for her support. The feisty Desdemona from earlier in the play would have done so. There is a sense that she is broken, unable to fight the victim narrative into which she has been cast. Perhaps the double abandonment by her father (see line 51) and her husband is too much to bear (see also notes on line 111 and on Act 4, Scene 3, line 23).

110. *water* tears.
111. *Lay on my bed my wedding sheets* The symbolic significance of this is heartbreaking. She is reminding Othello of their happy marriage in the hope of reviving it. Instead, tragically, the 'marriage' bed she prepares will be her deathbed.

Desdemona

O, heaven forgive us!

Othello

               I cry you mercy, then.

I took you for that cunning whore of Venice

That married with Othello. – You, mistress,   95

That have the office opposite to Saint Peter

And keeps the gate of hell!

[Re-enter EMILIA.]

You, you, ay you!

We ha done our course; there's money for your

   pains.

I pray you turn the key, and keep our counsel.   100

[Exit.]

Emilia

Alas, what does this gentleman conceive?

How do you, madam? How do you, my good lady?

Desdemona

Faith, half asleep.

Emilia

Good madam, what's the matter with my lord?

Desdemona

With who?   105

Emilia

Why, with my lord, madam.

Desdemona

Who is thy lord?

Emilia

            He that is yours, sweet lady.

Desdemona

I have none. Do not talk to me, Emilia;

I cannot weep, nor answers have I none

But what should go by water. Prithee, to-night   110

Lay on my bed my wedding sheets – remember;

And call thy husband hither.

114. *meet* apt. It is worth asking how the actress should say the line *'Tis meet I should be us'd so, very meet*. Abuse victims may turn their anger at the abuser inwards, saying 'I deserved it; it was my fault', or surrendering because 'what's the point of fighting back?' On the other hand, it is possible to say this line passive aggressively, or even as a sarcastic aggressive protest, a vestige of the original Desdemona. (See Ellen Terry's point about Desdemona fighting back in the Introduction, p.xvii.)

115–16. *stick / The small'st opinion on my great'st abuse* base his largest doubt on my smallest fault.

121. *a child to chiding* new to being verbally abused in this way.

123. *bewhor'd her* named her as, treated her like, a 'whore'.
124. *despite and heavy terms* vicious and abusive insults.

127. Desdemona cannot even say 'whore' (see also lines 169–70). Note the immediate contrast with Emilia in the next line.

129. *callat* a woman with many sexual partners, a derogatory term for a woman who is considered to be promiscuous.

Emilia
    Here's a change indeed! *[Exit.]*
Desdemona
    'Tis meet I should be us'd so, very meet.
    How have I been behav'd, that he might stick   115
    The small'st opinion on my great'st abuse?

[Re-enter EMILIA *with* IAGO.*]*

Iago
    What is your pleasure, madam? How is't with you?
Desdemona
    I cannot tell. Those that do teach young babes
    Do it with gentle means and easy tasks.
    He might have child me so; for, in good faith,   120
    I am a child to chiding.
Iago
    What is the matter, lady?
Emilia
    Alas, Iago, my lord hath so bewhor'd her,
    Thrown such despite and heavy terms upon her
    That true hearts cannot bear it.   125
Desdemona
    Am I that name, Iago?
Iago
                 What name, fair lady?
Desdemona
    Such as she says my lord did say I was.
Emilia
    He call'd her whore. A beggar in his drink
    Could not have laid such terms upon his callat.
Iago
    Why did he so?   130
Desdemona
    I do not know; I am sure I am none such.
Iago
    Do not weep, do not weep. Alas, the day!

133. *forsook* sacrificed.

136. *Beshrew* curse.

138. *some eternal villain* the devil (the one standing before her in plain sight!).

140. *cogging, cozening* cheating, deceitful.
140. *office* promotion, i.e. exactly what Iago did it for. Emilia is intuitively perceptive here and lines 147–8.

144. *halter* a hangman's rope.

149. *companions* rogues.
149. *unfold* disclose.

152. *Speak within door* Be quiet! Shh! See also Othello's exit, line 31; both are keen to keep their 'domestic' life secret.
153. *such squire* low-life.
154. *seamy side without* inside out, with the dirty side showing.
155. *suspect me with the Moor* Emilia's words here indicate that she, too, was falsely slandered. (Iago continues to 'suspect' her, however.)

Emilia

    Hath she forsook so many noble matches,

    Her father, and her country, and her friends,

    To be call'd whore? Would it not make one weep?   135

Desdemona

    It is my wretched fortune.

Iago

                  Beshrew him for't!

    How comes this trick upon him?

Desdemona

                     Nay, heaven doth know.

Emilia

    I will be hang'd if some eternal villain,

    Some busy and insinuating rogue,

    Some cogging, cozening slave, to get some office,   140

    Have not devis'd this slander; I'll be hang'd else.

Iago

    Fie, there is no such man; it is impossible.

Desdemona

    If any such there be, heaven pardon him!

Emilia

    A halter pardon him! and hell gnaw his bones!

    Why should he call her whore? Who keeps her

        company?   145

    What place, what time, what form, what likelihood?

    The Moor's abus'd by some outrageous knave,

    Some base notorious knave, some scurvy fellow.

    O heaven, that such companions thou'dst unfold,

    And put in every honest hand a whip   150

    To lash the rascals naked through the world

    Even from the east to the west!

Iago

                  Speak within door.

Emilia

    O, fie upon them! Some such squire he was

    That turn'd your wit the seamy side without

    And made you to suspect me with the Moor.   155

161. *discourse of thought* thinking.

167. *foreswear* forsake.

169. *I cannot say 'whore'* The irony is that, in saying she cannot say it, she says it. This gives the actress playing Desdemona an intriguing opportunity. She can express all of Desdemona's abhorrence of the word and the act it names along with the shock and self-dislocation of hearing herself saying it. She could say it in a stunned innocent way, wondering at how the word came out of her mouth. She could also react to the fact that she *has* said it, as if trying something on that doesn't fit her but which has been thrust upon her. She could even say it as if considering the possibility of herself being this abhorred thing, which Othello insists she is (and Iago thinks all women are).

170. *abhor* appal.

171. *addition* title.

173. *humour* mood.

174. *does him offence* puts a strain on him.

175. *chide with* take it out on you.

176. *If 'twere no other!* That's not what is going on here! *It is but so, I warrant* Yes it is, I'm sure of it. Iago's brutal and unfeeling response to Desdemona's heartfelt plea is a reminder of his monumental cruelty. Essentially he is saying: 'Othello taking his anger out on you is nothing to worry about, get used to it. Oh, and stop crying and don't keep everyone waiting for dinner.' Add to this that he has caused this entire situation, destroyed a happy marriage because he envied its daily beauty and is complicit in Othello's plan to murder her (as mere collateral damage in his revenge on Othello and Cassio; he doesn't even dislike her), and you have one of the most chillingly amoral characters in stage history.

178. *stay the meat* wait for dinner.

Iago

You are a fool; go to.

Desdemona

               O God! Iago,
What shall I do to win my lord again?
Good friend, go to him; for, by this light of heaven,
I know not how I lost him. Here I kneel.
If e'er my will did trespass 'gainst his love,   160
Either in discourse of thought or actual deed,
Or that mine eyes, mine ears, or any sense,
Delighted them in any other form,
Or that I do not yet, and ever did,
And ever will – though he do shake me off   165
To beggarly divorcement – love him dearly,
Comfort forswear me! Unkindness may do much;
And his unkindness may defeat my life,
But never taint my love. I cannot say 'whore';
It does abhor me now I speak the word;   170
To do the act that might the addition earn,
Not the world's mass of vanity could make me.

Iago

I pray you be content; 'tis but his humour.
The business of the state does him offence,
And he does chide with you.   175

Desdemona

If 'twere no other!

Iago

              It is but so, I warrant.

[Trumpets within.]

Hark how these instruments summon you to supper.
The messengers of Venice stay the meat.
Go in, and weep not; all things shall be well.

[Exeunt DESDEMONA and EMILIA.]

[Enter RODERIGO.]

179–247. The scene closes in prose, as befits a comic interlude. Iago and Roderigo are better comic relief than the actual (and brief) Clown scenes. This is partly because Shakespeare has concentrated the action on an unusually limited number of characters, and done without a sub-plot. The play relies on pacy intrigue and acceleration towards a catastrophe, so extended Clown scenes would have dispersed tension and been a deceleration and a distraction. The clowning is made of part of the intrigue instead. It is also important that Iago is a Clown (as the Devil character often was in mediaeval drama): his character debases, belittles and mocks the higher and nobler aims of humanity.
180. You haven't treated me honestly or fairly or been true to the promises you made me. All of the characters who have had dealings with Iago would probably agree with Roderigo's sentiment here.
182. *daff'st me with some device* put me off with some excuse.
184. *conveniency* what is needed.

189–90. *your words and performances are no kin together* You're all talk and no action.

192–3. *wasted myself out of my means* bankrupted (financially ruined) myself.
194. *half* easily.
194. *votarist* nun.

196. *expectations* encouragements.
196. *comforts of sudden respect* promises of receiving her attentions.

200. *scurvy* underhand.
201. *fopt* duped.

How now, Roderigo!

Roderigo

I do not find that thou deal'st justly with me.   180

Iago

What in the contrary?

Roderigo

Every day thou daff'st me with some device, Iago; and
rather, as it seems to me now, keep'st from me all
conveniency than suppliest me with the least advantage of hope. I will indeed, no longer endure it; nor 185
am I yet persuaded to put up in peace what already I
have foolishly suffer'd.

Iago

Will you hear me, Roderigo?

Roderigo

Faith, I have heard too much; for your words and
performances are no kin together.   190

Iago

You charge me most unjustly.

Roderigo

With nought but truth. I have wasted myself out of
my means. The jewels you have had from me to deliver
to Desdemona would half have corrupted a votarist.
You have told me she hath receiv'd them, and return'd 195
me expectations and comforts of sudden respect and
acquaintance; but I find none.

Iago

Well; go to; very well.

Roderigo

Very well! go to! I cannot go to, man, nor 'tis not very
well; by this hand, I say 'tis very scurvy, and begin to 200
find myself fopt in it.

Iago

Very well.

Roderigo

I tell you 'tis not very well. I will make myself known
to Desdemona. If she will return me my jewels, I will

206. *I will seek satisfaction of you* challenge you to a duel.

207. *You have said now.* Is that it, have you finished?

208. *protest intendment* assert my intentions.

209. *mettle* spirit, bravery.

212. *exception* objection.

214. *It hath not appear'd* That's not how it's looked to me.

221. *devise engines for my life* scheme to end my life.

227. *Mauritania* a region of North Africa.
228. *his abode be linger'd* his stay is delayed.
229–30. *determinate* effective. Note the increase of pace as the end of Act 4 approaches. Iago has to bring all the elements of his plot to a speedy conclusion (which he does with great skill and daring) or Othello and Cassio will elude him.

give over my suit and repent my unlawful solicitation; 205
if not, assure yourself I will seek satisfaction of you.

Iago

You have said now.

Roderigo

Ay, and said nothing but what I protest intendment
of doing.

Iago

Why, now I see there's mettle in thee; and even from
this instant do build on thee a better opinion than 210
ever before. Give me thy hand, Roderigo. Thou hast
taken against me a most just exception; but yet, I
protest, I have dealt most directly in thy affair.

Roderigo

It hath not appear'd.

Iago

I grant, indeed, it hath not appear'd; and your suspicion 215
is not without wit and judgment. But, Roderigo, if thou
hast that in thee indeed, which I have greater reason
to believe now than ever – I mean purpose, courage,
and valour – this night show it; if thou the next night
following enjoy not Desdemona, take me from this 220
world with treachery, and devise engines for my life.

Roderigo

Well, what is it? Is it within reason and compass?

Iago

Sir, there is especial commission come from Venice to
depute Cassio in Othello's place.

Roderigo

Is that true? Why, then Othello and Desdemona return 225
again to Venice.

Iago

O, no; he goes into Mauritania, and taketh away with
him the fair Desdemona, unless his abode be linger'd
here by some accident; wherein none can be so determinate as the removing of Cassio. 230

236. *a harlotry* a derogatory term for a female sex worker.
237. *honourable fortune* reinstatement.
238. *his going thence* his leaving.
238. *fashion* manipulate.

240. *second* support (like a second in charge).

244. *put it on him* do for him, kill him. Roderigo agrees to murder Cassio simply to have the opportunity for adultery with Desdemona. It is testament to Iago's extraordinary manipulation of people's weaknesses (here Roderigo's lust for Desdemona) that Roderigo goes along with this implausible plot. (Or perhaps Shakespeare himself is stretching the limits of reality here.)

Roderigo

How do you mean removing of him?

Iago

Why, by making him uncapable of Othello's place –
knocking out his brains.

Roderigo

And that you would have me to do?

Iago

Ay, an if you dare do yourself a profit and right. He 235
sups to-night with a harlotry, and thither will I go to
him – he knows not yet of his honourable fortune. If
you will watch his going thence, which I will fashion
to fall out between twelve and one, you may take him
at your pleasure. I will be near to second your attempt, 240
and he shall fall between us. Come, stand not amaz'd
at it, but go along with me; I will show you such a
necessity in his death that you shall think yourself
bound to put it on him. It is now high supper-time,
and the night grows to waste. About it. 245

Roderigo

I will hear further reason for this.

Iago

And you shall be satisfied. *[Exeunt.]*

SCENE 3

This scene is known as the Willow Scene. Othello roughly orders Desdemona to bed. As Emilia prepares her, Desdemona sings a sad 'willow' song of a forsaken woman and they talk of love, women, death, and their contrasting views of marriage. Emilia's view of marriage is realistic, even cynical; Desdemona's is innocent, romantic, childlike. Emilia partially sees what is going on, whereas Desdemona is in shock and denial, reflected in her child-like regression. There is a contrast here between the sexually aware Emilia and the sexually innocent Desdemona, but also Emilia does not see that Desdemona's life is in danger. Emilia makes a strong case for the rights of wives.

7. *on th'instant* right now!

7–8. *forth-with* at once. Note the snappy imperatives (lines 7–8), reflecting Othello's anger and emotional disconnection from his wife.

10. *gentler* calmer.

11. *incontinent* immediately.

15. *nightly wearing* nightdress.

SCENE 3

Cyrus. The citadel.

Cyprus. The citadel.

[*Enter* OTHELLO, DESDEMONA, LODOVICO, EMILIA,
and Attendants.]

Lodovico
   I do beseech you, sir, trouble yourself no further.
Othello
   O, pardon me; 'twill do me good to walk.
Lodovico
   Madam, good night; I humbly thank your ladyship.
Desdemona
   Your honour is most welcome.
Othello
   Will you walk, sir? O, Desdemona!   5
Desdemona
   My lord?
Othello
   Get you to bed on th' instant; I will be return'd forth-
   with. Dispatch your attendant there. Look 't be done.
Desdemona
   I will, my lord.

    [*Exeunt* OTHELLO, LODOVICO, *and Attendants.*]

Emilia
   How goes it now? He looks gentler than he did.   10
Desdemona
   He says he will return incontinent.
   He hath commanded me to go to bed,
   And bade me to dismiss you.
Emilia
                Dismiss me!
Desdemona
   It was his bidding; therefore, good Emilia,
   Give me my nightly wearing, and adieu.   15
   We must not now displease him.

18. *So would not I* I don't feel that.

19. *checks* rebukes.

22. *All's one.* Who cares? It doesn't matter anymore. (Note Desdemona's dazed, dreamy state.)

23–4. *If I do die before thee … same sheets* This is a chilling premonition for Desdemona (and for the audience) of her death; it symbolically connects (via the sheets) marriage and death.

24. *you talk* how you chatter. Emilia speaks to Desdemona as if to a child in this scene.

25. *Barbary* a Moor (Berbour/Araby was the home of the Moors). Shakespeare's choice of word 'Barbary' here has the additional connotation of 'barbarian' (literally beyond civilisation) and continues the theme of outsiders and how non-European non-Christian cultures were judged to be 'uncivilised'.

27. *'willow'* the symbol of forsaken lovers.

35. *proper* handsome. This line was once reassigned in a classic edition of the play to Emilia because it reflects her husband's 'This Cassio's a proper man' (Act 1, Scene 3, line 388) and seems more suited to Emilia's frank sexuality than Desdemona's 'purity'. Some scholars have argued that Shakespeare made a mistake in giving the line to Desdemona; others have similarly objected to Desdemona's extended sexual banter with Iago at Act 2, Scene 1, lines 117–62. But if we accept that Desdemona is both sexual *and* chaste then these lines do not appear out of character; the objections to this in effect condemn women simply for being sexual beings.

39. *touch of his nether lip* a kiss.

38–9. It was a custom to go on pilgrimage to the Holy Land to 'pay off' sins. Pilgrims normally sailed rather than walked there from Venice. The text continues in this scene to explore female sexual desire as both natural and problematic.

Emilia

    I would you had never seen him.

Desdemona

    So would not I: my love doth so approve him

    That even his stubbornness, his checks, his frowns –

    Prithee unpin me – have grace and favour in them.   20

Emilia

    I have laid those sheets you bade me on the bed.

Desdemona

    All's one. Good faith, how foolish are our minds!

    If I do die before thee, prithee shroud me

    In one of these same sheets.

Emilia

                            Come, come, you talk.

Desdemona

    My mother had a maid call'd Barbary: 25

    She was in love; and he she lov'd prov'd mad,

    And did forsake her. She had a song of 'willow';

    An old thing 'twas, but it express'd her fortune,

    And she died singing it. That song to-night

    Will not go from my mind; I have much to do   30

    But to go hang my head all at one side

    And sing it like poor Barbary. Prithee dispatch.

Emilia

    Shall I go fetch your night-gown?

Desdemona

    No, unpin me here.

    This Lodovico is a proper man.   35

Emilia

    A very handsome man.

Desdemona

    He speaks well.

Emilia

    I know a lady in Venice would have walk'd barefoot

    to Palestine for a touch of his nether lip.

Desdemona

    [Sings] The poor soul sat sighing by a sycamore tree,   40

48. *Lay by these* put aside the linen/clothes.

54. *It is the wind* This detail about the weather adds to the ominous atmosphere built up by the 'willow' song.

57. *couch* sleep
57. *moe* more.

59. *bode* foreshadow.

61. *in conscience* honestly.

62–3. *abuse their husbands / In such gross kind* are unfaithful to their husbands.

    Sing all a green willow;
Her hand on her bosom, her head on her knee.
    Sing willow, willow, willow.
The fresh streams ran by her, and murmur'd her
    moans;
    Sing willow, willow, willow;   45
Her salt tears fell from her and soft'ned the stones;
    Sing willow –
Lay by these –
    willow, willow. –
Prithee, hie thee; he'll come anon. –   50
    Sing all a green willow must be my garland.
Let nobody blame him; his scorn I approve –
Nay, that's not next. Hark! who is't that knocks?

Emilia
It is the wind.

Desdemona
[Sings] I call'd my love false love; but what said he
    then?   55
    Sing willow, willow, willow:
If I court moe women, you'll couch with moe men –
So, get thee gone; good night. Mine eyes do itch;
Doth that bode weeping?

Emilia
                'Tis neither here nor there.

Desdemona
I have heard it said so. O, these men, these men!   60
Dost thou in conscience think – tell me, Emilia –
That there be women do abuse their husbands
In such gross kind?

Emilia
            There be some such, no question.

Desdemona
Wouldst thou do such a deed for all the world?

Emilia
Why, would not you?

68. *Wouldst thou do such a deed for all the world?* The play's domestic (family) story is treated, like Ancient Greek tragedies, on a titanic scale.

69–70. *The world's a huge thing … a small vice* Emilia's reply to Desdemona's question reduces it to her own, more limited scale. This 'not for the world' question is echoed many times in the play.

72. *undo't* put it right.

73–4. *joint-ring* engagement ring.

74. *measures of lawn* lengths of fabric.

75. *petty exhibition* small sums, petty cash.

76. *ud's* God's.

78. *venture purgatory* risk going to Purgatory. Purgatory was the afterlife in which one experienced Hell but only for a limited time, until purged of sins. Shakespeare could be careless of such cultural details; his exotic locations are often England-in-disguise. However, in this case it fits: Venice was Catholic. (Belief in Purgatory, as a third alternative to Heaven and Hell, was heresy in Elizabethan and Jacobean Protestant England.)

85. *as many to th' vantage* as many more.

88. *slack their duties* men were guaranteed conjugal rights (especially to sexual relations) by marriage; Emilia reminds us that these rights also applied to women.

89. *pour out treasures into foreign laps* have sex with women who are not their wives.

91. *Throwing restraint* restricting our freedoms.

Desdemona

                No, by this heavenly light!   65

Emilia

Nor I neither by this heavenly light;
I might do't as well i' th' dark.

Desdemona

Wouldst thou do such a deed for all the world?

Emilia

The world's a huge thing.
It is a great price for a small vice.   70

Desdemona

Good troth, I think thou wouldst not.

Emilia

By my troth, I think I should; and undo't when I had
done it. Marry, I would not do such a thing for a joint-
ring, nor for measures of lawn, nor for gowns,
petticoats, nor caps, nor any petty exhibition; but for   75
all the whole world – ud's pity, who would not make
her husband a cuckold to make him a monarch? I
should venture purgatory for't.

Desdemona

Beshrew me, if I would do such a wrong for the whole
world.   80

Emilia

Why, the wrong is but a wrong i' th' world; and having
the world for your labour, 'tis a wrong in your own
world, and you might quickly make it right.

Desdemona

I do not think there is any such woman.

Emilia

Yes, a dozen; and as many to th' vantage   85
as would store the world they play'd for.
But I do think it is their husbands' faults
If wives do fall. Say that they slack their duties,
And pour our treasures into foreign laps;
Or else break out in peevish jealousies,   90
Throwing restraint upon us; or say they strike us,

92. *scant our former having* what we used to enjoy.
92. *despite* out of spite.
93. *galls* resentments.

96. *palates* appetites.

98. *sport* for the excitement.
99. *affection breed it* lust create it.
100. *frailty* moral weakness.
103. *use us well* treat (wives) with respect. All of Emilia's hardened experience of marriage and men/Iago and her bruised manifesto for the rights of wives emerges in this speech. She is like a grown woman teaching a girl about the harsh realities of life.
105–6. I pray that I never commit such immoral behaviour but improve myself by *knowing* it for what it is. Is Desdemona emerging, tragically too late, from a (childlike) sexual innocence? If so, the point is settled by this world-weary couplet. The whole of Act 4 is resolved in this couplet: it is the death of innocence (which Act 5 will play out).
106. *pick* learn.
106. *by bad mend* learn from bad ways.

Or scant our former having in despite;
Why, we have galls; and though we have some
   grace,
Yet have we some revenge. Let husbands know
Their wives have sense like them; they see and
   smell,   95
And have their palates both for sweet and sour
As husbands have. What is it that they do
When they change us for others? Is it sport?
I think it is. And doth affection breed it?
I think it doth. Is't frailty that thus errs?   100
It is so too. And have not we affections,
Desires for sport, and frailty, as men have?
Then let them use us well; else let them know
The ills we do their ills instruct us so.

Desdemona

Good night, good night. God me such uses send,   105
Not to pick bad from bad, but by bad mend!

[Exeunt.]

ACT 5 SCENE 1

Iago sets up Roderigo's murder attempt on Cassio, hoping both will die. Cassio wounds Roderigo; Iago wounds Cassio from behind. Believing Cassio is dead, Othello prepares to murder Desdemona. Lodovico and Gratiano cautiously investigate the street fight and Iago, pretending to help, finishes Roderigo off. Bianca arrives distressed and Iago blames the murder on her. Emilia adds insult to Iago's deception by calling Bianca a 'strumpet' then is sent off to tell Othello the news. This violent public street scene, dark, dangerous and uncertain, rushes us helter-skelter towards the play's deadly but quiet domestic conclusion.

1. *bulk* a projecting shop front.
2. *rapier bare* unsheathed sword.
2. *put it home* stab it 'to the hilt', i.e. kill with it.
3. *at thy elbow* with you (a phrase often used of the devil encouraging evil acts).
4. *It makes us or it mars us* A memorable expression of an exciting once-in-a-lifetime moment, which audiences would recognise from other plays. The idea is that fate offers us one dazzling opportunity to change and fulfil our entire lives if we seize it, but condemns us to disappointment and non-fulfilment if we fail to rise to that challenge. Iago is a daredevil, an exciting adrenaline-charged figure. When reading *Othello* we might consider whether the 'devil' has all the best action and the 'good' characters are dull by comparison.

11. *quat* pimple.
12. *angry* sore (like a pimple you've pulled at).

14. *Every way makes my gain* it's a win-win situation.
14. *Live Roderigo* i.e. if Roderigo survives.
15. *calls me to a restitution* claims compensation.
16. *bobb'd* trick'd.
19–20. *a daily beauty in his life ... makes me ugly* Iago is not just envious of Cassio's social grace and position but of the nobility of his character. The contrast with his own lack of all three of these 'daily beauties' has been rankling Iago since Cassio was preferred over himself for promotion at the start of the play. Note that after failing to be promoted Iago never considers trying to be more 'noble' in his own person.

ACT 5
SCENE 1 ·

Cyprus. A street.

[Enter IAGO and RODERIGO.]

Iago

    Here, stand behind this bulk; straight will he come.
    Wear thy good rapier bare, and put it home.
    Quick, quick; fear nothing; I'll be at thy elbow.
    It makes us or it mars us; think on that,
    And fix most firm thy resolution.   5

Roderigo

    Be near at hand; I may miscarry in't.

Iago

    Here, at thy hand. Be bold, and take thy stand.
       [Withdraws.]

Roderigo ·

    I have no great devotion to the deed;
    And yet he hath given me satisfying reasons –
    'Tis but a man gone. Forth, my sword; he dies.   10

Iago

    I have rubb'd this young quat almost to the sense,
    And he grows angry. Now, whether he kill Cassio
    Or Cassio him, or each do kill the other,
    Every way makes my gain. Live Roderigo,
    He calls me to a restitution large   15
    Of gold and jewels that I bobb'd from him
    As gifts to Desdemona;
    It must not be. If Cassio do remain,
    He hath a daily beauty in his life
    That makes me ugly; and besides, the Moor   20
    May unfold me to him; there stand I in much peril.
    No, he must die. Be 't so. I hear him coming.

[Enter CASSIO.]

23. *gait* walk.

25. *coat* an armoured shirt or vest.

Stage direction: *at a distance.* The reader is invited to consider where to stage Othello's entrance; the upper stage is one possibility.

35. *minion* hussy (insultingly meaning Desdemona).
36. *unblest fate hies* damnation hurries towards you.
37. *Forth of my heart* Get out of my heart!
37. *blotted* erased.
37–8. *blotted ... spotted* This rhyming couplet conveys finality, decisiveness and a calm murder method (*modus operandi*). But the murder Othello plans here involves blood, i.e. stabbing; elsewhere it is suffocation by pillow.
38. *spotted* stained, with the traditional connotation of evil. Perhaps Othello is thinking of that red-'spotted' handkerchief (see Act 3, Scene 3, lines 439–40).

Roderigo

    I know his gait, 'tis he. Villain, thou diest!

      [Thrusts at CASSIO.*]*

Cassio

    That thrust had been mine enemy indeed

    But that my coat is better than thou know'st.   25

    I will make proof of thine. *[Draws, and wounds*
      RODERIGO.*]*

Roderigo

    O, I am slain! *[*IAGO *stabs Cassio from behind in the*
      leg, and exit.]

Cassio

    I am maim'd for ever. Help, ho! murder! murder!

      [Falls.]

        [Enter OTHELLO *at a distance.]*

Othello

    The voice of Cassio. Iago keeps his word.

Roderigo

    O, villain that I am!   30

Othello

    It is even so.

Cassio

    O, help, ho! light! a surgeon!

Othello

    'Tis he. O brave Iago, honest and just,

    That hast such noble sense of thy friend's wrong!

    Thou teachest me – minion, your dear lies dead,   35

    And your unblest fate hies. Strumpet, I come.

    Forth of my heart those charms, thine eyes, are
      blotted;

    Thy bed, lust-stain'd, shall with lust's blood be
      spotted. *[Exit.]*

      [Enter LODOVICO *and* GRATIANO *at a distance.]*

Cassio

    What, ho! No watch? No passage?

41. *mischance* accident.
41. *direful* distressed.

45. *heavy* dark, clouded.
46. *may be counterfeits* may be a pretence, a trick. The streets of Cyprus are not as safe and well-policed as those of Venice.

50. *shirt* night shirt.
51. *noise* Note how Iago/Shakespeare gets voice and loud into one word. We expect him to ask 'whose voice?' but 'noise' describes the volume and nature of the voice as well.

55. *fellow* The audience knows Iago's name but these gentlemen do not – he is referred to as 'Othello's ancient'. This moment serves as a jolting reminder to us of Iago's (furiously resented) low status, obscurity and thwarted ambition. We might even read Iago as the play's tragic hero, and his inability to control this resentment as the *hamartia* (fatal flaw) from which the tragedy unfolds; it certainly drives Iago's plots from the first line of the play.

Murder! murder! 40
Gratiano
   'Tis some mischance; the voice is very direful.
Cassio
   O, help!
Lodovico
   Hark!
Roderigo
   O wretched villain!
Lodovico
   Two or three groan. 'Tis heavy night; 45
   These may be counterfeits; let's think't unsafe
   To come in to the cry without more help.
Roderigo
   Nobody come? Then shall I bleed to death.

[Re-enter IAGO with a light.]

Lodovico
   Hark!
Gratiano
   Here's one comes in his shirt, with light and weapons. 50
Iago
   Who's there? Whose noise is this that cries on murder?
Lodovico
   We do not know.
Iago
              Did not you hear a cry?
Cassio
   Here, here! For heaven's sake, help me!
Iago
                  What's the matter?
Gratiano
   This is Othello's ancient, as I take it.
Lodovico
   The same indeed; a very valiant fellow. 55
Iago
   What are you here that cry so grievously?

57. spoil'd, undone by villains As so many times in the play, the real villain is currently the devil in plain sight, the ever-present but ever-unsuspected Iago.

59. O me Oh my word. Iago is imitating (mocking) gentlemen's speech. He mocks and makes fun of gentlemen in the way that clowns often do in Shakespeare's plays and in this way provides 'clownish' entertainment and a degree of light relief otherwise in short supply in *Othello*.

62. What are you there? What kind of men are you?

66. O a sign to the actor to make the appropriate sound (here a groan).

68. Ho! murder! This revisits Iago's gleeful rabble-rousing of Act 1, but this time the tragic destruction and chaos will not be stopped by a Senate.

70. As you shall prove us, praise us Judge us by what we do. The gentlemen, cautious of the danger until now, step forward. Note the alliteration 'prove' and 'praise', succinctly fusing together two distinct ideas by linking the sounds.

73. I cry you mercy. Please accept my apologies. (Another gentlemen's expression; Iago is still gleefully mocking their gentility.)

Cassio

Iago? O, I am spoil'd, undone by villains!
Give me some help.

Iago

O me, Lieutenant! What villains have done this?

Cassio

I think that one of them is hereabout,   60
And cannot make away.

Iago

O treacherous villains! –
[*To* LODOVICO *and* GRATIANO] What are you there?
Come in, and give some help.

Roderigo

O, help me there!

Cassio

That's one of them.

Iago

O murd'rous slave! O villian!   65

[Stabs RODERIGO.*]*

Roderigo

O damn'd Iago! O inhuman dog!

Iago

Kill men i' th' dark! Where be these bloody thieves?
How silent is this town. Ho! murder! murder!
What may you be? Are you of good or evil?

Lodovico

As you shall prove us, praise us.   70

Iago

Signior Lodovico?

Lodovico

He, sir.

Iago

I cry you mercy. Here's Cassio hurt by villains.

Gratiano

Cassio!

83. *notable* infamous.

87. *garter* sash.

90. *trash* Iago is fond of this belittling put-down (see also Act 2, Scene 1, line 297).

94. *countryman* compatriot.

Iago

How is't, brother? 75

Cassio

My leg is cut in two.

Iago

Marry, heaven forbid!

Light, gentlemen. I'll bind it with my shirt.

[Enter BIANCA.*]*

Bianca

What is the matter, ho? Who is't that cried?

Iago

Who is't that cried! 80

Bianca

O my dear Cassio!

My sweet Cassio! O Cassio, Cassio, Cassio!

Iago

O notable strumpet! Cassio, may you suspect

Who they should be that have thus mangled you?

Cassio

No. 85

Gratiano

I am sorry to find you thus; I have been to seek you.

Iago

Lend me a garter. So.

O, for a chair, to bear him easily hence!

Bianca

Alas, he faints! O Cassio, Cassio, Cassio!

Iago

Gentlemen all, I do suspect this trash 90

To be a party in this injury.

Patience awhile, good Cassio. Come, come;

Lend me a light. Know we this face or no?

Alas, my friend and my dear countryman

Roderigo? No – yes, sure; O heaven! Roderigo. 95

Gratiano

What, of Venice?

101. *a chair* a stretcher.

104. *said* done.

107. *Save you your labour* Don't bother, keep your hands off!
108. *malice* argument, quarrel.
109. *None in the world; nor do I know the man* Cassio (as was Othello) is of an honest and trusting nature and Iago is mocking him for it. Should a General be more wary? If Cassio had been less condescending about his promotion rival Iago as a potential enemy, less complacent about his own superiority, he might have been more suspicious of the dangerous hostilities caused by his position and success (including with Desdemona's affections, in contrast to Roderigo). Perhaps Cassio, with his 'daily beauty', wasn't paranoid enough.

112. *gastness* aghast-ness, ghastlinesss.

115–6. *guiltiness will speak / Though tongues were out of use* Her actions and body language will show that she is guilty.

Iago

Even he, sir; did you know him?

Gratiano

Know him! Ay.

Iago

Signior Gratiano? I cry your gentle pardon;
These bloody accidents must excuse my manners,
That so neglected you.

Gratiano

I am glad to see you.   100

Iago

How do you, Cassio? – O, a chair, a chair!

Gratiano

Roderigo!

Iago

He, he, 'tis he. *[A chair brought in.]*
O, that's well said; the chair.
Some good man bear him carefully from hence;   105
I'll fetch the General's surgeon. *[To* BIANCA*]* For you,
    mistress,
Save you your labour. – He that lies slain here,
    Cassio,
Was my dear friend. What malice was between you?

Cassio

None in the world; nor do I know the man.

Iago

[To BIANCA*]* What, look you pale? – O, bear him out
    o' th' air.   110

    *[*CASSIO *and* RODERIGO *are borne off.]*

Stay you, good gentlemen. – Look you pale,
    mistress? –
Do you perceive the gastness of her eye? –
Nay, an you stare, we shall hear more anon. –
Behold her well; I pray you look upon her.
Do you see, gentlemen? Nay, guiltiness will speak   115
Though tongues were out of use.

117. *'Las* Alas

119. *'scap'd* escaped.

121. *Alas good gentleman ... good Cassio* For the wordly Emilia, both men are equally good. Her response shows the non-judging generosity of her heart and the limitations of her judgement.

122. *This is the fruits of whoring* the result of their relationship with Bianca. Iago is trying to set Bianca up for Roderigo's murder and Cassio's attempted murder.

126. *charge* order.

128–9. *I am no strumpet ... thus abuse me* The List of Characters (p.1) supports Bianca's assertion: a courtezan is a high-class 'escort' – a woman who provides company for men which *may* include sexual services. But 'I am no strumpet' is also Bianca's defiance in the face of Iago's slander. She is certainly, as we have seen, 'honest' in her feelings for Cassio.

129. *Foh!* an expression of disgust.

130. *dress'd* bandaged.
131. *tell's* tell us.

135. *fordoes me quite* ruins me.

[Enter EMILIA.*]*

Emilia
'Las, what's the matter? What's the matter, husband?
Iago
Cassio hath here been set on in the dark
By Roderigo and fellows that are 'scap'd.
He's almost slain, and Roderigo quite dead.   120
Emilia
Alas, good gentleman! Alas, good Cassio!
Iago
This is the fruits of whoring. Prithee, Emilia,
Go know of Cassio where he supp'd to-night. –
What, do you shake at that?
Bianca
He supp'd at my house; but I therefore shake not.   125
Iago
O, did he so? I charge you go with me.
Emilia
Fie, fie upon thee, strumpet!
Bianca
I am no strumpet, but of life as honest
As you that thus abuse me.
Emilia
                As I! Foh! Fie upon thee!
Iago
Kind gentlemen, let's go see poor Cassio dress'd. –   130
Come, mistress, you must tell's another tale.
Emilia, run you to the citadel,
And tell my lord and lady what hath happ'd.
Will you go on afore? *[Aside]* This is the night
That either makes me or fordoes me quite.   135

[Exeunt.]

SCENE 2

In their bedroom, Othello overcomes a last-minute reluctance to kill Desdemona. Despite her lack of confession, he suffocates her. The dying Desdemona forgives Othello, who justifies the murder to Emilia as punishment for adultery. Emilia begins to recognise Iago's evil plot and boldly calls for help. Montano, Gratiano and Iago enter. Emilia accuses Iago, who tries to silence her. Emilia reveals the true story of how Cassio got the handkerchief. Othello finally recognises Iago as the 'demi-devil' behind the false accusations and attacks him. Iago kills Emilia and escapes. Othello is confronted with the truth of his tragic crime and accepts his soul is damned. Lodovico investigates and Iago refuses to explain. Lodovico arrests Othello, who kills himself. Lodovico orders Cassio to severely punish Iago and leaves to take the news to Venice.

1. *It* i.e. her adultery; *is the cause* gives Othello the 'legal' case for his actions.
1. *soul* Othello speaks to his 'soul' as characters do in the Bible. This, along with the references to Greek mythology, add tragic grandeur to these fatal moments.
3. *I'll not shed her blood* Othello's murder method is clearly suffocation at this point.
5. *alabaster* pale stone used for monuments. This perhaps also anticipates Desdemona's lifeless corpse.
7. Othello puts out the bedroom light and will then extinguish the light of Desdemona's life. The first literal snuffing out of a candle foreshadows the second metaphorical 'snuffing out' of Desdemona's life.
8. *flaming minister* a torch (of fire) (see line 12).
12. *Promethean heat* fire. Prometheus stole fire from the gods and gave it to mortals, changing the course of human history (Greek mythology). This may also anticipate that Othello will be horribly punished for his crime, as Prometheus was.
13. *pluck'd thy rose* taken her life, murdered her – but note how attracted he still is by Desdemona (the rose is a traditional emblem of beauty and love).

22. *It strikes where it doth love* a Bible reference – whom God loves, he strikes (Hebrews 12.6). Are we watching a jealous fool 'playing God' or the tragic flaw of a great man?

25. *Will you come to bed, my lord?* This line – and Othello's subject-changing reply, *Have you pray'd?* (line 26) – have been acted in vastly different ways since 1603.

SCENE 2

Cyprus. The citadel.

[DESDEMONA in her bed. Enter OTHELLO with a light.]

Othello

It is the cause, it is the cause, my soul –
Let me not name it to you, you chaste stars –
It is the cause. Yet I'll not shed her blood,
Nor scar that whiter skin of hers than snow,
And smooth as monumental alabaster.   5
Yet she must die, else she'll betray more men.
Put out the light, and then put out the light.
If I quench thee, thou flaming minister,
I can again thy former light restore,
Should I repent me; but once put out thy light,   10
Thou cunning'st pattern of excelling nature,
I know not where is that Promethean heat
That can thy light relume. When I have pluck'd thy
    rose,
I cannot give it vital growth again;
It needs must wither. I'll smell thee on the tree.   15

[Kissing her.]

O balmy breath, that dost almost persuade
Justice to break her sword! One more, one more.
Be thus when thou art dead, and I will kill thee,
And love thee after. One more, and that's the last:
So sweet was ne'er so fatal. I must weep,   20
But they are cruel tears. This sorrow's heavenly;
It strikes where it doth love. She wakes.

Desdemona

Who's there? Othello?

Othello

Ay, Desdemona.

Desdemona

Will you come to bed, my lord?   25

257

26. *Have you pray'd* Christians believed that if you didn't pray before death your soul would not go to Heaven.

28. *bethink yourself* call to mind, remember.

30. *Solicit for it straight* pray for forgiveness straightaway.

33–4. *I would not kill thy unprepared spirit ... thy soul* i.e. won't leave her unprepared for death and God's Judgement. Note the careful consideration Othello still has for Desdemona, despite his murderous intent. It suggests an internal struggle between his enduring love for her and his Iago-poisoned sense of betrayal; of his images of Desdemona as 'pure' and 'whore'.
34. *forfend* forbid.

35. *Ay* Othello and Desdemona repeat this word in a kind of hypnotised call and response formula, each with a different feeling – see lines 24, 27, 35, 43 and 54) until her murder. Here its use is menacing.

38. *Humh!* a menacing sound; the actor must decide how to say it.

42. *loves I bear to you* loving you more than God.

Othello

Have you pray'd to-night, Desdemona?

Desdemona

Ay, my lord.

Othello

If you bethink yourself of any crime
Unreconcil'd as yet to heaven and grace,
Solicit for it straight.

Desdemona

      Alack, my lord,   30
What may you mean by that?

Othello

Well, do it, and be brief; I will walk by.
I would not kill thy unprepared spirit;
No, heaven forfend! – I would not kill thy soul.

Desdemona

Talk you of killing?

Othello

      Ay, I do.

Desdemona

        Then heaven   35
Have mercy on me!

Othello

     Amen, with all my heart!

Desdemona

If you say so, I hope you will not kill me.

Othello

Humh!

Desdemona

And yet I fear you; for you're fatal then
When your eyes roll so. Why I should fear I know
  not,   40
Since guiltiness I know not; but yet I feel I fear.

Othello

Think on thy sins.

Desdemona

     They are loves I bear to you.

44. *That death's unnatural that kills for loving* Nobody should be killed for loving someone.

47. *portents* bad omens.

50. *handkerchief* Othello has been preparing himself to murder Desdemona since the scene began. Here he accuses her of giving his handkerchief to Cassio. She denies it and says Cassio (since stabbed by Iago) will bear her out. Note how important the handkerchief is, how insulted he is by her giving it away, and how it is this that finally sends him over the edge (see line 65).

52. *Send for the man and ask him* Othello doesn't send for Cassio as she pleads, (mistakenly) believing that Cassio has been murdered. But he could have sent to check Iago's insinuations many times before – and never did.

53. *Take heed of perjury ... death-bed* You will damn yourself to hell if you lie (on your death bed) and do not confess your sins.

56. *article* accusation against her (as in a court of law).

57. *choke* smother (a foreshadowing of her death).

59. *I say, amen* Is Othello playing God again?

Othello

    Ay, and for that thou diest.

Desdemona

    That death's unnatural that kills for loving.
    Alas, why gnaw you so your nether lip?   45
    Some bloody passion shakes your very frame.
    These are portents; but yet I hope, I hope,
    They do not point on me.

Othello

    Peace, and be still.

Desdemona

                 I will so. What's the matter?

Othello

    That handkerchief which I so lov'd and gave thee   50
    Thou gav'st to Cassio.

Desdemona

             No, by my life and soul!
    Send for the man and ask him.

Othello

                 Sweet soul, take heed,
    Take heed of perjury; thou art on thy death-bed.

Desdemona

    Ay, but not yet to die.

Othello

             Yes, presently.
    Therefore confess thee freely of thy sin;   55
    For to deny each article with oath
    Cannot remove nor choke the strong conception
    That I do groan withal. Thou art to die.

Desdemona

    Then, Lord have mercy on me!

Othello

                 I say, amen.

Desdemona

    And have you mercy too! I never did   60
    Offend you in my life; never lov'd Cassio
    But with such general warranty of heaven

63. *token* a love token (the handkerchief).

64–8. *By heaven ... handkerchief* Before this reminder, Othello was 'calm' and killing Desdemona was (to him) a sort of ritual justice and sacrifice; now he is in a murderous rage.

72. *us'd thee* i.e. as a sexual partner. Note Othello's insistence on sex as a predatory act, a woman as a thing to be used; he isn't jealous of her loving or being loved.

77–8. *Had all his hairs ... stomach for them all* If he'd had as many lives as hairs on his head, I would have killed them all. This is another Biblical reference (Psalm 40. 12), lending heroic scale to Othello's avenging fury. Note also the pun on 'hairs' and 'heirs', which suggests how deeply his manhood is threatened – here by the idea of Cassio begetting heirs on his wife.

79. *betray'd* Again, Othello misinterprets Desdemona's intentions here: she means Cassio has been plotted against; he assumes her distress reveals that he is her lover.

As I might love. I never gave him token.
Othello
By heaven, I saw my handkerchief in's hand.
O perjur'd woman! thou dost stone my heart,   65
And mak'st me call what I intend to do
A murder, which I thought a sacrifice.
I saw the handkerchief.
Desdemona
                              He found it, then;
I never gave it him. Send for him hither;
Let him confess a truth.
Othello
                              He hath confess'd.   70
Desdemona
What, my lord?
Othello
That he hath – ud's death! – us'd thee.
Desdemona
How? unlawfully?
Othello
                    Ay.
Desdemona
He will not say so.
Othello
                    No, his mouth is stopp'd;
Honest Iago hath ta'en order for't.   75
Desdemona
O, my fear interprets! What, is he dead?
Othello
Had all his hairs been lives, my great revenge
Had stomach for them all.
Desdemona
Alas, he is betray'd, and I undone!
Othello
Out, strumpet! Weep'st thou for him to my face?   80
Desdemona
O, banish me, my lord, but kill me not!

82. *Down, strumpet* Othello pushes Desdemona down onto the bed, where he plans to strangle her. This moment also provides a sexually suggestive image that once caused uproar in audiences, particularly during periods when interracial relationships were actively discouraged.

86. *Being done, there is no pause* I've started so I'll finish.

89. *lord* Othello; *Lord Lord* God, God! Desdemona says the prayer she is denied at line 87.

90. *My lord, my lord!* This spooky echoing of Desdemona's death line has considerable potential for dramatic staging. The two speeches could even overlap, with 'lord' being uttered by the two women at the same time. One refers to God, the other to Othello. While Othello has certainly been 'playing God' with Desdemona's life, this contrast between the God Desdemona prays to and the merciless murdering husband could not be more marked.

94. *So, so* Some productions show Othello stabbing Desdemona here. It horribly fulfils his promise at Act 4, Scene 1, line 125.

99. *she* i.e. Emilia.

Othello

  Down, strumpet.

Desdemona

  Kill me to-morrow; let me live to-night.

Othello

  Nay, an you strive –

Desdemona

  But half an hour!   85

Othello

  Being done, there is no pause.

Desdemona

  But while I say one prayer!

Othello

  It is too late.   *[Smothers her.]*

Desdemona

  O lord, Lord, Lord!

Emilia

  [Within] My lord, my lord! what, ho! my lord, my
     lord!   90

Othello

  What voice is this? Not dead? not yet quite dead?
  I that am cruel am yet merciful;
  I would not have thee linger in thy pain.
  So, so.

Emilia

  [Within] What, ho! my lord, my lord!   95

Othello

  Who's there?

Emilia

  [Within] O, good my lord, I'd speak a word with
     you!

Othello

  Yes – 'tis Emilia – by and by. She's dead.
  'Tis like she comes to speak of Cassio's death;
  The noise was high. Ha! no more moving?   100
  Still as the grave. Shall she come in? Were't good?
  I think she stirs again. No. What's the best?

104. *My wife! … no wife* Othello's murderous rage is finally subsiding and he begins to realise what he has done. This marks a key point in the *denouement* (outcome) of the tragedy and the first horrifying glimmer of his *anagnorisis* (recognition).

105. *unsupportable* unbearable.

106–7. *Methinks … affrighted globe* Shakespeare's audiences believed that great changes in human affairs were reflected by natural events such as eclipses. But here, as Othello points out, there is the *absence* of any such signal; the murder is ordinary, domestic, deadly quiet; the chaos and cataclysm is all within himself.

108. *yawn* gape.

108. *alteration* her death.

111. *curtains draw* i.e. around the bed (possibly a stage direction). Shakespeare's theatre company presented the play in front of 3,000 people at the outdoor Globe and later in front of 750 people at the new indoors, candle-lit Blackfriars. This domestic scene would most likely be more effective in the more intimate setting of the Blackfriars.

112–14. *with thee now? … What, now?* such repetition is common when a speaker is in shock.

116. *error of the moon* disorders on Earth were believed to caused by disorders in the heavens, and vice versa (see note to lines 106–7).

117. *She comes more nearer earth than she was wont* The Moon ('She') is much closer to the Earth than usual.

118. *mad* the word 'lunatic' derives from the long-held belief that 'lunar' (i.e. moon) activity caused madness.

121. *Cassio kill'd!* The uncomprehending repetitions (and broken lines) continue to show Othello in shock.

If she come in she'll sure speak to my wife.
My wife! my wife! what wife? I have no wife.
O insupportable! O heavy hour!   105
Methinks it should be now a huge eclipse
Of sun and moon, and that th' affrighted globe
Did yawn at alteration.

Emilia

   [Within] I do beseech you that I may speak with you.
      O good my lord!

Othello

I had forgot thee: O, come in, Emilia.   110
Soft, by and by. Let me the curtains draw.
Where art thou?

        [Unlocks the door.]

        [Enter EMILIA.]

        What's the matter with thee now?

Emilia

   O, my good lord, yonder's foul murders done!

Othello

   What, now?

Emilia

   But now, my lord.   115

Othello

   It is the very error of the moon;
   She comes more nearer earth than she was wont,
   And makes men mad.

Emilia

   Cassio, my lord, hath kill'd a young Venetian
   Call'd Roderigo.

Othello

         Roderigo kill'd!   120
   And Cassio kill'd!

Emilia

        No, Cassio, is not kill'd.

122. *out of tune* gone awry.

124. *O, falsely, falsely murder'd* (see also lines 129 and 131–2) A Jacobean audience would have been terrified by Desdemona's three 'posthumous' speeches. They believed in ghosts, and for a corpse to start speaking would have been shocking. The appearance of Banquo's ghost in *Macbeth* is a similar representation of how 'the afterlife' and the supernatural was seen to intrude on the natural world. For modern audiences of the play, Desdemona's words could be interpreted on a psychological level as the repressed intuitions or conscience of Othello. But also suffocation is an imprecise form of murder – and some signs of life including speech could linger.

132. *kind* If Desdemona means gentle and caring, this is a 'divinely' forgiving speech from one just murdered. If she means 'behaving in line with his true nature' it is tragic reminder of Othello's lost (flawed) greatness and the love he has thrown away. Either way this is a moment of audaciously brilliant drama. By contrast, the moment when the tragic figure of King Lear sees his dead daughter Cordelia breathe post-mortem was a perception limited to one (grief-deranged) character; here the whole audience witnesses it.

Othello

Not Cassio kill'd! Then murder's out of tune,
And sweet revenge grows harsh.

Desdemona

O, falsely, falsely murder'd!

Emilia

O Lord, what cry is that?

Othello

That! what?   125

Emilia

Out and alas! that was my lady's voice.
Help! help, ho! help! O lady, speak again!
Sweet Desdemona! O sweet mistress, speak!

Desdemona

A guiltless death I die.

Emilia

O, who hath done this deed?   130

Desdemona

Nobody. I myself. Farewell.
Commend me to my kind lord. O, farewell!

[She dies.]

Othello

Why, how should she be murder'd?

Emilia

Alas, who knows?

Othello

You heard her say herself it was not I.

Emilia

She said so. I must needs report a truth.   135

Othello

She's like a liar gone to burning hell:
'Twas I that kill'd her.

Emilia

O, the more angel she,
And you the blacker devil!

139. *folly* sexual promiscuity.

139–40. The exchange here between Othello and Emilia deploys to brilliant effect a technique from classical Greek theatre called *stichomythia*. This refers to a sharp line-by-line dispute between two characters who take up, and throw back, the opponent's words. It makes for exciting theatre, and its fast pace and use of the opponent's speech against them may usefully be compared to a rally in tennis. Here it is the structure of Othello's sentence that is repeated and hurled back at him. *Stichomythia* was used to mark moments of high tension, and these two lines mark the climax of Emilia's recognition of Othello's fault. Note also her use of 'thou' (line 140) to the social superior she has called 'my lord' earlier in this scene, showing her complete loss of all respect for him.

141. *false as water* a proverb. Note the continuation of the *stichomythia* in Emilia's echo reply.

143. *top her* lie on top of her, have sex with her.

150–3. Othello's comparison here is characteristically on an epic scale. (He compared his revenge in similarly titanic terms in Act 3, Scene 3, lines 458–65.) He thinks of himself in terms of vast natural forces and the play tells his and Desdemona's domestic marriage story on that same epic scale.

152. *chrysolite* topaz.

Othello

She turn'd to folly, and she was a whore.

Emilia

Thou dost belie her, and thou art a devil. 140

Othello

She was false as water.

Emilia

                    Thou art rash as fire to say

That she was false. O, she was heavenly true!

Othello

Cassio did top her; ask thy husband else.

O, I were damn'd beneath all depth in hell

But that I did proceed upon just grounds 145

To this extremity. Thy husband knew it all.

Emilia

My husband!

Othello

Thy husband.

Emilia

That she was false to wedlock?

Othello

Ay, with Cassio. Nay, had she been true, 150

If heaven would make me such another world

Of one entire and perfect chrysolite,

I'd not have sold her for it.

Emilia

My husband!

Othello

Ay, 'twas he that told me on her first. 155

An honest man he is, and hates the slime

That sticks on filthy deeds.

Emilia

                    My husband!

Othello

What needs this iterance, woman? I say thy
   husband.

159. *made mocks with* made a mockery of.

163. *pernicious* wicked.
165. *She was too fond of her most filthy bargain* This racist insult, calling him a 'filthy bargain', throws back at Othello the 'filthy' he uses about Desdemona's alleged misdeeds at lines 156–7.

169. *Peace, you were best* You had better shut up! Women are frequently bullied into silence in this play. In this scene Emilia finally speaks out, even as Othello and Iago threaten her – and ultimately loses her life for doing so. It is dangerous for anyone to speak the truth in this play (both Othello and Cassio make themselves vulnerable by their trusting and open natures), but evidently for a woman to do so is fatal.
169–73. Othello uses the formal and distancing 'you' to Emilia; she responds with 'thee', showing her lack of respect. She is speaking down to a murderer and a fool (see line 171), not up to a General and her mistress's lord.
170–1. *Thou hast not half that power ... hurt* You can't hurt me half as much as I am by seeing her dead.
171. *gull ... dolt* dupe, fool.
175. *The Moor* We must consider why Emilia uses this term here rather than 'The General'. 'The Moor' sets Othello again as the outsider, both in terms of country of origin and his ethnicity. This marks Emilia's alienation from him, shocked by the murder of her mistress, an understandable reaction though (under the impact of this shock) a primitive one, not free from racism. (It also marks the way Othello's action has tragically lost the outsider all the hard-won acceptance and honour of Venetian society.) Emilia embodies the limitations of her society and under stress expresses them, just as when she turned on Bianca and called her a strumpet (Act 5, Scene 1, line 127). Nevertheless, she will in this final scene attain a tragic grandeur and redemption in her rejection of Iago and defence of her mistress's 'honesty'. She dies for truth and against lies.

Emilia
O mistress, villainy hath made mocks with love!
My husband say that she was false!
Othello
He, woman; 160
I say thy husband; dost understand the word?
My friend, thy husband – honest, honest Iago.
Emilia
If he say so, may his pernicious soul
Rot half a grain a day! He lies to th' heart.
She was too fond of her most filthy bargain. 165
Othello
Ha!
Emilia
Do thy worst:
This deed of thine is no more worthy heaven
Than thou wast worthy her.
Othello
Peace, you were best.
Emilia
Thou hast not half that power to do me harm 170
As I have to be hurt. O gull! O dolt!
As ignorant as dirt! Thou hast done a deed –
I care not for thy sword; I'll make thee known,
Though I lost twenty lives. Help! help, ho! help!
The Moor hath kill'd my mistress! Murder! murder! 175

[Enter MONTANO, GRATIANO, IAGO, and Others.]

Montano
What is the matter? How now, General!
Emilia
O, are you come, Iago? You have done well,
That men must lay their murders on your neck.
Gratiano
What is the matter?
Emilia
Disprove this villain, if thou be'st a man: 180

273

182. *I know thou didst not; thou'rt not such a villain* Emilia is about to experience a tragic recognition (or *anagnorisis*, as Aristotle called it).

184–5. *I told him what I thought ... apt and true* a succinct summary of the play! Iago (and his schemes) function here exactly as Aristotle says the Plot in a tragedy should: they have fully unfolded the hero's tragic flaw *in action* through misfortune, reversal and recognition. This is probably why *Othello* has been called the most Aristotelian of Shakespeare's tragedies. (See also the section on Plot versus character in the Introduction, pp.xiv–xv.)

185. *apt* fitting, appropriate.

191. *charm your tongue* be quiet, with the suggestion that women talk too much.

He says thou told'st him that his wife was false.
I know thou didst not; thou'rt not such a villain.
Speak, for my heart is full.

Iago

I told him what I thought, and told no more
Than what he found himself was apt and true.   185

Emilia

But did you ever tell him she was false?

Iago

I did.

Emilia

You told a lie – an odious, damned lie.
Upon my soul, a lie – a wicked lie.
She false with Cassio! Did you say with Cassio?   190

Iago

With Cassio, mistress. Go to, charm your tongue.

Emilia

I will not charm my tongue; I am bound to speak:
My mistress here lies murdered in her bed.

All

O heavens forfend!

Emilia

And your reports have set the murder on.   195

Othello

Nay, stare not, masters: it is true, indeed.

Gratiano

'Tis a strange truth.

Montano

O monstrous act!

Emilia

Villainy, villainy, villainy!
I think upon't. I think – I smell't. villainy!
I thought so then. I'll kill myself for grief.   200
O villainy, villainy!

Iago

What, are you mad? I charge you get you home.

203. *let me have leave to speak* Greek (and Shakespearean) tragedy gave women a voice they did not have in any other public forum (albeit a voice written and acted by males).

206. *O! O! O!* a sign to the actor to howl (or roar, see line 207).

213. *match was mortal to him* Brabantio's grief over Desdemona's marriage to Othello was fatal to him (i.e. killed him).

214. *Shore his old thread atwain* sheared or cut his life's thread, i.e. killed him. The reference is to the classical Fate Atropos whom the Ancient Greeks believed cut the thread of one's life at death. Here it is Brabantio's grief at 'losing' his daughter that acts the part of Atropos, first driving him mad then killing him. Note the function of Act 5 as a denouement, (unhappily) resolving all the issues of the play, including this father-daughter theme with its sympathy for the old bereft (and in Act 1 not very sympathetic) father.

217. *reprobance* damnation.

219. *act of shame* adultery.

221–5. We find out the 'true' origin of the handkerchief – a gift from Othello's father to his mother. We are left to think about the physical as well as the symbolic attributes of the handkerchief. Shakespeare's audience would have recognised it as a symbol of the familiarly tragic position of women, suffering for male wrongdoings. They might also share Othello's view of it as magical, actually causing the tragedy.

Emilia

Good gentlemen, let me have leave to speak.
'Tis proper I obey him, but not now.
Perchance, Iago, I will ne'er go home. 205

Othello

O! O! O! *[Falls on the bed.]*

Emilia

        Nay, lay thee down and roar;
For thou hast kill'd the sweetest innocent
That e'er did lift up eye.

Othello

[Rising]   O, she was foul!
I scarce did know you, uncle. There lies your niece,
Whose breath indeed these hands have newly
   stopp'd. 210
I know this act shows horrible and grim.

Gratiano

Poor Desdemona! I am glad thy father's dead.
Thy match was mortal to him, and pure grief
Shore his old thread atwain. Did he live now,
This sight would make him do a desperate turn, 215
Yea, curse his better angel from his side,
And fall to reprobance.

Othello

'Tis pitiful; but yet Iago knows
That she with Cassio hath the act of shame
A thousand times committed; Cassio confess'd it; 220
And she did gratify his amorous works
With that recognizance and pledge of love
Which I first gave her; I saw it in his hand.
It was a handkerchief, an antique token
My father gave my mother. 225

Emilia

O God! O heavenly God!

Iago

Zounds, hold your peace.

228–43. Emilia finally gives the true version of events, for which, Iago kills her.

229. *as liberal as the north* as freely (and bitingly cold) as the north wind. She suggests that a woman's voice (i.e. one that articulates female concerns) is elementally hostile to male ears.

242. *coxcomb* numbskull, fool.

242–3. *What should such a fool/ Do with so good a wife?* The crux of the matter; the audience surely asks the same question. Scholars have argued about whether Desdemona is *positively* pure *or negatively* passive (and everything in between) or *both* at different stages of the play. Edward Pechter, like Kernan and others, argued that she represents the beliefs the play impresses upon us and therefore that her unjust death registers a kind of despair of these – a despair at the futility of (and even of the survival of) human goodness in the world.

244. *stones* thunderbolts. Again, Othello notes that nature is *not* acting in accord with the tragic events unfolding on Earth (see also lines 106–7 and 116).

Emilia
'Twill out, 'twill out. I, peace!
No, I will speak as liberal as the north.
Let heaven and men and devils, let them all,   230
All, all, cry shame against me, yet I'll speak.

Iago
Be wise, and get you home.

Emilia
                                                    I will not.

[IAGO offers to stab his wife.]

Gratiano
Fie! Your sword upon a woman?

Emilia
O thou dull Moor! That handkerchief thou speak'st
    of
I found by fortune, and did give my husband;   235
For often with a solemn earnestness –
More than indeed belong'd to such a trifle –
He begg'd of me to steal it.

Iago
                                        Villainous whore!

Emilia
She give it Cassio! No, alas, I found it,
And I did give't my husband.

Iago
                                        Filth, thou liest.   240

Emilia
By heaven, I do not, I do not, gentlemen.
O murderous coxcomb! What should such a fool
Do with so good a wife? *[The Moor runs at IAGO;*
    MONTANO and others disarm the Moor. IAGO kills his
    wife and escapes.]

Othello
Are there no stones in heaven but what serves for the
thunder? Precious villain!   245

249. *notorious* obvious, out and out, absolute.

249–50. *Take you this weapon ... Moor* Othello did have a weapon at the start of the scene so could have stabbed Desdemona at line 94.

255. *puny whipster* whipping boy, whippersnapper.

256. *honour* A soldier should not lose or give up his sword; it was considered a dishonour to do so. But Othello realises the 'dishonour' of losing his sword no longer matters. Nothing does. His real dishonour was to be so completely duped by Iago.

259–60. *play the swan / And die in music* There is a tradition that a swan 'sings' before it dies, hence the expression 'swan song' meaning a farewell performance. Emilia literally dies 'in music' because she is singing this song as she bids farewell to life. This is not a realistic text (it would be weird 'in real life' for Emilia to sing out her last breath) but it is terrific theatre. As a stage representation of a woman's 'swan song' it engenders a suitably eerie emotion, and its link to the Willow Scene conveys her poignant connection with Desdemona and their shared fate: killed by their husbands.

265. *sword of Spain* Spain (and Spanish steel) was famous for its high-quality sword-manufacture (Spain was the greatest military power in the world during Shakespeare's lifetime).

265. *ice-brook's temper* of hardened and tempered steel.

270. *naked* unarmed, without a sword.

Gratiano

  The woman falls; sure he hath kill'd his wife.

Emilia

  Ay, ay. O, lay me by my mistress' side.

Gratiano

  He's gone, but his wife's kill'd.

Montano

  'Tis a notorious villain. Take you this weapon,
  Which I have here recover'd from the Moor.   250
  Come, guard the door without; let him not pass,
  But kill him rather. I'll after that same villain,
  For 'tis a damned slave.

      [Exeunt MONTANO, GRATIANO, *and others.]*

Othello

  I am not valiant neither –
  But every puny whipster gets my sword.   255
  But why should honour outlive honesty?
  Let it go all.

Emilia

  What did thy song bode, lady?
  Hark, canst thou hear me? I will play the swan,
  And die in music. *[Sings]* Willow, willow, willow. –   260
  Moor, she was chaste; she lov'd thee, cruel Moor;
  So come my soul to bliss, as I speak true;
  So speaking as I think, alas, I die.

      [She dies.]

Othello

  I have another weapon in this chamber;
  It was a sword of Spain, the ice-brook's temper.   265
  O, here it is. Uncle, I must come forth.

Gratiano

  [Within] If thou attempt it, it will cost thee dear;
  Thou hast no weapon, and perforce must suffer.

Othello

  Look in upon me, then, and speak with me,
  Or, naked as I am, I will assault thee.   270

279. *butt* where the sword stops, i.e. with himself as its target.

280. *very sea-mark of my utmost sail* the final point of my life's journey. Once again, Othello describes himself in terms of a vast ocean, a huge natural force.

282. *a rush* a reed.

285. *compt* Judgement Day – a time (recognised by Judaism, Islam, Christianity and Zoroastrianism) when God judges all souls and rewards or punishes them.

291–2. *roast me in sulphur ... liquid fire* signs of burning in Hell (eternal damnation).

297. *viper* i.e. Iago, with an allusion to Satan in the Garden of Eden (as described in the Book of Genesis), who appears as a serpent to tempt Eve to disobey God. Desdemona's Eve-like innocence is part of why Iago's schemes succeed. She and Othello hardly knew each other; their love and romance was based on romantic storytelling, not experience of how relationships between men and women work in the real world. In this sense the critic William Empson saw Iago as an agent of truth. Yet the tragic naïvety of Othello and Desdemona is part of their grandeur and nobility; we feel the pity and terror of their fall and at best only grudgingly acknowledge Iago's destructive corrections. We certainly don't admire his cruelty, deceitfulness and hatred. The paranoid little hell he makes of their Eden is fallen indeed.

[Re-enter GRATIANO.]

Gratiano
 What is the matter?
Othello
     Behold, I have a weapon;
 A better never did itself sustain
 Upon a soldier's thigh. I have seen the day
 That with this little arm and this good sword
 I have made my way through more impediments 275
 Than twenty times your stop. But, O vain boast!
 Who can control his fate? 'Tis not so now.
 Be not afraid though you do see me weapon'd;
 Here is my journey's end, here is my butt,
 And very sea-mark of my utmost sail. 280
 Do you go back dismay'd? 'Tis a lost fear;
 Man but a rush against Othello's breast,
 And he retires. Where should Othello go?
 Now, how dost thou look now? O ill-starr'd wench!
 Pale as thy smock! When we shall meet at compt, 285
 This look of thine will hurl my soul from heaven,
 And fiends will snatch at it. Cold, cold, my girl!
 Even like thy chastity. O cursed, cursed slave!
 Whip me, ye devils,
 From the possession of this heavenly sight. 290
 Blow me about in winds, roast me in sulphur,
 Wash me in steep-down gulfs of liquid fire.
 O Desdemona! Dead! Desdemona! Dead!
 O! O!

*[Enter LODOVICO, MONTANO, CASSIO carried in a
chair, and Officers, with IAGO prisoner.]*

Lodovico
 Where is this rash and most unfortunate man? 295
Othello
 That's he that was Othello – here I am.
Lodovico
 Where is that viper? Bring the villain forth.

298. *towards his feet* i.e. to see a devil's cloven hooves.

302–3. *I am not sorry neither ... happiness to die* This is a curious response, perhaps, to Othello's failure to kill Iago, but he goes on to suggest that mortal life itself is a better punishment. The audience might think of the equivalent character – Mephistopheles – in Marlowe's *Doctor Faustus*, who says of every moment of his existence: 'This is hell, nor am I out of it.'
305. *practice* plotting.

314. *demi-devil* half man, half devil.
316. *Demand me nothing ... you know* Iago's frank retort indicates that Othello should have known the truth; and that only he can be blamed for failing to see through Iago's lies. Shakespeare's paired contrast of innocence *versus* frank realism in Iago/Othello (as of Desdemona/Emilia) does not necessarily side with the innocents. Iago's cynical world-weary wisdom has its own value. Shakespeare's audiences would have been familiar with the playwright's examinations of how naïvety is not only punished in this world but *ought to be* punished, however sympathetic the innocents are. General Othello should not have judged others – least of all Iago – by his own honest face. Emilia's feisty response in the Willow Scene to the male chauvinism of her marriage and her husband's world is surely preferable to Desdemona's passive acquiescence.
318. *pray* i.e. to avoid *eternal* damnation. Prayer would send Iago to Purgatory, which was just as bad but not eternal.

Othello

    I look down towards his feet – but that's a fable.
    If that thou be'st a devil, I cannot kill thee.

                [Wounds IAGO.*]*

Lodovico

    Wrench his sword from him.   300

Iago

    I bleed, sir; but not kill'd.

Othello

    I am not sorry neither: I'd have thee live;
    For, in my sense, 'tis happiness to die.

Lodovico

    O thou Othello, that was once so good,
    Fall'n in the practice of a damned slave,   305
    What shall be said to thee?

Othello

                    Why, any thing:
    An honourable murderer, if you will;
    For nought I did in hate, but all in honour.

Lodovico

    This wretch hath part confess'd his villainy.
    Did you and he consent in Cassio's death?   310

Othello

    Ay.

Cassio

    Dear General, I never gave you cause.

Othello

    I do believe it, and I ask your pardon.
    Will you, I pray, demand that demi-devil
    Why he hath thus ensnar'd my soul and body?   315

Iago

    Demand me nothing. What you know, you know.
    From this time forth I never will speak word.

Lodovico

    What, not to pray?

318. *Torments will ope your lips* Torture will make you speak the truth. The end of Iago's story is retained from the source Cinthio (whereas Othello's is completely changed). Shakespeare's text from here to the end invites us to compare our righteous (savage) indignation to those on stage and what punishments we would sanction for Iago's deeds. Do we agree with the civilised Venetian gentlemen Gratiano and Lodovico in wishing extreme tortures on Iago? We should certainly wonder whether Cassio wishes to, because only *he* has the authority to impose them.

327. *discontented paper* letter of complaint.

330. *nick* just in time (i.e. the 'nick of time').

331. *pernicious caitiff* despicable villain.

334. *even now* just now.
336. *wrought to his desire* suited his plot.
336. *O fool! fool! fool!* This moment combines Othello's *anagnorisis* – the tragic recognition of his awful folly in trusting Iago (rather than Desdemona) – with his *peripeteia* (action directed for a good purpose ending in disaster, i.e. by seeking to right the wrong of his wife's perceived unfaithfulness, he annihilated that love). Aristotle would doubtless also note with approval that Othello's triple recognition (his folly, Iago's villainy, Desdemona's honesty) and the disaster coincide. Four short words – that brief 'O' and the thrice repeated 'fool' – capture the enormity of this moment.
338. *upbraids* harangues, tells off.
339. *upon the watch* while on guard.
340. *cast* cast off, relieved of his post.

Gratiano
                    Torments will ope your lips.
Othello
  Well, thou dost best.
Lodovico
  Sir, you shall understand what hath befall'n,   320
  Which, as I think, you know not. Here is a letter
  Found in the pocket of the slain Roderigo;
  And here another: the one of them imports
  The death of Cassio to be undertook
  By Roderigo.   325
Othello
  O villain!
Cassio
                  Most heathenish and most gross!
Lodovico
  Now here's another discontented paper,
  Found in his pocket too; and this, it seems,
  Roderigo meant t' have sent this damned villain;
  But that, belike, Iago in the nick   330
  Came in and satisfied him.
Othello
                              O thou pernicious caitiff!
  How came you, Cassio, by that handkerchief
  That was my wife's?
Cassio
                  I found it in my chamber;
  And he himself confess'd it even now
  That there he dropp'd it for a special purpose   335
  Which wrought to his desire.
Othello
                              O fool! fool! fool!
Cassio
  There is besides in Roderigo's letter,
  How he upbraids Iago that he made him
  Brave me upon the watch; whereon it came
  That I was cast; and even but now he spake,   340

342. *set him on* urged him on, encouraged him.

343. *forsake* leave.

345. *slave* note the insistence on Iago's low social status.

346–7. *cunning cruelty ... hold him long* method (of torture) to extend his suffering. Shakespeare's text here follows the Italian source story and is not an unusual legal response in 'civilised' Christian society at the time, where torture was used to extract confessions. So Lodovico's sadistic suggestions for the 'devil' who ended his young cousin's life and marriage are understandable, but is a character's response which the audience is invited to compare with its own.

348. *close prisoner rest* under arrest and closely guarded.

355. *nothing extenuate* no excuses.

356–8. *must you speak ... not easily jealous* How accurate is Othello's self-assessment here?

357. *wisely* in moderation.

359. *Perplexed in the extreme* provoked beyond endurance.

360. *base Indian, threw a pearl away* Othello could be attempting to explain his own misjudgement by aligning himself with another maligned and misunderstood outsider. Native Americans did not view the Earth's natural resources as belongings to be sold, so did not recognise the monetary value of 'precious' stones. 'Base Indian' is used here as a symbol for the 'unbeliever' not appreciating the divinity of Christ, and suggests a racist stereotype.

362. *melting mood* weeping.

364. *med'cinable gum* the fragrant (and expensive) sap of an Arabian tree. A mixture of Christian and Arab elements is used to describe the tragic Othello weeping. Othello is again asking the audience to sympathise with his position as 'outsider'.

367. *traduc'd* insulted.

368. *circumcised dog* Othello uses a racist slur, to refer to himself as a Muslim (circumcised) soldier.

370. *period* time, conclusion.

After long seeming dead, Iago hurt him,
Iago set him on.

Lodovico

You must forsake this room and go with us.
Your power and your command is taken off,
And Cassio rules in Cyprus. For this slave,   345
If there be any cunning cruelty
That can torment him much and hold him long,
It shall be his. You shall close prisoner rest
Till that the nature of your fault be known
To the Venetian state. Come, bring away.   350

Othello

Soft you; a word or two before you go.
I have done the state some service, and they know't –
No more of that. I pray you, in your letters,
When you shall these unlucky deeds relate,
Speak of me as I am; nothing extenuate,   355
Nor set down aught in malice. Then must you speak
Of one that lov'd not wisely, but too well;
Of one not easily jealous, but, being wrought,
Perplexed in the extreme; of one whose hand,
Like the base Indian, threw a pearl away   360
Richer than all his tribe; one of whose subdu'd eyes,
Albeit unused to the melting mood,
Drops tears as fast as the Arabian trees
Their med'cinable gum. Set you down this:
And say besides that in Aleppo once,   365
Where a malignant and a turban'd Turk
Beat a Venetian and traduc'd the state,
I took by th' throat the circumcised dog,
And smote him – thus.

[He stabs himself.]

Lodovico

O bloody period!

Gratiano

              All that is spoke is marr'd.   370

374. *great of heart* courageous (but also great-hearted, a 'great' man, a tragic figure).

374. *Spartan dog* a bloodhound or bloodthirsty man (Sparta, the rival city to Athens in the classical Greek world, had notoriously savage dogs).

375. *fell* cruel, wicked.

375. *the sea* Note how Iago is here linked with the same elemental force as Othello (see, for example, Act 1, Scene 2, lines 26–8).

376. *tragic* This is a moment of self-conscious awareness of tragedy as the play concludes. Jacobean (like Ancient Greek) audiences shared such self-consciousness (awareness of the genre which one is witnessing).

377. *thy work* called a 'demi-devil' by Othello (line 314), Iago now becomes Tragedy itself, working against human beings.

378. *hid* i.e. behind a curtain.

379–80. *seize upon the fortunes ... succeed on you* Othello and Desdemona's wealth passes on to Lodovico as Desdemona's uncle and closest living relative.

380–2. *To you, Lord Governor ... O, enforce it!* A hint to Cassio to be firm in applying discipline and the rule of law.

383. *straight aboard* take ship immediately.

384. *heavy act* grim and depressing deed.

Othello

    I kiss'd thee ere I kill'd thee. No way but this –
    Killing my self, to die upon a kiss.

       [Falls on the bed and dies.]

Cassio

    This did I fear, but thought he had no weapon;
    For he was great of heart.

Lodovico

    [To IAGO*]*   O Spartan dog,
    More fell than anguish, hunger, or the sea!   375
    Look on the tragic loading of this bed.
    This is thy work. – The object poisons sight;
    Let it be hid. Gratiano, keep the house,
    And seize upon the fortunes of the Moor,
    For they succeed on you. To you, Lord Governor,   380
    Remains the censure of this hellish villain;
    The time, the place, the torture – O, enforce it!
    Myself will straight aboard; and to the state
    This heavy act with heavy heart relate. *[Exeunt.]*

Theme and character index

HONESTY (APPEARANCE AND REALITY)
The word 'honest' is used a total of fifty-two times in the play, first by Iago (as an insult) and then sixteen more times by him, always dishonestly. Brabantio uses the word once (properly), rejecting Roderigo as a suitor for his daughter; Othello nineteen times, the first and last to name Iago; Cassio, Emilia and (always honest) Desdemona use the word three times each. The word has a gendered history, explored in the play: in general use, it refers to things being what they seem; for women the word is used to describe them as 'faithful' to their husbands.

Key scenes: 1.1 49 and 98; 1.3 284, 294 and 396; 2.1 199; 2.3 6, 129, 165, 235, 254, 313, 320 and 321–347; 3.1 21–22, 39–40; 3.3 5, 50, 103–129, 224–227, 243, 259 and 371–389; 4.1 263; 4.2 12–19, 40-45 and 69; 5.1 128–129 and 316; 5.2 156–157, 162 and 256

MANHOOD AND MASCULINITY
General Othello cuts a heroic 'manly' figure in Venice in Act 1, his impressive military record overcoming the racism in that society. Iago despises everything except his (and Othello's) 'trade of war' (Act 1, Scene 2, line 1); for Iago, calmness under artillery fire and despising women and their domestic world go hand in hand. 'Would you would bear your fortune like a man!' is Iago's response to Othello's seizure in Act 4, Scene 1, line 63. Iago does not consider Cassio a 'real' man; he mocks his Florentine graces and calls him 'a great arithmetician', a theorist who 'never set a squadron in the field' (Act 1, Scene 1, lines 19 and 22). Othello is comfortable, accepted and renowned in his man's world of soldiering, but marriage with a Venetian lady is a potential threat to his manhood. Under Iago's careful manipulations, Othello becomes husband as domestic abuser and murderer.

Key scenes: 1.1 8–33; 1.3 76–94, 335 and 388–398; 2.3; 3.3 (especially 377); 3.4 89–100; 4.1 63–92 and 113–134; 4.2 208–210; 4.3 34–39 and 85–106 (husbands); 5.2 180–295

WOMEN AND MARRIAGE, LOVE AND SEX

A rebel marriage changes the status quo in Act 1, meeting with Brabantio's fury. Othello wins Desdemona with a romantic life story, marries her into *his* love story then (under Iago's influence) 're-tells' her as a 'strumpet' (Act 4, Scene 2, line 86) and finally decides that her story must end. Shakespeare invites the audience to consider how far the play's *marriages* – where the husband legally owns the wife – differ from Bianca's professional relationships with men. For Iago, sex is comically crude ('making the beast with two backs' – Act 1, Scene 1, line 117), a means to use women and a source of possessive paranoia. For Othello (before Iago's lies) and Desdemona (throughout) sex is romantic. For Roderigo it is a conquest. For Cassio it is a courtly game he mis-plays. For Bianca it is a profession, except in regard to Cassio, whom she touchingly loves. For Emilia sex is an asset to be traded like any other.

Key scenes: 1.1; 1.2; 1.3; 2.1; 3.3; 3.4; 4.1; 4.2 1–178; 4.3; 5.1 79–133; 5.2 1–243

DESDEMONA'S HANDKERCHIEF

This is the key prop of the play and the ultimate theatrical prop. It serves as a token of Desdemona's nursing and femininity and a symbol of her wedding sheets/marriage. The handkerchief was Othello's first gift to Desdemona; she loves and talks to it, a 'sign' of her/their love. Rather brilliantly, Iago manipulates this sign for *his* audience and it becomes symbolic of Desdemona's betrayal of Othello and 'dishonest' nature. Othello tells two romantic stories of the origins of the handkerchief that don't add up: one to intimidate Desdemona and the other to justify her murder.

Key scenes: 3.3 284–326, 439–446; 3.4 20–26, 50–75 and 176–189; 4.1; 5.2 50–52, 64–70, 224–225, 234–238 and 332–336

BRABANTIO

This sophisticated Venetian senator is friend and charming host to Othello until his daughter falls in love with him. He then becomes a hysterically possessive father, explaining her 'disobedience' through racist accusations of bewitchment, drugs and black magic.

Key scenes: 1.1 83–184; 1.2 56–100; 1.3 47–293; 5.2 212–217

OTHELLO

A renowned army general of royal descent, who escaped slavery and prizes his bachelor freedom. He wins Desdemona's affections with his thrilling life story, but even his wedding night does not distract him from army duties. He is an outsider accepted by the Venetian state because of his talent. His personal stability breaks down in Cyprus.

Key scenes: 1.2; 1.3 47–300; 2.1 177–210; 2.3 1–11 and 151–247; 3.3 29–290 and 331–484; 3.4 28–95; 4.1; 4.2 1–100; 5.1 29–38; 5.2
See also: 1.3 395–398 (Iago's assessment of him) and (close references) 1.2 21–22; 2.1 282–285; 2.3 193–197; 3.3 264–267 and 458–464; 5.2 39–40

DESDEMONA

She is accused of, and tragically punished for, sexual corruption and misrepresenting feelings, yet she is the only main character innocent of both. Iago insinuates and Othello accepts her corruption. Cassio calls her 'The divine Desdemona' (Act 2, Scene 1, line 72).

Key scenes: 1.3 170–300; 2.1 72–210; 2.3 8–24 and 237–246; 3.3 1–89 and 278–290; 3.4 1–166; 4.1 211–262; 4.2 23–178; 4.3; 5.2 1–132

IAGO

Iago is the play's formal antagonist, not just the ringleader of the *charivari* (see Introduction, p.iv), but on Cyprus his schemes drive the plot to the end. As Shakespeare's most duplicitous villain, he is a reworking of the blunt honest soldier who would have been familiar to Jacobean audiences – a character who tells it like it is and to your face.

Key scenes: 1.1; 1.2 1–59; 1.3 294–400; 2.1 96–306; 2.3 6–374; 3.3 35–259 and 301–484; 3.4 103–137; 4.1; 4.2 117–247; 5.1; 5.2 143–243 and 297–382

EMILIA

Emilia is a waiting woman and army wife whose final action redeems her accidental guilt in supporting Iago's scheme. Like Iago, Emilia is a realist but without his viciousness.

Key scenes: 2.1 95–162; 3.1 41–55; 3.3 1–29 and 291–322; 3.4 20–28, 96–104 and 129–164; 4.2 1–32 and 97–179; 4.3 10–104; 5.1 113–134; 5.2 90–264

CASSIO

Cassio is Othello's lieutenant and a courteous gentleman-soldier, until drunkenness reveals his incapability and deep-seated class prejudice. Cassio lacks the strength of character to refuse alcohol or keep Iago in his place, an issue that remains at the end of the play.

Key scenes: 1.1 20–33; 1.2 36–55; 1.3 388–394; 2.1 26–306; 2.3 1–320; 3.1 1–55; 3.3 1–34 and 110–144; 4.1 103–166; 5.1 22–110; 5.2 294–374

RODERIGO

Roderigo is sexually jealous and racially abusive of Othello while lusting after his wife. He is barely confident enough to challenge Cassio for her. He is perhaps the only character who falls prey to Iago's scheming that we don't feel sorry for.

Key scenes: 1.1; 1.2 55–59; 1.3 301–378; 2.1 211–279; 2.3 124–144 and 347–367; 4.2 179–247; 5.1 1–111

BIANCA

Bianca is a female companion (courtesan) for the 'gentleman' class. Her profession is a 'female escort' but her love relationship with Cassio is not as a sex worker, at least as far as she is concerned.

Key scenes: 3.4 167–199; 4.1 145–160; 5.1 79–135

THE 'TURK' ('OTTOMITES')

Shakespeare painstakingly researched Venetian government and puts the 'Moor' centre-stage, but 'the Turk' remains the 'general enemy' off it. The real general enemy within surely reveals himself when 'honest' Venetian Iago says *he* is 'a Turk' *if* what he says isn't true (Act 2, Scene 1, line 114).

Key scenes: 1.3 1–49, 211 and 221–234; 2.1 10–29, 109–114 and 199–200; 2.2 1–3; 2.3 158–160; 5.2 365–369